THE KISSING RABBI

LUST, BETRAYAL, AND A
COMMUNITY TURNED
INSIDE OUT

A NOVEL BY

ANDY BECKER

The Kissing Rabbi
Lust, Betrayal, and a Community Turned Inside Out

A Novel By Andy Becker

Tree of the Field Publishing
Gig Harbor, Washington
www.andybecker.life

TREE OF THE FIELD
——— PUBLISHING ———

ISBN: 978-1-7336698-2-5
Library of Congress Control Number: 2020922227

Disclaimer: This novel is entirely a work of fiction with elements of humor and satire. While the story may resemble a composite of *Me Too* reports in the press or may be inspired by actual events, the characters in all respects, including, but not limited to, their actions, interactions, speech, thoughts, ideas, and circumstances, are entirely imagined.

PRAISE FOR
THE KISSING RABBI

Andrew Becker writes with humor and considerable charm. The Kissing Rabbi is a wholly original novel that will leave readers wanting more from Becker. Five stars.

Gregg Olsen
New York Times bestselling author

So you want to hear the real story of Rabbi Mishegas Dreidel? The whole schmeer is a story as old as Jerusalem and as new as today's politics. The young rabbi, his wife, and nine kids show up in Destiny, Oregon filled with missionary zeal. He opens a synagogue in their basement, builds his flock, earns its trust, borrows a million dollars from a friendly banker for a towering house of worship, and off he goes to repair the world.

Part of that mission includes unwanted advances with women of the temple, questionable synagogue financial dealings kept secret, and a steadfast refusal to admit anything done wrong. This story is told with just the right touch of satire, humor, insight, and the hope it won't happen again.

Bob Hill
Award-winning Louisville Courier-Journal
columnist and author

*With a wry sense of humor and colorful cast of characters
(in fact, you probably know people like them), Becker dissects the
lamentable fall from grace of a well-intended shepherd turned
wolf. A witty and timely parable that keeps you wondering how
some people never seem to learn from their mistakes.
Entertaining and reflective.*

Larry Fowler
Award winning author

*The Kissing Rabbi humorously shines a light on a dark and heavy
subject—narcissistic abuse by a religious authority figure. This story
is a real page-turner and very relatable—highly recommended!*

Yitz Epstein
Life coach and host, Narcissism Recovery Podcast

You don't have to be Jewish to enjoy Andrew Becker's novel,
The Kissing Rabbi! *Meet Rabbi Mishegas (Mishy) Dreidel who
establishes a Jewish community in the Christian Destiny County
area while building a magnificent synagogue from a simple set-up
in his basement, but even the holy can fall from grace. You won't
be able to stop reading because you will want to know what's
going to happen to the rabbi, his wife, and nine kids in a world of
Jewish courts, close-knit families, and loyal supporters. Go inside
the secret and hidden world of ultra-orthodox Judaism to see how
power corrupts and how sexual harassment
can destroy a community.*

Patty Lesser
Author of *Sister Innocent* and several novels

A little bit of light pushes away a lot of darkness.

- Jewish Proverb

CONTENTS

IN THE
BEGINNING

S o you want to hear the real story of Rabbi Mishegas Dreidel, "The Kissing Rabbi"? You want the whole *megillah*? The day is long, and the tasks are many. Are you sure you don't have to be somewhere? This story has so many twists and turns, not to mention bumps and bruises, and it won't go away, like a pain in your gut.

The Kissing Rabbi, as he became known when it all went viral, wasn't originally viewed as a wannabe Casanova lusting after every woman he met. A young, doe-eyed, long-bearded, black-hatted rabbi commands a certain respect. How could anyone have predicted his future infamy?

Our beloved rabbi ultimately failed so miserably at turning his libidinal thoughts into action that he imagined himself the real victim. He claimed that his punishments and his humiliation, though thoroughly self-inflicted, exceeded his crimes. But let's not put the *schmeer* before the bagel. The point is this: a person is not born a *schlemiel*. And for that *schlemiel* to turn into a real *schmuck* takes even more doing.

They say a person's destiny is written on Rosh Hashanah, the Jewish New Year—who shall live and who shall die, who by fire, who by sword, who by wild beast, and who by earthquake. But Divine Providence can only afford the individual an opportunity to perform a *mitzvah*, a good deed, or commit a transgression. How is it that we zig when we should have zagged?

But is it right to recount a rabbi's missteps, foibles, and ultimate, tragic downfall without mentioning all the good that he accomplished? Foremost, let's acknowledge that Rabbi Mishegas Dreidel was a loving father to his nine kids. God bless all the rabbis who raise wonderful children. The children, may God bless them, who have honest fathers, should learn from their fathers' examples. And the others, God bless them double, should not be stigmatized by their fathers' sins. Unfortunately, in the ultra-orthodox world, the sins of the father are visited upon the children, especially when it comes time to arrange the *shidduch*, a match between a prospective bride and groom. The mother of the unfortunate child, whose father, heaven forbid, strayed from the holy path, is going to suffer some real *tsuris*, heartbreak and trouble, when it comes to finding a good match for her child.

Stigmatized or not, every child, even those raised in an ultra-orthodox fashion with rabbis as fathers, will have many opportunities to make their own mistakes. This is the human condition since Adam and Eve made the choice to partake of the Tree of Knowledge, the first exercise of free will gone awry. If our eldest progenitors, born into a perfect world, could stumble out of the gate, why did we expect that our beloved rabbi would never trip and fall? But let's not start philosophizing about the Tree in the Garden. There's only so much whiskey in the bottle.

Let's start the story before the Kissing Rabbi was kissing anyone—when, brimming with enthusiasm, with a young wife and a first child in tow, he rented his first house in our little garden, Destiny County, Oregon. Rabbi Dreidel, "Mishy" to his family and closest friends, belonged to a sect of Jews called TUCAS, an acronym for Torah, Understanding, Compassion, Atonement, and Solidarity. Their mission was to provide outreach to unaffiliated Jews worldwide from their home neighborhood in New York.

Rabbi Dreidel was delighted to find a spacious, three-bedroom house in Destiny County with a daylight basement that would serve as his first synagogue. It was located in a nice neighborhood—affordable, upper-middle-class, but not too upscale—on the south side of town near a Navy base. What a bargain compared to New York, New York. So spacious! So cheap!

Rabbi Dreidel dove headfirst into his holy mission, meeting all the nearby Jews that he could find and inviting himself to their homes. He even ran through the phone book cold-calling last names that included the syllables Farb, Man, Gold, Stein, or any combination thereof. When he hit a mark, the Jewish person on the other end of the phone call struggled to turn away his exuberance and disappoint him, or worse, invite the wrath of the Almighty. Saying "yes" often invited a different type of wrath:

"*Who's* coming over? You *agreed* to this?"

"What was I supposed to do, say no to a rabbi?"

"Who is this exactly?"

"That rabbi we met last Passover at Rob's house."

"They're ultra-orthodox. Our house isn't kosher; we won't be able to offer them anything!"

"It's okay. They just want to introduce themselves."

"Why are we doing this? We've never had a rabbi over to our house."

"They're new. They want to come and meet us."

"Okay, but you better help me pick up. And hide the shrimp in the crisper!"

"They're not going to look inside the damn refrigerator."

"Just hide the shrimp! What time are they coming?"

One call, one introduction, often led to another, sometimes several. Rabbi Dreidel consistently offered any Jewish man *tefillin*, black leather boxes with leather straps. Highly observant Jewish men wrap *tefillin* on their non-dominant arms and around their heads to pray once a day. If the man had never previously wrapped *tefillin*, the rabbi joked that he was giving the man a bar mitzvah. Bar mitzvah boys who are orthodox commence daily prayers wrapped in *tefillin* straps when they reach that milestone. The rabbi explained solemnly that praying daily with *tefillin* was one of the Torah's greatest mitzvahs because it focused on God's assurance that reward will follow observance.

Carefully and gently, Rabbi Dreidel wrapped one of the straps around the uninitiated's arm and placed the other around his head. Once all strapped up, the rabbi gave the man a cheat sheet of the *tefillin* prayer on a laminated piece of paper, faced the man eastward, and told him to read. After the man stumbled and mumbled his way to the prayer's conclusion, the rabbi unwrapped and removed the straps. He wound them up around their two little boxes and put them away in their velvet purse with Hebrew letters. He did so gently, with kindness, humor, and joy.

And so *nu*? Now what, sweet young rabbi? Now that he had given the man of the house a "bar mitzvah" by wrapping *tefillin*, the rabbi continued to listen, love-bomb, and establish intimacy. After some mild flattery, a smile, and a joke, he would ask his new acquaintance to talk about himself, his history with Judaism, level of observance, and prior experiences as a Reformed or Conservative Jew. The young rabbi just cared that you were Jewish, regardless of your background. He quickly learned how to read the cues.

Ah, this new friend had a personal issue to unload. The young rabbi was ready to listen. He only had to say, "I am here for you, I hear you, I know what you mean, tell me more," or "I feel we have a real connection." A highly charged, intimate conversation soon followed.

As the conversation progressed, a relationship formed. The rabbi appeared truly devout, talking about Judaism with great enthusiasm and energy. Jumping to the next level, the rabbi asked, "Would you like to come *daven*, that's our word for praying, on Shabbos? I would be honored if you would come for a Shabbos dinner. First, we'll do services in our makeshift, downstairs synagogue, and then we can really enjoy a beautiful Shabbos meal together: Israeli salad, gefilte fish, and matzah ball soup, just for starters, and then chicken and potato kugel, all kosher. How's the Friday after next? We start davening at 6:30 p.m."

Before you knew it, the rabbi's new "friend," perhaps a little nervously, *schlepped* his family to enjoy a beautiful Shabbos dinner with Rabbi Mishegas and his young family. The rabbi telephoned each week with invitations to attend services every Shabbos; in fact, the rabbi explained, he needed ten men, a *minyan*, to read the Torah on Shabbos. He needed you, yes you, to help him out. And he promised you a special honor, an *aliyah*, a blessing as the Torah is read.

"Can you please come?"

First, you prayed in the makeshift, basement synagogue, then you feasted upstairs. There, you enjoyed a luxurious spread on a handsomely decorated, white table-clothed dining room table. It was a real, five-course meal, delicious as represented. Of course, the meal came with prayers welcoming the Shabbos, blessing God, blessing the wine, blessing the challah, and then yet another sermon between the soup and the chicken. More prayers followed after the meal, all enthusiastically performed by the young rabbi, seemingly for your soul's personal, spiritual benefit.

The rabbi made it clear that your Jewish soul was his primary concern. He gave you the opportunity to get closer to God. His missions were to get a minyan every Shabbos and to find the Jews in the Destiny County area who were unaffiliated. He was creating a Jewish community of joy, observance, celebration, and lighting sparks of spirituality—how could you argue against it? And how could you laugh at his greater mission—to hasten the Redemption, when *Moshiach*, the Messiah, would come so that a new, holy era would reign upon the earth. Sure, it seemed unlikely and farfetched, but who were you to tell him it wasn't going to happen?

As it turned out, Rabbi Dreidel's experience of the "real world" was limited. Things that you and I take for granted—how to rent a house, buy a car, obtain health insurance or operate a lawn mower—were challenges for the young rabbi and his wife. Their naiveté and helplessness charmed many of the more secular and assimilated Jews they met. Who didn't want to help a young couple with a baby? The Jews of Destiny County were only too happy to offer advice and assistance.

Rabbi Dreidel's business model was simple. By helping each unaffiliated, poor *schlepper*, any lost soul he could find, connect to God, Rabbi Dreidel forged a relationship. Sooner or later that relationship also adhered to the family's pocketbook. And if you can't trust an orthodox rabbi, who can you trust? Thank you, Almighty God, for creating the 501(3)(c) corporation—religious, tax-exempt, and all donations accepted! Here's the web page to input your credit card that allows for monthly, automatic donations. May God bless you and keep you holy! Thank you, God, for cash, and thank you, God, for checks! It's a mitzvah to give, so give as much as you like. It says in our prayer book that God will bless those who establish a synagogue in which to pray.

The young couple found a home in Destiny County, started a synagogue, reached out, and were ablaze with their mission to rekindle a spark of Judaism in so many spiritually snoozing Jews. Over the next decade, Rabbi Mishegas Dreidel, seemingly slowly— but more like the hare than the turtle—built a Jewish community.

What was the rabbi's payoff for all of his outreach and hard work, the nonstop calling, meeting, hosting, teaching, praying, counseling, and schmoozing? He became the main character in a world that he created, where he enjoyed great respect, admiration, and eventually, even love and devotion. He appeared genuine, beyond reproach or criticism, and powerful in his Jewish fiefdom, where he starred as the benevolent oracle and final word for all things Jewish. He basked in the glory of God, the Torah, and a community of his own construction.

In what seemed like the time needed to recite the *Kaddish*, a prayer of mourning, he'd personally met one hundred Jews, then two hundred, then three, then five, then a thousand. Who knew that a thousand Jews lived in Destiny County? His list of donors grew bit by bit. Some gave a little and some gave a lot. The more you gave, the more honored you were with special *aliyot* and blessings when you came to religious services. The more you came, the more often you were invited to Shabbos dinner, and the more you felt a kinship, a friendship, and a spiritual connection to your new, young, holy friend. You had never before enjoyed a one-on-one, face-to-face friendship with a rabbi.

The young couple started a preschool, and the rabbi's wife sponsored and led her own "Soup, Salad, and Torah" woman's group. She taught Torah, baking challah, and decorating for the Jewish holidays. Everyone marveled at how she did it, constantly engulfed by the chaos of new babies and little kids. She birthed a new gift from God almost every two years; God bless her and bless God! Following little Rivka in short order were Reuben, Shimon, Asher, Yitzhak, Ephraim, Hannah, Chaya, and the latest baby, Menachem Mendel.

They raised their children to be future rabbis and the future wives of rabbis.

The kids ran helter-skelter through the shul on Shabbos, all dressed up in their little fancy party dresses and their suits and ties. Members of the community embraced the children, and the kids felt well-loved and special. But their house was always full of strangers, so it was natural that they, while polite, were sometimes shy with the latest dinner guest or new member of the congregation.

Rabbi Dreidel was in constant motion, like his namesake, the spinning top. He visited Jews here, there, and everywhere, taught evening classes, "Lox, Bagel, and Learn" lunchtime classes in lawyers' conference rooms, and put on grand events for every Jewish holiday. If a Jew, God forbid, landed in a hospital, jail, or mental institution in Destiny County, Rabbi Dreidel rushed there as quickly as he could, regardless of the hour, *tefillin* in hand.

In a little more than a decade from the day he set foot in Destiny County, Rabbi Dreidel created a great miracle. It was born with generous donations from the Jews of Destiny County. It also required a giant loan from a local bank. Its chief loan officer was a born-again Christian who loved Jews.

After a lot of nudging and arguments with the contractor and subcontractors, there it stood: a beautiful synagogue. The chapel's high ceiling and stained-glass windows complemented a tall, hand-carved wooden ark housing the Torah. Outside of the chapel stood a foyer, a cozy office for the rabbi, two multipurpose classrooms, and a spacious community hall with a commercial-sized kosher kitchen! The vacant lot next to the rabbi's house was vacant no longer.

Yes, the new Jewish Center of Destiny County was grandiose, with a mortgage of over a million dollars, probably more than the community could afford. But how was the rabbi going to grow a Jewish community without a proper and attractive synagogue? How was traditional Judaism going to compete with the well-funded Reformed

Temple's version of assimilated, watered-down Judaism across town? And Rabbi Dreidel wasn't done yet. As soon as the old lady in the house next door to the synagogue died or moved, he was going to snap up that property too, and build a proper *mikvah*, a ritual bathhouse. It would be used for conversions, for ritual baths before weddings, and for menstrual purity. With the synagogue and the *mikvah* side by side, highly observant Jews would move to the neighborhood, and faster than you could say *Shema Yisrael*, the Jewish Center of Destiny would grow and thrive, forever a light unto the world! And let us all say it together, "Amen!"

THE RED-HEADED
BIKINI BARISTA

The Bikini Cafe—a coffee drive-thru near the Navy base that featured bikinied servers—is where Lacey Johnson met her husband, Gerald, an enlisted serviceman. Lacey was a striking, red-headed barista. Gerald was a customer who tipped liberally. They married in a week; sometimes the stars aligned.

Gerald felt completely intoxicated by Lacey's shapely physical attributes coupled with her outgoing and flirtatious personality. She was a sexy redhead in her revealing, pink halter-neck bikini. But what got him was her long, red hair, girl-next-door face, and big eyes with full eyebrows that gave her a wonderfully innocent look.

Lacey, for her part, fell for a trim guy in a uniform. The crisply ironed Navy uniform and Gerald's calm manner signified trust and stability to her, attributes that were absent in her family. He seemed like such a sincere, stand-up guy. On their first date, he didn't grab at her shapely legs or lovely bosoms, like a lot of guys. She made the first moves, inviting his kiss and his touch, placing his hand where she thought he might want to put it.

He was assigned to a Navy carrier that was set to sail in ten days. Rather than wait for a six-month reunion, they flew to Las Vegas and tied the knot. On the plane, Lacey told Gerald for the first time that she was Jewish. Gerald's only comment was, "You don't look Jewish."

Once Gerald's ship came back to port, Lacey and Gerald adjusted to housing on base. Lacey quit her job at the Bikini Cafe and volunteered on the base. She became a part-time, lay counselor for the Navy. They soon started a family; a son was born after a year. Lacey found a second home on base at a makeshift Jewish Chapel. There, she made friends with the handful of military Jews who came for services. They celebrated their son's bris (ritual circumcision) at the chapel on base in a traditional Jewish ceremony.

Rabbi Hazzarai officiated. His Navy assignment as a chaplain included pastoral duties for all the enlisted sailors at the big base near Destiny County. Because he was a rabbi, he also tended to the Jews at the base, enlisted and civilian, and their families. There were not a lot of them. Rabbi Hazzarai found that the Jews in the military were often from less-observant, less affluent backgrounds. They liked to gather for the Jewish holidays, perhaps to enjoy an extra day off duty. He wasn't a charismatic pulpit rabbi, but he did the job adequately, and the military Jews didn't expect much, so he met their expectations.

Was it strange to see an orthodox rabbi, bearded and wearing his broad-brimmed black hat, like other TUCAS rabbis, as a Navy chaplain? After all, what was an orthodox rabbi doing in the Navy, a place that is not exactly a hotbed of highly observant Jews? Well, a man had to eat, didn't he, and feed his kids? Rabbi Hazzarai and his wife were still in their thirties, but they already had five kids, all little darlings. They had a roof over their heads, thanks to the United States Navy. When God commanded a Jew to be fruitful and multiply, He didn't say everywhere except in Navy housing.

Rabbi Hazzarai didn't really know what to think when he met Lacey Johnson. She didn't *look* Jewish. She looked like a real *shiksa*, like a glamorous pin-up girl. The rabbi didn't expect her to attend services regularly, unfairly categorizing her as a "once in a blue moon" Jew, based on her looks. But she attended services and classes frequently, volunteered with setup and cleanup, clearly wanted to learn, and she was willing to incorporate religious practices into her day-to-day life. Most importantly, she was a mom who wanted to raise her kids Jewish. *True*, thought Rabbi Hazzarai to himself, *she married a goy, a non-Jewish Navy guy with tattoos, but with the birth of her child, she brought a Jew into the world, a true blessing.*

So, how did Rabbi Hazzarai get mixed up in introducing Lacey Johnson to Rabbi Dreidel? What ended up not kosher months later, according to the newspaper articles that went viral, started out innocently enough, and all for the sake of kosher meat.

Rabbi Dreidel organized a delivery of kosher meat once a week to his house. The big, mega-grocery store in Portland with a kosher butcher sent a van to Destiny County with individual orders of kosher meat. You could email your order as late as Monday night each week, and the store delivered the orders each Wednesday. The boxes, packed with ice and meat, sat outside Rabbi Dreidel's house on a table under an overhang to allow for easy pickup.

Lacey grew up in a house with parents who enjoyed nice, fat, greasy strips of bacon on their BLTs, cheese on their burgers, and a killer clam dip recipe. Her marriage and baby boy inspired her to take a spiritual plunge into her long-neglected and unstudied Jewish heritage. In childhood, Judaism to Lacey mostly meant parents who argued about everything. In other words, when they argued, which happened frequently, their voices got quite loud, a style inherited from their immigrant parents. Personal insults and criticisms bounced back and forth like a ping pong ball. Lacey didn't want her children exposed to that. She was determined to create a mentally healthy and positive home environment for her son and her husband.

Just like the Polar Bear Club jumped into the Willamette River on the first day of the secular New Year, Lacey Johnson's marriage and the birth of her son sparked her leap into a world of Judaism. Just like her husband had to obey the rules of the military in his career, she was going to observe the rules of Judaism in her home. She would give her children the spiritual foundation that she never had. Lacey told herself that she could face these new challenges with the help of the Almighty, blessed be He.

Kashrut, or the laws of kosher, include many dietary laws about what foods observant Jews are permitted to eat and how they must be prepared. The main rules are found in the Torah, but the devil is in the details, and many of the rules were part of an oral tradition that was eventually codified. That happened after the rules were argued about in the Mishnah and the Talmud, books longer than the federal tax code.

To this day, arguments persist among the most learned rabbis concerning what should and shouldn't be certified as kosher. What the ultra-orthodox can eat is not based on what looks and tastes most tasty, but on other complicated criteria altogether. Not only that, the best scholars, religious and secular, say the rules are not logical, scientific, or even health-related, but exist simply to require the obedience of the Jewish people to the word of God.

In other words, when God said no cheeseburgers and no shrimp cocktails, that's the rule, period, and no exceptions. Whether you want to wonder about the reason for it or not is up to you. But you have to obey the rules to stay kosher, whether you think they make sense or not.

The rules seemed overwhelming to Lacey at first. She had to separate meat and dairy, not just milk and cheese, but butter too. She needed two sets of dishes, two sets of pots and pans, two sets of forks and knives, and don't forget the serving spoons, spatulas, and ladles. She had to look for symbols on every packaged box of processed food to make sure there weren't any non-kosher ingredients. Even some beers, wines, and alcohols were kosher and some weren't, sometimes just because one company bothered to get certified kosher while another did not. Although all the laws came down from Mount Sinai with Moses in one day, the Jews spent several thousand years figuring them out, and not without arguments. This is why the Jews of TUCAS started the religious educations of their children at age three. There was a lot to learn.

Lacey figured she'd start with kosher meat. She wasn't sure what kosher meat was exactly, but she knew, thanks to Rabbi Hazzarai's giving her Rabbi Dreidel's cell number, where to get it.

"Hi, I'm Lacey Johnson. I got your phone number from Rabbi Hazzarai."

"Oh sure. He called and said you'd call me. Nice to meet you. You're interested in picking up kosher meat at our house. Text me your email address, and I'll email you the order form and our address in town. The meat usually arrives at our house around nine-thirty or so on Wednesday mornings. Just park next to our driveway, and there's a little table under an overhang on the side of our garage."

Not exactly a sexy phone call. That started later.

THE MATURE
JEWISH LADY

When Rabbi Dreidel appeared out of nowhere, Gloria Epstein thought, *Where's this going to lead? We never even belonged to the Reformed Temple.*

She and her husband, Benjamin, were Jewish and identified as such, but they did not practice or attend anything. Her Jewish identity was ingrained in childhood. Mrs. Epstein grew up in a Jewish neighborhood in Brooklyn, but that was a long time ago. When their kids were Sunday school age, the Epsteins preferred staying at home on Sundays rather than *schlepping* to yet another kid activity. They worked hard, and their careers were busy and demanding; they wanted a day to sleep in. This was mellow Oregon, not hustling New York.

Mrs. Epstein really enjoyed her life. She and her husband were financially set. Three of their four children were grown, married, and out of the house. Three grandchildren lived in Portland, and they saw them frequently. Mr. Epstein, now in his early seventies, stopped working for a large environmental company, but he didn't like sitting at home watching TV. After six months, he went back to work for the same company full-time.

Mrs. Epstein retired years ago from a cosmetics business that she built from the ground up. She sold her company when its success started to burn her out. Retirement suited her. She loved her house and her privacy. She decorated with a tasteful touch—modern, classy, and comfortable but not overstated.

Their house was surrounded by tall evergreen trees, but it still had a vista of town from the expansive porch that bordered a patio, herb garden, and large lawn. All the houses in the area sat on at least five acres. Mrs. Epstein's sat on ten. She loved her grandkids, cooking, dinner parties, barbequing in the summer, and occasional travel.

She really didn't care about religion. She liked her Jewish heritage and culture, but when the kids wanted a Christmas tree and decorations, she thought, *Why not, what's the big deal?* They usually brought in a little Christmas tree that Mr. Epstein cut down from their own property. They also lighted Chanukah candles. She liked making potato latkes and brisket for a Chanukah party that they usually celebrated with longtime friends who had kids around the same ages as theirs. Religious practice in a synagogue was not a part of the Epsteins' lives.

Given that history, she surprised herself when she accepted an invitation to a Shabbos dinner with Rabbi Dreidel and his wife, Abigail. Since Mrs. Epstein was retired, her schedule was open. Her husband said, "Sure, why not?" and she shrugged and figured, *what the heck. It was just a dinner.* She fully disclosed that she and her husband were poor candidates to become involved in the basement synagogue.

At the Shabbos dinner, she liked the young couple's charm

and youthful energy. She felt an immediate connection with Abigail, notwithstanding they had nothing in common other than coming from New York. She enjoyed playing a tried and true funny tickle game with the Dreidel's eldest daughter, Rivka. Mrs. Epstein's tickle game worked better on Rivka than on her own grandchildren. In short, the Epsteins, and especially Mrs. Epstein, enjoyed themselves immensely with the Dreidels.

One thing led to another, and Gloria Epstein became a close auntie or second grandmother to all the Dreidel children. There was a new one every two years, pretty much like clockwork. With every new baby, Abigail very much appreciated the attention Mrs. Epstein gave to the other kids, which afforded her quality time with the infant. Gloria also volunteered to help Abigail prepare her "Soup, Salad, and Torah" events for the ladies.

Before long, Abigail, a young mother in her thirties, opened up to Gloria, a lady over seventy. One long phone conversation led to many more, after the kids went to bed. They talked about raising kids, each other's background in New York, shopping, table decorations for dinner parties and Jewish holidays, and eventually, a subject that Gloria found fascinating—the sex lives of orthodox women.

Their discussions of this subject started with questions about head coverings and wigs, as Gloria always thought it might be fun to buy a wig but never did. Abigail was required to wear a wig or head covering, like a scarf, under Jewish ultra-orthodox rules requiring modesty. Gloria told Abigail that she thought her wig was sexy! Abigail was flattered and a little embarrassed, but she welcomed the compliment.

"Listen," Gloria asked, "why should anyone dress unattractively? If a man is truly devout, shouldn't he be able to discipline himself? Isn't he going to be out and about in the world where women are dressed in every conceivable manner?"

"Modesty," explained Abigail, "doesn't mean ugly or unattractive. You can cover the hair on your head and the skin on your arms and legs and still be shapely. Think about it. Isn't what's left to the imagination more interesting?"

"But," asked Gloria, "isn't the point of covering everything up so that men will not think about you sexually? Why not make yourself as ugly as possible, if you want to avoid inciting lust in men?"

"That's not how it works," continued Abigail. "Our rules and customs about modesty increase the sexual desires of our husbands rather than stunt them. Every time we have sex," she said, lowering her voice like she was sharing a secret, "it's like our honeymoon all over again. It's like eating chocolate pudding. If you have it for breakfast, lunch, and dinner, it's not delicious or special. In our case, the proof is in the pudding, isn't it? We have been blessed with so many kids."

The rules were broader than just sexual intercourse. During menstruation, Abigail explained, she could not have any contact with her husband. They couldn't even pass objects directly to each other. When her period was finished, Abigail, like all the other orthodox ladies of the TUCAS sect, worldwide, had a method to check for any more bleeding in her vagina. She inserted a cloth with her fingers up her canal to look for any spots. If she found one, she had to wait a week. If she wasn't sure about the color of the spot on the cloth, she took a picture of it and emailed it to a special rabbi who rendered a judgment. After Abigail was clear of any discharge for a full seven days, she then had to go to the mikvah, the ritual bath in Portland, before she and the rabbi could even touch, let alone sleep in the same bed or have sex. By that time, they hadn't had sex for at least two weeks! The rabbi's sermon that Shabbos was going to be inspired! In the back of his mind, he had to be thinking about that chocolate pudding!

Well, thought Mrs. Epstein, *if this is what works for you, whatever floats your boat.* Still, she was skeptical.

She asked Abigail, "During your period, don't you sometimes just need a hug? Maybe you had a rough day?"

"Well," said Abigail, "that's when it's good to call family, or someone like you, who I consider my family here in Destiny County. If you are around and I need a hug, I know I can count on you to give me one."

"By the way," Abigail told her breathily, "did you know that sex on the Holy Shabbos is a double mitzvah?"

Oh boy, thought Gloria, *I guess more than the challah is going to rise Friday night.*

"One mitzvah is to be fruitful and multiply," explained Abigail, "but there's another one for the husband to sexually satisfy the wife. As tired as I may be from the kids, the Shabbos preparations, and Shabbos dinner, we are also commanded to enjoy the Shabbos. Need I say more?"

THE LADY CPA

Sarah Shofar was a certified public accountant—a contemporary Jewish professional woman. As a modern woman of valor, she juggled children, marriage, and career, successfully keeping all the balls in the air.

When she was at college, she had married another aspiring accountant named Elmer Smith, a goy, a real "white bread." Not only wasn't he Jewish, but he didn't know the difference between a matzah ball and a challah. It wasn't his fault. He had no exposure to Jewish people before Sarah.

Elmer looked clean-cut and all-American. In contrast, Sarah had a Semitic, dark-haired look. He found her looks extremely earthy and sexy. Her Jewish background felt exotic and rich to him. He wondered if all Jewish women were as sensual in the bedroom as she. He decided that he didn't really like white bread. He preferred rye. Bring on the challah, the bagel, and the macaroon. And for her part, she found out that she liked a guy who wasn't hairy, but was masculine and still felt smooth. She preferred white bread, imagine that! Their attraction led to matrimony. Despite the differences in their backgrounds, their lusty sex life sustained their marriage.

The couple always thought it was funny that her name sounded so Jewish and his sounded like that of a Midwestern farmer. Although a goy, to whom everything Jewish started out as a mystery, Elmer was always supportive of raising their kids Jewish, an issue that they had discussed and agreed upon after he proposed marriage. He wisely intuited it would be a deal-breaker if he objected. At the time, he didn't really care, because he didn't have any religious background. Neither of his parents attended church.

As they settled into work and started their family in Destiny County, Sarah checked out the Reformed Temple. The membership people wanted to see their tax returns and other financial information. That seemed uncomfortably intrusive to Sarah, in part because they were really just scraping by in their CPA practice and even had some negative months. She was a little embarrassed that they weren't earning more and didn't want to share that information with anyone.

She rationalized putting off the Reformed Temple's request for the financials by telling herself that she didn't even know if her family was going to like it there. She resented their focus on money, recognizing the irony of her feelings when she worked with money numbers every day. The temple membership person she talked to acted like Sarah had to buy the damn car even before they offered her a test drive. Who buys a car without kicking the tires? This was not the welcoming environment she was looking for.

Sarah and her husband wanted to project a certain image. They bucked the trend of accountants dressing down to "business casual." She wanted upscale clients, so she dressed the part. She spent ample time at the Nordstrom and two boutique stores at the local mall.

Elmer also wore a suit or sport coat and tie every day. Both Sarah and Elmer looked trim, like up-and-comers, even though they were more than forty years old and, perhaps, should already have arrived. Sarah wasn't sure how her image of millennial prosperity would fit with an orthodox synagogue whose customs dated back centuries. But she decided to check out the only alternative to the Reformed Temple in Destiny County—the Jewish Center run by Rabbi Dreidel.

Rabbi Mishegas Dreidel was friendly and energetic, and he told Sarah and Elmer that he really wanted them to come pray and learn just for the sake of Judaism. He never even mentioned money and was far too polite and deferential to ask about their tax returns. He love-bombed them. That made the choice easy, even though Sarah had misgivings about whether women were second-class citizens in an orthodox shul. Women were not allowed on the *bima*, the raised platform where only men read the Torah. Women also sat segregated from men. The rabbi's wife wore a wig. Sarah knew he was not allowed to shake hands with women or even touch a woman in any way if that woman was not his wife. There were times when the rabbi couldn't even touch his wife. These stringent rules and customs, many of which Sarah was learning about for the first time, seemed very foreign. Still, Sarah chose the Jewish Center of Destiny County for her family. Rabbi Dreidel welcomed them with enthusiasm and joy. She wanted her family to go where they were welcomed.

Sarah also wanted their two boys and one girl to each have a bar and bat mitzvah. She was delighted when Rabbi Dreidel immediately invited the kids to start Hebrew School on Sundays. The Sunday school was small. The rabbi and his wife, Abigail, ran the program. They devoted a lot of individual attention to each child, and Sarah's kids didn't complain about going there, which meant to Sarah that they actually liked Sunday school. She certainly hadn't as a kid. She distinctly remembered complaining about Sunday school over and over again to her parents. Rabbi Dreidel's Sunday Hebrew school was far superior to Sarah's experience growing up. The kids learned Hebrew and much more about Judaism than she ever did. Sarah put aside her reservations about the rabbi's traditional brand of Judaism and put her trust in him. Rabbi Dreidel appeared so sincere and dedicated.

Around six months before the oldest boy's bar mitzvah, Rabbi Dreidel started one-on-one classes with him and encouraged the family to attend more services. The Friday night Shabbos service was much shorter than the marathon on Saturday morning that stretched into the afternoon, with a lunch and more prayers after services. Either Sarah or Elmer went straight home from the office to pick up the kids for Friday night services, usually still wearing their professional attire.

As it turned out, Elmer really started to enjoy the Shabbos services, especially Rabbi Dreidel's sermons. He became very interested in Judaism and developed a spirituality that he previously didn't know existed. He and Sarah also started attending once-a-week "Lunch and Learn" classes taught by Rabbi Dreidel on the Kabbalah, mystical Judaism, hosted by another accountant in a nearby office conference room.

In short, Sarah Shofar's family enjoyed and participated in far more Judaism than they ever imagined they would when Elmer agreed to raise the children Jewish. They started to buy kosher meat, light candles at home on Shabbos, and experiment with turning off their electronics from sundown Friday night through Saturday night. Turning off their TV, phones, and computers was a major adjustment, but Sarah delighted in how the family spent more time interacting and bonding. She loved her husband's newfound interest in Judaism. They credited Rabbi Dreidel for the spirituality that enriched their family life.

Sarah always liked talking to Rabbi Dreidel. He always complimented the kids, which Sarah found so flattering that sometimes his compliments made her blush. The rabbi told her that this one was "a little *mensch*" (a real person) and that one possessed a real "*yiddishe kup*" (a Jewish mind), making her feel that she had hit the jackpot with her kids. The rabbi also spent more time with her going over the one-on-one course of study and prayers that he wanted the kids to master. When she had a religious question about the kids' homework, Rabbi Dreidel responded with detailed explanations. She started to ask questions in the lunch and learn sessions. She felt very connected to the rabbi. She assumed that he spent more time explaining things to her than her husband because she was the Jewish parent in the family. She didn't object to the extra attention. In fact, she enjoyed it.

When the rabbi told her, one day, in a meeting about her son's bar mitzvah, that he thought they had a special connection, she felt flattered. He told her that he felt he could talk to her very openly about things. She agreed.

Sarah knew that, if an orthodox rabbi was not allowed to even shake hands with a woman who wasn't his wife, he certainly wasn't allowed to look down her blouse, which he appeared to be doing that day. She instantly looked away from catching him peeking at her breasts. She felt flushed with embarrassment and immediately tried to put the incident out of her mind. When that didn't work, she thought that men will be men and that she shouldn't have been leaning over.

After a moment or two, Sarah realized the rabbi was doing more staring than peeking. She found it impossible to process what was happening; it squarely conflicted with her holy image of him. Because she couldn't process it, she put it out of her mind. How big a deal was it anyhow?

Like no man ever looked at my tits before? she thought. *C'mon,* she told herself, *give me a break.*

What she couldn't put out of her mind was a conversation on the phone a few days later that started with Rabbi Dreidel asking if he could talk to her privately. He had called to reschedule a one-on-one study session for her upcoming bar mitzvah boy. He first asked if she would agree that what he was about to say would be kept strictly confidential—that he had something important he wanted to discuss with her. She said, of course, she was a CPA and was used to keeping things confidential.

"This is very personal information," Rabbi Dreidel said in a serious tone. "You have to promise not to share it with anyone, not even Elmer and especially not ever with Abigail."

Sarah felt a bit dizzy. She was expecting to talk about her son's bar mitzvah studies, not about keeping secrets from Elmer and Abigail. The rabbi sounded so intense, like it was a matter of life and death.

"Yes, Rabbi, I'm here in the kitchen by myself. The kids are upstairs and Elmer is watching football. You're free to speak."

"Only because we have a special friendship," the rabbi went on, "is why I can tell you this. It's hard for me to admit, but I can confide in you. It's snowballed and seems to be getting worse. Abigail is not interested in certain things, in bed that is. I am experiencing problems with arousal."

"What?" exclaimed Sarah, trying to buy herself time to consider what she had just heard. "I don't understand. What are you talking about?"

"Abigail and me, we just can't manage in bed anymore. I am not fulfilling my duty as a husband."

Sarah didn't trust what she was hearing. She was dumbfounded that her rabbi was discussing sex. She was astonished that he shared such shocking and private details. She was surprised that his marriage even had an intimacy issue, when the couple always gave the impression of a perfect marriage.

"Abigail," Sarah responded, "always talks about how your faith and mission together has led to such a strong marriage. She always says you're a wonderful father and how thrilled she is by the shul you have built here."

"Yes, yes," Rabbi Dreidel went on. "But she's always so disinterested at night, even on Shabbos. Sometimes, I can't even get excited when I want to. We are in a terrible rut that has turned me off.

"It means I can't fulfill the mitzvah of making her happy and satisfied," the rabbi continued, sounding needy.

Sarah felt overwhelmed and underwater.

"Let me be more specific about how you might help," said the rabbi, while Sarah thought, *Please don't!*

"I am wondering," Rabbi Dreidel asked, "if you could give me some pointers about how I can interest her in different positions or, something I want to try, but she won't hear about it—oral sex. I know that would help me with my problem. You have to understand, the way we were raised, this is something she won't really talk about. It's causing friction in our marriage. I'm desperate."

"Abigail works so hard with all the kids and classes and the shul," Sarah offered. "Every marriage, maybe every relationship, has its ups and downs..."

"I knew you'd understand," Rabbi Dreidel interjected, sounding relieved. "Perhaps, another time, you can give me advice, from a beautiful woman's viewpoint, about what's stimulating, about what I can do to get my wife more excited."

"I'm an accountant, not a sex therapist," blurted Sarah. "Have you talked to a therapist?"

"Yes, I talked online to someone who works with TUCAS rabbis. It was no use," he said.

After a minute of stunned silence from Sarah, the rabbi asked, "Are you still there? Sarah?"

"Uh, yes, I'm still here. But I have to go," Sarah said. "Elmer and the kids are shouting to me from the other room," she said, making up an excuse. "Goodbye."

When she abruptly ended the phone call, Rabbi Dreidel realized that he had surprised her. She seemed taken aback, but he felt great.

She just needs time to think about things, he said to himself.

Leaning back in his office chair, he fantasized about Sarah. He felt his own sexuality, spirituality, intellect, and knowledge pulsing through his veins. He could meet Sarah in his office with the shades pulled down. She would show him everything he yearned to experience. Maybe he would send her a few texts asking a few more questions about how to excite a woman. He thought about doing her with her skirt hiked up and her bra pulled down. He thought about what oral sex might feel like.

Back at her house, Sarah sat staring at her turned-off cell phone trying to figure out what had happened. She found Elmer in the den watching a football game.

"What's wrong?" he asked as soon as he saw the shock on Sarah's face and tears in the corners of her eyes. He clicked off the game.

She went over the entire phone call.

"He seemed like a confused, teenage boy," Sarah said, sitting next to Elmer on the couch. "It's crazy!"

After thinking for a minute or two, Elmer said, "We have to meet with him."

"God, no!" she replied.

But as she and her husband spoke more about the bizarre phone call and how different it was from the rabbi's usual behavior, she agreed to go with Elmer to confront him.

Elmer was firm, upset, and clear when they met with the rabbi in his cluttered office. He told the rabbi that his telephone conversations were not acceptable behavior. The rabbi was entirely apologetic. He teared up. He made a mistake. He said he had a schoolboy crush on Sarah that was wrong. He crossed a line. He asked that they please accept his apology.

"Please," he begged, "don't tell Abigail anything about this. It would kill her."

He was sorry for making Sarah uncomfortable, and he wouldn't repeat what he did. He knew it was wrong, and he obviously misunderstood the phone conversation. He thought she wanted to help him. Would they please believe that his intentions were good?

Sarah sat uncomfortably throughout the meeting. She was so eternally grateful that Elmer took the lead. Elmer felt the apology was sincere. Elmer felt that he had stood up for his wife and resolved the situation, at least for the time being. He and Sarah would take a break from Rabbi Dreidel and reassess their participation in the Jewish Center of Destiny County.

THE LESBIAN
MOTHER

Sarah's son wasn't the only youngster studying with Rabbi Dreidel. Selma Braun's granddaughter, Nancy, was another. Mrs. Braun was a widow, living on a modest, union pension and social security, but she always donated a little something to Rabbi Dreidel whenever she could. The rabbi reminded her of her grandparents, who were much more observant than her parents.

Her grandparents died when she was little, but she had memories of her grandfather's beard, which looked like a witch's Halloween broom, much like the rabbi's. Her parents didn't speak Yiddish, but her grandparents did, so her heart melted a little whenever Rabbi Dreidel spoke a bit of Yiddish. She didn't practice Judaism much, but, from afar, she loved rabbis, Jewish people, and Israel. While Mrs. Braun remained unaffiliated with a synagogue for years, her Jewish heritage was immensely important to her. Most of all, she wanted her only grandchild, Nancy, to have a bat mitzvah.

Nancy lived in Destiny County with her mother—Mrs. Braun's daughter—Dorothy, who had a female partner. Dorothy was always a little chubby, and, in her mother's view, underperformed her intellectual capacity. She had been an average student, but Mrs. Braun thought she was very smart and never made the most of herself because of a poor self-concept. She was never one of the popular girls in school. She was the shy type who hung back for fear of embarrassing herself. Maybe being on the social outs, thought Mrs. Braun, snowballed into a bit of a depression for her daughter, deflating her prospects in life.

Dorothy's ex-husband was a real dud and a good-for-nothing, a *schlemiel* who didn't pay child support and didn't visit Nancy. He could go to hell; what a *schmuck*.

In contrast, Dorothy's girlfriend was a real partner and a wonderful person. She got along great with Dorothy—Nancy liked her and vice versa. *Well*, thought Mrs. Braun, *you have to go along with the times.* They had a stable relationship, *thank God.* Mrs. Braun originally thought they were just friends, but it made sense when they came out. Mrs. Braun felt glad when Dorothy's girlfriend moved in with her. *Finally,* she thought, *here is a person who fully appreciates my Dorothy.*

The couple was not religious and didn't attend shul at all, but Dorothy acceded to her mother's request to bring Nancy to Rabbi Dreidel's shul for Sunday school and Bat Mitzvah lessons. Mrs. Braun was delighted. She told Dorothy that she would pay for the Hebrew lessons and the bat mitzvah.

To mollify her daughter's concerns about bringing her daughter to an orthodox synagogue when the mother was gay, Mrs. Braun promised to have a forthright discussion with Rabbi Dreidel about her daughter's sexual orientation and partner. She would make sure it wasn't a problem for her partner to attend Nancy's bat mitzvah.

The conversation indeed occurred, although awkwardly. Mrs. Braun just blurted out that her daughter was gay and that her daughter's partner, at times, might drop off and pick up Nancy at the synagogue.

Rabbi Dreidel thanked Mrs. Braun for the information and told her that he already had intimated as much. He first met Dorothy when she was visiting Mrs. Braun, and he had dropped off a box of Matzah for Passover. The rabbi told her that his focus was on Nancy, helping her learn the Torah in-depth, conveying a love of Judaism, and fulfilling the requirements of a bat mitzvah. Rabbi Dreidel made clear that he could not endorse certain behaviors, but that he welcomed all Jewish people to the synagogue, including Mrs. Braun's daughter. Dorothy's partner was also free to attend the bat mitzvah and other services.

A famous passage in Leviticus, read on each Yom Kippur, the all-important Day of Atonement, condemns homosexual sex as an "abomination." But it doesn't say anything about lesbianism. Orthodoxy generally frowns on lesbianism as an outgrowth of decadent behavior in Godless societies, like the idol-worshipping Romans. However, in the grand tradition of the great Talmudic Rabbis, who knew how to split hairs better than corporate tax attorneys, today's orthodox rabbis draw distinctions between Jews with "proclivities" and Jews who commit certain acts. They say that no one should be stigmatized, and a homosexual man should not be cast out, as long as he doesn't advertise a penchant for anal or other forms of same-sex practices.

In fact, according to this view, endorsed by many orthodox rabbis, a homosexual man may serve as a full member in good standing of an orthodox congregation. This includes being counted as one of ten men needed for a "*minyan*," a quorum, during services, giving the Priestly Blessing on certain holidays, serving as a witness in the Beis Din, the religious court, and even coming up on the *bima* for a blessing during the Torah reading on the Sabbath. These holdings, however, do not apply to lesbian women, who are disqualified from all of these activities, not on the basis of their sexual *orientation*, but due to their gender.

Confusing? I'll tell you confusing. Confusion is when the rabbi, who genuinely cares about the bat mitzvah girl learning Judaism, forgets his marital obligations and starts texting salty messages of a heterosexual nature to the girl's lesbian mother. Now, that's confusing!

That was certainly the case for Dorothy. She didn't believe in organized religion, and she had lost interest in heterosexuality during her failed marriage to a guy who turned out to be a bona fide louse. Despite the confusion, Dorothy decided that she didn't want to make waves, so she didn't tell her mother about the rabbi's weird text messages.

His initial texts to Dorothy were strikingly similar to those he wrote to Sarah, the lady accountant and the mom of Nancy's classmate. At first, Rabbi Dreidel texted about lessons and study times, but soon he began discussing matters best left for sex therapists and psychologists.

Initially, Dorothy was drawn into the text messages. She thought that, perhaps, her same-sex orientation might make the rabbi think she could be more objective about his questions involving the female anatomy and female sexuality. Maybe she was someone safe for him to talk to. In other words, Dorothy did not immediately interpret any of the spicy things she read on her phone as indicating a sexual interest in her. She gave the rabbi the benefit of the doubt.

This feeling was photo-bombed to smithereens when Rabbi Dreidel sent her a selfie of himself lying on a bed with the top buttons of his shirt undone.

Whoa! Dorothy's mind exploded, *what's going on here?* The meaning of this text message, with the caption, "thinking of you," could not be misinterpreted.

Dorothy didn't know what to do. She didn't know what to think. This was an "OMG!" moment. Did her lesbianism make the rabbi think she was promiscuous? Had she dressed provocatively, in some way, or said something inappropriate in response to his text messages about sexually arousing his wife? Panic flooded Dorothy.

She wasn't going to share this message or the other texts with her mother. The bat mitzvah was coming up soon, and the invitations were already mailed out. Nancy had worked too hard for mom to blow the whole thing up. She was Dorothy's first consideration. She didn't want to tell her partner about it, either. If she told her, she would demand to see the picture the rabbi texted. She would immediately explode if she saw it, and they would argue about what to do about it. She knew her partner's strong views about sexual harassment. Her partner wasn't one to ignore bad behavior. She would demand to see all the text messages. She would demand an immediate apology from the rabbi, and who knows what else. She might want to hire an attorney. It could lead to canceling the bat mitzvah.

First things first. Dorothy deleted the text message and photo and then deleted all of the rabbi's other texts about female anatomy and sexuality. She then texted Rabbi Dreidel, telling him to stop texting her. That text backfired. It led to rapid-fire texts from Rabbi Dreidel asking her, "What's wrong, can you call me, are you mad at me and why don't you text back?"

All in all, there were twenty text messages in less than five minutes. Another thirty texts followed over the course of the next two days.

Dorothy decided she simply wouldn't text any further with Rabbi Dreidel. She would muscle through the final arrangements and study sessions for her daughter's bat mitzvah. She would make sure her partner or Nancy was with her whenever she might be in the same room as Rabbi Dreidel. When it was time to pick Nancy up from bat mitzvah classes, she would text her daughter to wait outside.

Rabbi Dreidel couldn't hurt her over the phone, thought Dorothy. The rabbi hadn't touched her, and he wasn't going to, especially with her guard up. The whole idea of the rabbi having sex with her was so absurd! All that had happened, she rationalized, was an exchange of inappropriate words. The rabbi turned out to be just another yucky, sick, horny guy who picked on her the way other loser guys had picked on her.

They say, she thought to herself, *if you can't stand the heat, stay out of the kitchen.*

She was going to stay out of the kitchen and any other room with Rabbi Dreidel unless the room had at least one other person in it. She was not religious, but she said to herself, "*Thank God,* this will all be over soon. *Please God,*" she prayed, "save me from more text messages." She then added, "*Amen!*"

THE HOT
COOKIE

So, dear reader, Rabbi Mishegas Dreidel went off the rails with his telephoning and texting, *nu*? Maybe you are thinking he is obviously going a little (or a lot) "mental." But so far, no harm, no foul, right? No big deal, right?

Wrong! Once Rabbi Mishegas Dreidel cracked open the door to thinking that he could seek a solution by "talking" to other women about his "intimacy issues," he didn't just peek into the room. Texting and talking weren't enough. He swung the door open wider. He stuck one foot in and then the other. What about some touching, too? Some hugging? A little kiss?

Now, let's consider that a Reformed rabbi can hug all the members of the congregation with all kinds of hugs. A Reformed rabbi may engage in sympathy hugs, friend hugs, how-good-it-is-to-see-you hugs, a pat on the back hug, the one-armed hug, the keep some distance and reach over hug, a long hug, a strong hug, and you-name-it hugs—all kosher hugs! Kosher hugs for the Reformed rabbi evoke friendliness, love, inclusiveness, and kindness. When it comes to hugs for the Reformed rabbi, an appropriate hug shows warmth and spirituality. In the midst of the hug with a Reformed rabbi, neither the clerical hugger nor the lay "huggee" is thinking about sexy parts of the body.

The ultra-orthodox rabbi, in sharp contrast, is strictly limited in whom he can touch of the opposite sex. He can touch his spouse, parents, sisters, daughters, and granddaughters, but he is strictly prohibited from touching any other woman who is past the age of menstruation (God forbid)! Now, if it's okay for the Reformed rabbi to hug and touch and shake hands with everybody, what gets the orthodox rabbi in such piping hot water for the same behavior?

Well, let's take the example of a handshake. What possibly could go wrong with a handshake, you ask? Ah, a handshake held a little too long, or maybe with a certain accompanying glance, may become an actual encounter with affection and sexuality, at least, according to the horny old rabbis of yesteryear who came up with the rules. And remember, they made the rules for sexually repressed, misogynistic men who already had created rules for women to cover their hair, legs, and arms.

Maybe they knew that rabbis, who spent so much of their time studying creation, including the miracle of the "birds and the bees," and the sometimes lusty stories of the Torah, might feel their own instruments of human procreation stirring or (God forbid) saluting. *Oy vey*, the touch of a hand might make the blood boil! Much better to tamp down those feelings by prohibiting touch by persons who should not touch and by putting the women in wigs and covering up their beautiful bodily parts. In other words, the learned, holy rabbis decided to legislate female modesty. After all, why should people who should not be touching, touch each other? That might lead to more touching (God forbid)!

Despite conforming to these rules and their underlying rationalizations for four decades of his life, Rabbi Mishegas Dreidel did a little touching. He wasn't supposed to. *Nu?* It happened. He succumbed to the beauty of a young woman. He hugged her. He smelled her uncovered hair. Ooh! What a smell! He kissed the side of her face (so soft!) and was going for a kiss on her neck, or maybe even the lips, when she escaped from his embrace. This was more than a handshake. This was more than a hug. It wasn't a crime, but it broke the rules shockingly enough that the beautiful young woman reported the incident to her mother.

The mother, Peggy Cohen, was a financially struggling motivational speaker, life coach, and published author. She was a divorcee who went back to school, got her master's degree in psychology, and created her own career. She adored her daughter, Miriam, a sensitive and introspective college student. They were best friends in many ways, having moved far away from Peggy's husband, Miriam's dad, when Miriam was in elementary school.

Peggy learned to be assertive, and some might say, even a little pushy, albeit with charm, in order to eke out a living as a speaker, life coach, and counselor. She discovered her passion, which was empowering other women in business and corporate settings. Her book, *Stand Out! How Women Lead as Leaders*, did not earn her the national fame and fortune that she hoped for, but it was well-reviewed, feathering her resume for individual and corporate clients. Sexual harassment, diversity training, and assertiveness training were prime subjects that she included in her talks and workshops. She also counseled women individually about how to achieve their goals with confidence and assertiveness.

Peggy attended synagogue several times a year, doing her best to find somewhere to go for the High Holidays—Rosh Hashanah and Yom Kippur. She found Rabbi Dreidel that way; she was another unaffiliated Jew who needed a synagogue to sporadically attend and to *schlep* her daughter to.

Why do many non-observant Jews suddenly feel a compulsion to attend services with their children on the High Holy Days? Why do they suddenly flock to synagogue two or three times a year? Do they go out of guilt, or do they feel an obligation toward their children? For Peggy, she sincerely wanted a spiritual connection on the High Holy Days.

The Jewish Center of Destiny County and Rabbi Dreidel fit the bill. The rabbi welcomed her without any mention of upfront payments or financial commitments. She contributed a little something by check annually. Peggy, as a motivational speaker, also felt a kindred spirit with Rabbi Dreidel. She identified with his struggle to pay the bills of the synagogue, his public speaking, even when his sermons were poorly attended, and his consistent, ongoing outreach. She also saw him as a possible referral source for clients, and Peggy was not shy about promoting herself and singing her own praises to the rabbi. But most of all, she saw Rabbi Dreidel as a holy rabbi, a spiritual being, whose sincere mission, above and beyond all else, was spreading Torah and Judaism.

When Rabbi Dreidel traveled to New York to attend an annual convention of rabbis of his TUCAS sect, Peggy asked him if he could possibly find the time to visit her brother in the hospital. He was getting intensive treatment for stomach cancer. Peggy's daughter, Miriam, was attending college in New York and frequently visited her uncle. But the uncle didn't have a rabbi, and it would make Peggy feel better if Rabbi Dreidel met and prayed with him.

The rabbi said he would make a point of it and took all the details, including the hospital information and Miriam's cell number. He also said he would regularly include her brother's name during the prayer for health and healing during the Holy Shabbos. Visiting the sick fell right smack in the rabbi's wheelhouse as a *mitzvah*, good deeds done from a religious duty.

Rabbi Dreidel wandered off from his TUCAS convention in short order to visit Peggy's brother. As he was leaving, he crossed paths with Peggy's daughter, Miriam, who had just arrived to visit her uncle. He joyfully greeted her with a big hug.

"Miriam, I just saw your uncle. How are you?"

She was an attractive young woman. The hug went on a little too long. The rabbi breathed the shampoo scent of Miriam's hair and kissed Miriam on the side of her face before loosening his embrace.

Miriam automatically returned the hug before she had time to think how odd it was. But during the hug, it started to feel weird. She asked herself whether Rabbi Dreidel was supposed to hug anyone. The hug itself was too close, lasted too long, and conveyed an undeserved emotion. She didn't really know the rabbi very well. He was her mother's "friend." They didn't have an independent relationship. When she tried to leave the hug, the rabbi kissed her on her face. This was clearly over the line. She felt flushed.

Miriam, although flustered, was also a quick thinker. "Rabbi, thank you for visiting," she said, hurriedly trying to move on. "I'll tell my mom you came."

"Listen," said Rabbi Dreidel, "let me make sure I've got the right phone number for you from your mom."

By this time, Miriam mentally processed that an ultra-orthodox rabbi like Rabbi Dreidel wasn't supposed to hug women, let alone kiss them. The way he hugged her felt so weird. She could not believe that he had just kissed her. The weirdness fully sank in.

Sensing her discomfort, Rabbi Dreidel said, "Listen, I'd like to talk to you. Perhaps we could go for coffee after your visit? I can wait right here."

"No, I won't have time, sorry," replied Miriam, nervously looking down, "I am running late to class already. Goodbye."

She turned and strode off in the direction of her uncle's room.

"That's okay," the rabbi called after her, "I'll phone you later."

As soon as Miriam visited her uncle and left the hospital, she called her mom.

"He did what?" Peggy exclaimed. She was shocked. "Tell me again how it happened." Miriam uncomfortably repeated what had happened.

"I am going to call him," Peggy said.

"Mom, don't. Really. I'm fine. Nothing happened."

"Something happened. He hugged and kissed you! Okay, I am going to think about it and call you later."

Peggy obsessed about it for two days and two sleepless nights. In the meantime, Rabbi Dreidel burned up Miriam's cell number, calling and texting her repeatedly, asking to get together for coffee. Miriam didn't return the rabbi's texts or calls. She didn't want to tell her mom what he was doing, but she finally let her know.

That pushed Peggy over the edge. She called Rabbi Dreidel and demanded, "Why are you hugging and texting my daughter?"

He didn't deny what happened. Instead, he immediately apologized. He explained that he had some issues that he was working on and begged for Peggy's understanding. This was the rabbi's explanation to Peggy:

"I must have been affected by visiting your brother in his hospital bed. I felt highly emotional and hugged Miriam without thinking. I hope she will forgive me. I hope you will forgive me. I know I can tell you this, because we have always had a special rapport.

"Maybe you have experience or at least an understanding of this kind of thing in your job as a life coach. I am having some difficult intimacy issues in my marriage, and I have been very lonely.

"Miriam is so nice and innocent that I just hugged her without thinking. This doesn't excuse my behavior, but I hope you will keep it between us. I have been calling Miriam," he lied, "because I wanted to apologize."

Peggy's training and work as a life coach gave her insight into the world of apologies and incidents of sexual harassment. To Peggy, an apology, first and foremost, had to be utterly sincere. Rabbi Dreidel sounded sincere, although Peggy wondered if the rabbi's ongoing calling and texting to Miriam were for an apology or because he wanted sex with her.

His explanation for the ongoing texting didn't feel right in Peggy's *kishkas*. He just confessed that what he did was wrong. He hugged and kissed, although he didn't mention the kissing part. A hug and a kiss did not rise to the level of a sexual assault, not exactly. But it was off-the-charts behavior for an ultra-orthodox rabbi. The rabbi just admitted that he had some sort of psychological issue; that admission was in his favor and added a high degree of contrition to the apology. Most importantly, it seemed certain that the behavior was not going to be repeated.

Maybe, thought Peggy, giving Rabbi Dreidel the benefit of the doubt was the right thing to do. Maybe he had a weak moment and just lost his head. Miriam was a beautiful, Jewish girl.

"Rabbi, I don't want you to call or text Miriam anymore."

"I won't, not a problem. The TUCAS convention ends tomorrow, and I fly back. But, please, can you tell her for me that I apologize? I hope she won't hold it against me. I hope you will also give me a break and keep this between ourselves."

"Well, what is your problem?"

"Can I confide in you, completely confidentially? You can't discuss what I am going to say with anyone. Can you promise me that? Maybe you can help me understand some things."

"I am listening," responded Peggy, softening her tone and very curious.

"In my marriage, and this is hard to talk about, my needs are not being met. I am starved for physical intimacy, but at the same time, I am having problems with arousal.

"There are things I want to do of an intimate nature that my wife refuses to try. She won't try even once. She acts horrified when I even try to talk about it. I don't know what to do, physically, to interest my wife. She lays there all covered up and like a cold piece of herring. I don't get excited. I think I need a woman's advice."

"You have nine kids. I don't think you need my advice," replied Peggy.

"That's not the point," said the rabbi, "I am still young and vital, with more drive than ever."

"This is not my area of expertise, but I think a sex therapist or psychologist might be worth pursuing."

Rabbi Dreidel clicked his tongue. "You see, that's the problem. In my circles, as a TUCAS rabbi, seeing a sex therapist isn't done, unless it's a childless marriage. I've worked with an online psychologist who works with TUCAS, but it hasn't helped.

"I thought that just talking to a special woman, like you, about my intimacy questions and issues, confidentially of course, would help. You are an attractive woman who is more modern and knows about these things."

"Rabbi, let me stop you right there," replied Peggy. Alarm bells went off for Peggy with the word, "attractive."

"This is clearly not my area. I am not the right person to help you. If you want, I can give you some names of couples counselors or psychologists in the area. There are some Jewish ones who are pretty good."

The discussion went on for another hour. Rabbi Mishegas pressed to confide his "intimacy issues" with Peggy, but her internal gauge convinced her that Rabbi Mishegas had a screw loose, and she was better off deflecting and rejecting his entreaties. Privately, she was up in the air as to whether she and Miriam would ever again attend the Jewish Center of Destiny County. For sure, she thought, I am going to take a time-out from Rabbi Mishegas Dreidel.

TEXTING

Rabbi Mishegas Dreidel and his wife, Abigail, stepped out of their house to retrieve their family's box of kosher meat. It was delivered to their driveway along with those for other members of the community.

Who pulled up as the rabbi and his wife were *schlepping* their boxes into the house? None other than Lacey Johnson, the Navy wife, with whom Rabbi Dreidel previously had talked on the phone.

Lacey wore a stylish, low-cut, sleeveless blouse. She liked to look fashionable. She was used to boys and men staring at her breasts, no matter what clothes she wore. The cleavage she showed wasn't even close to what she revealed when she wore bikini tank tops as a barista.

In other words, she considered her manner of dress that day attractive, but not overly provocative. She dressed how she wanted. The way she dressed expressed a certain freedom. That particular day she hadn't dressed with any specific thought in mind. She hadn't expected to meet an ultra-orthodox rabbi and his wife. She just came to pick up her kosher meat. Was this a chance encounter, or had the stars aligned?

Rabbi Dreidel acted as friendly as possible with every new Jewish man or woman he met. Greeting, welcoming, smiling, and making small talk comprised his DNA as a rabbi whose mission depended on outreach. He wanted to bring Judaism to every encounter. Rabbi Dreidel was not going to avoid Lacey because she was good-looking. However, he found himself instantly smitten. He strained his eyes to look away from her chest area as he introduced himself and Abigail.

"Wasn't it easy to order your kosher meat and find our house?" Rabbi Dreidel schmoozed, noticing her long red hair, clear skin, pretty face, big eyes, and luscious lips.

"Yes, it was," smiled Lacey. As she bent down to pick up her box, her breasts were more exposed. Rabbi Dreidel caught himself trying to look away but also straining to see as much as possible. His self-consciousness was compounded because his wife was standing there.

Lacey asked if the rabbi's congregation included other young families like hers. She said it was hard being Jewish in the military, especially when there were no other Jews at the base with whom to socialize who were around the same age. The rabbi and Abigail told her that they knew one young couple who recently had moved to the area and also were looking for friends their age. The conversation only lasted a few minutes.

Later that day, alone in his office, as he opened his mail and prepared a bank deposit of contributions, the rabbi couldn't stop thinking about those breasts. His libido prompted him to search her name on social media. He pretended that he needed to screen Lacey before calling the other young couple to share her contact information.

Bingo. Lacey had numerous pictures and posts on Facebook and Instagram.

He found pictures of Lacey in other low-cut clothing and compulsively stared at her breasts. His mouse let him zoom in. He shamefully admired her trim figure. In one picture, she wore a bikini at the beach. He loved her legs! He knew consciously, as he clicked around, that his behavior was pitiful, atrocious, awful, and sinful. This knowledge reverberated deep in his soul. He hated what he was doing, but Rabbi Dreidel simply couldn't help himself. The sin was right there, unavoidable and incontrovertible. He promised himself that he would double the intensity of his prayers during *Mincha*, the daily afternoon prayers, to calm his disturbed psyche.

Lacey's social media posts included a blog about being a Navy wife who met her husband when she worked at the *Bikini Cafe*. It explained that they got married in a week.

When he read the blog, Rabbi Dreidel felt even more feverish. He decided that Lacey Johnson, based on her skimpy, barista attire, must be a sexually free woman. That was his polite way of mentally labeling her as promiscuous—exactly the kind of person he needed to talk to about his "intimacy issues."

The rabbi told himself he was fighting his *yetzer hara*, his evil inclinations. He sought an understanding of female sexuality, he rationalized, not to honor his own sexual needs and urges, but to improve the quality of his relationship with Abigail.

He dwelled upon remembered passages of Kabbalah, the book of Jewish mysticism, which talks of sacred kissing before intercourse. Of course, the Kabbalah was referring to the great love between God and the Jewish people being aroused by prayer, not sexual arousal between a husband and wife. But Rabbi Dreidel felt his physicality like a dog in heat. His mind engaged in mental gymnastics to allow his forbidden thoughts while feeling disgusted about himself.

He scrolled his smartphone to Lacey's phone number. He texted her an emoji of a man with a beard and a yarmulke, saying, "Nice to meet you!"

Immediately, Lacey texted back a headshot of herself smiling and wearing a Navy baseball cap with the message, "You rang?"

Within days, Rabbi Dreidel and Lacey were regularly texting and talking to each other on the phone. Lacey wanted to know what it would take for her husband to convert to Judaism. She told Rabbi Dreidel that Rabbi Hazzarai, the Navy rabbi at the base, didn't seem too keen on the idea of her husband converting. She complained that Rabbi Hazzarai didn't even want to discuss it. Unknown to Lacey, Rabbi Hazzarai was following the Jewish custom of rejecting a potential convert three times to test the sincerity of the interest in conversion.

Rabbi Dreidel, in contrast to his colleague, was only too happy to respond to Lacey's questions. He freely discussed the elements of conversion, including a commitment to follow all the commandments, immersion in a *mikvah*, a ritual bath, and the importance of circumcision. As it turned out, Lacey's husband had never been circumcised, an important requirement.

The rabbi also gave Lacey contact information for the other young Jewish family. He confirmed they would be happy to meet and looked forward to her call. Rabbi Dreidel explained that the husband and wife had gone through a lengthy conversion. He told Lacey that this was an example of a couple who made a commitment to live a completely kosher, Jewish life.

The subject of her husband's possible conversion opened the door to discussing Lacey's marriage and her desire for a greater spiritual connection with her husband. This was her larger goal. She felt that the way she met her husband and got married so quickly emphasized their physical love. She wanted a more spiritual and deeper connection. "Do you know what I mean?" Lacey asked the rabbi.

Boy, he sure did!

"It's so amazing we met," the rabbi told her enthusiastically. "I want, more than anything, exactly what you want. I am so happy to talk to you about this."

"Really?" asked Lacey.

"I am also striving to achieve greater intimacy in my marriage. I want to improve an unexplored physical compatibility to complement our spiritual relationship."

"What do you mean, exactly?" asked Lacey.

"Perhaps," he proposed, "I can counsel you from a Jewish perspective on spiritual intimacy, and you could confidentially provide me advice on physical intimacy from a woman's point of view?"

"Of course," Lacey readily agreed.

Thus began a telephone relationship that included phone calls, voice mails, texting, and emails. Rabbi Dreidel, again and again, went over the line in the same manner he had with Dorothy and Sarah. What was said exactly? Things got "X" rated. The bottom line is that the clumsy attempts by the beloved rabbi to achieve his "intimacy" goals were recorded on someone else's cell phone.

The blessed rabbi demonstrated an almost pornographic curiosity about the female anatomy. What he wanted to know, more than anything else, were the mechanics of female genitalia and arousal. Should we fault him? He had lived in yeshiva dormitories from the age of thirteen until he was married. Even before that, from the age of three, Rabbi Dreidel attended *Cheder*, a religious school focused on teaching Torah and Hebrew, attended only by other boys. All of the emphasis in his elementary school was on religious study, with only a rudimentary study of secular subjects. There was a distinct lack of sex education. His family never talked about sex openly.

This rigid gender divide extended to the synagogue, where segregated seating for the opposite sexes was strictly enforced. Rabbi

Dreidel's dating experience was also limited, allowing for only a few supervised meetings with his potential wife before their wedding.

To be clear, Rabbi Dreidel was not a raving sex addict. He simply lived a life of sexual deprivation and ignorance that was drowning him, choking him, and making him crazy. A drowning and choking man is going to gasp desperately for air and flail for anything he can grab.

The blessed rabbi wanted Lacey to tell him how he could induce his wife to masturbate him because that would turn him on. To Rabbi Dreidel, masturbation was a religiously forbidden practice that was equated with murder if *he* did it, but not if his wife did it. The lack of an outlet for his overwhelming, sexual urges created feelings of guilt, frustration, and worthlessness.

Abigail was not averse to sex, although she felt some shame about her physical body and sexual responses. Who wouldn't, when raised in a culture that required her to cover her arms, her legs, and wear wigs to cover her hair? She never questioned the rules. She rationalized that this is how it was and how it was meant to be by the Holy One, blessed be He. Men just wanted sex more, so it was wise for women to cover up.

At this point in her life, with nine kids running around, and all her other responsibilities, when it came to the bedroom, Abigail would prefer to be left alone. She certainly was not going to try any of the things Rabbi Dreidel suggested. If he wanted to have sex, he could do it at the appointed times, as they always had. They were not going to experiment. She didn't want to reject him, but what she really wanted was a good night's sleep.

Rabbi Dreidel felt he could not talk about his "issues" with Abigail, but he could discuss all matters of female sexuality with Lacey. All of his thoughts found their way, in exquisite detail, to Lacey's cell phone through his emails and text messages. What Rabbi Dreidel was unable to say on the phone, due to feelings of shame and embarrassment, he was able to text and email.

Lacey, in a decision she later regretted, tried to help Rabbi Dreidel, but she soon realized he had crossed a line. She tried several serious conversations, falling back on her training and experience as a lay counselor on the Navy base.

"Rabbi," she exhorted, "I think you need to get professional help."

"But you are helping me, and I you," he pleaded to Lacey.

She explicitly told him that he had gone too far. He disagreed. He pleaded. He cajoled. She deflected. The conversations went down a rabbit hole.

Lacey started to roll her eyes at messages that continued to light up her cell phone. She was not going to text about female masturbation and oral sex. She texted back, "TMI," and it was clearly too much information, but that did not stop the tone and tenor of the messages; in fact, it did the opposite. The rabbi's messages increased, with him begging for her help and understanding.

He claimed the best intentions.

"Don't you understand that I am melding the spiritual with the physical?" he texted.

"This would fulfill the *mitzvah* of pleasing my wife in the bedroom," he emailed.

Lacey started to shudder at each new message.

She wrote, "PLEASE STOP TEXTING ME!"

He stopped for a while, but then he started emailing that they should meet to discuss things.

"Please," he wrote, "you are the only one I can talk to. We have a special affinity."

Then he texted, "We agreed to help each other confidentially."

Lacey emailed, Lacey texted, and Lacey left a voicemail. She made her position abundantly clear, repeating, "PLEASE STOP EMAILING ME. PLEASE DON'T CALL ME. PLEASE STOP TEXTING ME."

Rabbi Dreidel couldn't stop, but she could. She would not respond any longer. She would ask Rabbi Hazzarai, who was also a TUCAS rabbi, what to do. If she confided in him, she thought, he would get the message to Rabbi Dreidel to cut it out.

FRUM

Hezekiah Miller and his wife, Rachel, didn't start out Jewish. They converted after growing up as evangelical Christians. They were raised in a rural area outside Salem, Oregon. Hezekiah's Christian fundamentalism led him to explore Judaism. Before they were Hezekiah and Rachel, they were Buddy and Faith. Buddy worked construction. Faith did not work outside the home. Instead, she gave birth to three sons in short order: Zachariah, Nathaniel, and Caleb.

The couple decided that secular school was too infused with corrupt ideas; they would homeschool their children. As Buddy worked full-time, and his time off work was devoted to Christianity, this task fell to Faith. Unfortunately for the kids, Faith lacked the discipline and creativity to teach effectively. She followed their Christian homeschool teacher's manual without any improvisation, variation, or pizazz. The children were bored. They trailed their peers.

Buddy put himself in charge of the boys' religious education, and he told Faith that their children's solid, spiritual foundation was their priority. As long as the boys possessed strong Christian values, their academics would come along in due time—if it were meant to be, by their Lord and Savior, ~~Jesus Christ~~.

Buddy wasn't just religious, his religiosity drove him. He attended church and bible study like clockwork, but that wasn't enough. He also studied the gospels in his spare time, and he even wrote a Christian-themed science fiction book, *The Ghost Christ*. It was a fantasy adventure in which the main character is transported from a sleepy rural town in America into space. There, he learns to battle demons from other dimensions while relying on his faith in ~~Jesus~~. Buddy felt on-guard against evil in his everyday life, just like his main character.

The exhilaration of seeing his book in print, especially as he identified with his own protagonist, soon died down. Initially, he felt like a hero—he, Buddy, had written a Christian book! He magically imagined a laudatory career as a Christian writer spreading the Word of Christ to rural communities.

However, after a year of disappointing online sales and hardly any sales in Christian bookstores, Buddy felt rejected as an author and as a Christian. He questioned the meaning of his life. His sense of religious importance still resided within him, but it was not as widely recognized by others as he wanted. He was searching for something more. His work in construction paid the bills, barely, for his young family. He knew God put him on earth for a greater purpose. He prayed to live righteously so that God's purpose would manifest itself to him.

Buddy's best friend in their bible study group shared his affinity for the Old Testament and studying the roots of their religion. He suggested that they drive together to Salem to attend a real Jewish synagogue led by a young, orthodox rabbi named Moishe Cohnmen.

Rabbi Cohnmen came from the same TUCAS organization as Rabbi Dreidel and Rabbi Hazzarai. He was accustomed to the occasional born-again Christian attending his synagogue.

Buddy was blown away by the rabbi's sermon, which discussed that week's Torah portion, *Pinchas*. In the first part of the story, Pinchas kills a couple when he sees them publicly fornicating, a brazen sin. For his trouble, Pinchas gets elevated to the priesthood. For good measure, Pinchas's righteous action also ends a plague.

The rabbi explained in his sermon that a true zealot is an utterly selfless individual who is only passionately concerned about what God wants and not his own feelings or prejudices. Buddy heard that spiel like a thunderbolt from heaven. He felt that Rabbi Cohnmen was a messenger from God who called directly to him. Buddy pictured himself as a modern-day Pinchas. Then and there, he decided to become a Jew.

Buddy's newfound enthusiasm for Judaism scared his wife Faith, but she knew Buddy was a righteous man and husband. He always treated her with love and respect. Just as she followed the Christian teacher's homeschooling manual to the letter, she followed the new dictates of her husband. She saw how important it was for Buddy. She saw how excited he was to finally find his calling.

Before you knew it, Buddy and Faith asked their family and friends to call them Hezekiah and Rachel, and they were, to the best of their knowledge, the only Jews (even though they weren't officially converted yet) in their rural area. All their spare money went to the purchase of Jewish things, including all the Jewish prayer books and bibles they could afford.

Hezekiah prayed daily with a Tallit, a Jewish prayer shawl, and he wrapped himself in *tefillin* every day, recited prayers upon awakening, prayed three times a day, and prayed again upon going to bed. He wore a *tallit katan*, a smaller prayer shawl with specially twined and knotted fringes, as an undergarment. Hezekiah also wore a yarmulke all the time.

On Shabbos, he dressed like an ultra-orthodox rabbi. He sported a large-brimmed black hat and white shirt and tie. He also wore a long, black jacket that came down to his knees and was tied in front with a black sash. Rachel wore a scarf to cover her hair, long-sleeved blouses, and skirts down to her ankles. They ate kosher; they attended services and went to shul every Jewish holiday. They were more observant, and to their own observations, much more Jewish than most Jews!

It wasn't easy for their parents and immediate family members to accept the changes in their names, holiday celebrations, and practices. At first, their families thought they were becoming Jews for ~~Jesus~~ Hezekiah and Rachel had been the most Christian of all the relatives of their respective families. Now, they no longer recognized ~~Jesus~~ as their Lord and Savior. That rubbed some of their parents and siblings the wrong way.

After close to two years of study and Jewish observance, Rabbi Cohnman sponsored the couple to appear before the Beis Din, a religious court in San Francisco that consisted of three orthodox rabbis. The fix was in. Rabbi Cohnman had already told the other rabbis how hard and long Hezekiah and Rachel had worked to reach this moment and about all the sacrifices they had made. They were serious and sincere.

After they answered the questions from the panel of rabbis, Hezekiah and Rachel got the good news—they were Jews! The Beis Din officially certified their conversions with an ultra-orthodox stamp of approval.

After this incredible achievement, instead of taking it a little easier in their religious observance, the couple became *frum*—religious Jews who exceed the requirements of strict Jewish laws and

UNLIKELY STORY CONVERSION HAS
TOO MANY WRONG DETAILS

customs. Hezekiah was inspired to devote himself to even more study of Torah, prayers, and observance of the mitzvahs. He even walked more upright at shul and around his coworkers. He was proud to be frum. He loved posting Jewish messages on social media. He found kindred spirits there, especially when it came to defending Israel and condemning Israel's foes.

Not long after their conversions, Hezekiah and Rachel moved to the County of Destiny, where there were more Jews and where they thought it would be easier to be frum. Hezekiah found a job as a construction worker, and the family rented a home that allowed them to walk to the synagogue on Shabbos. Rabbi Dreidel counted on Hezekiah to attend every Friday night and Saturday morning service to make up the *minyan*, one of the ten men needed for important, communal prayers. Rabbi Dreidel introduced Lacey Johnson to Hezekiah and Rachel. They were around the same age. They started to socialize.

In the year Hezekiah spent attending Rabbi Dreidel's shul, he had two conflicts with the rabbi. Their first little argument concerned money, or perhaps, better stated, the lack of it.

Ever since Hezekiah moved his family to the County of Destiny, he was earning more, but, unfortunately, all of their living expenses, especially the rent on their house, was much higher. In short, they were poor. They lived as pious and devout Jews, but, as they say, you can't make a stew out of faith. Hezekiah put what he could, which wasn't much, in the synagogue's *pushke*, its community funds.

Rabbi Dreidel, who ran a Jewish Center that was always in debt, was frustrated that the family was consuming way more than it was contributing. The children all had voracious appetites. Rabbi Dreidel saw them stuff themselves each Kiddush luncheon and every holiday sit-down meal. The preschool had to double its snack budget once Hezekiah and his family moved to town.

Rabbi Dreidel tried to nudge Hezekiah to give a set monthly amount. This was impossible on the earnings of a construction worker whose hours were seasonal and cut to the bone in stormy weather.

Another time, the rabbi, with a holiday approaching, directly asked Hezekiah for a contribution to dent the budget for the observance, which included a nice meal for the congregation. Before you could say *Shema Yisrael*, the two got into an argument about what the Talmud said about tithing. Hezekiah thought he knew more than the rabbi; the rabbi thought Hezekiah questioned his religious authority. The upshot: both felt insulted, and the rabbi got only a token, and to his mind, meaningless, contribution.

The second conflict occurred on Simchas Torah, the joyous holiday that celebrates reaching the end of that year's cycle of Torah readings and beginning again. Rabbi Dreidel encouraged a great deal of drinking to lubricate the celebration, which focused on dancing with the Torah during the evening service. On Simchas Torah, the Torah is carried about the synagogue seven times, with all the men in the congregation given a chance to dance holding a Torah. To kick things off, Rabbi Dreidel downed an entire Kiddush cup of a kosher Canadian whiskey before the first prayer. He filled all the men's little plastic cups before and after each round of prayers and songs for each of the seven dances with the Torah. He kept filling his own cup, too. Before long, the rabbi was snockered.

In the middle of the service, Rabbi Dreidel started pushing away the panels of the *mechitza*, the dividers that separated where the men and women sat. It wasn't hard to do, because the *mechitza* sections, six-foot-high wooden panels with frosted glass on top, sat on rollers. Moving them simply required pushing the panels to the back of the synagogue. Rabbi Dreidel, in his drunken exuberance, wanted to include the women in the Simchas Torah dancing. Less intoxicated men followed his lead.

Hezekiah did not try to stop Rabbi Dreidel from pushing the *mechitza* away, but he felt deeply troubled. He was not only embarrassed by Rabbi Dreidel's intoxication, which he viewed as unseemly, but pushing away the *mechitza* violated Jewish law! He believed, unequivocally, that Jewish law required the *mechitza* to remain up, and that the women, who were not allowed to carry or dance with the Torah scrolls, should remain separated from the men during the dancing.

Between the drinking and the removal of the *mechitza*, Hezekiah felt Rabbi Dreidel had sullied the holy synagogue and brought sin to the congregation.

Hezekiah complained to Rachel about the rabbi. She repeated his comments to others, including Lacey, during one of their frequent, Sunday morning conversations at Rachel's kitchen table.

This was all Lacey needed to hear to finally unburden herself. This is how the conversation went:

Rachel: "Hezekiah feels Rabbi Dreidel got way too drunk on Simchas Torah."

Lacey: "What exactly did he do?"

Rachel: "He got falling down drunk and moved the dividers between the women's side and the men's side to the back of the room."

Lacey: "Why?"

Rachel: "He was drunk and wanted the women to dance."

Lacey: "Weird."

Rachel: "No one said anything. Everyone is so devoted to him. Everyone does whatever he wants."

Lacey: "Well, I'm not."

Rachel: "Not what?"

Lacey: "Doing what he wants."

Rachel: "What? What is he doing? Did he hit on you?!"

Lacey: "Not exactly."

Rachel: "What?"

Lacey: "I don't know if I should tell anyone."

Rachel: "Tell me! You can tell *me*!"

Lacey: "You can't believe what he texted me. I told him to stop."

Rachel: "What?"

Lacey: "He has sex questions. I don't know what to think."

Rachel: "What kind of sex questions?"

Lacey: "Well, I guess he is having arousal problems with Abigail. He says he wants to improve his sex life."

Rachel: "No!"

Lacey: "You should see his text messages. Oh my God. He has lots of questions about sex."

Rachel: "Oh my God! Show me!"

Lacey: "Well, here's one." She handed over her phone.

Rachel: "Oh my God!" handing the phone back, like it was a piece of burning coal.

Lacey: "Here, look at this one." Lacey handed the phone back to Rachel again.

Rachel: "Oh my God! He's out of his freaking mind! And this is our rabbi?!"

Lacey: "He definitely needs some help. I told him, in no uncertain terms, to stop harassing me."

Lacey felt relieved that she had shared the rabbi's text messages with someone, but she didn't want their conversation to go any further. They agreed that the rabbi needed to get help but didn't think he would.

Rachel convinced Lacey that they should share the things on her phone with Hezekiah. He would know what to do. Of course, he wouldn't do anything unless Lacey agreed.

THE
ATTEMPTED
COUP

Hezekiah felt a rush of emotions when he saw the text messages and emails between Rabbi Dreidel and Lacey. First, he experienced a clear sense of "Ah-ha!" and "I told you so!" He felt vindication for his criticisms of Rabbi Dreidel. He always suspected that Rabbi Dreidel wasn't a holy rabbi, exemplified by the problems with the *mechitza* on Simchas Torah. Now he had his proof. He felt that the material on Lacey's phone was his Pinchas moment, a test of his own religious zeal. Perhaps God had chosen him for this. He had to expose Rabbi Dreidel for the fraud that he was. Rabbi Dreidel was un-kosher!

The rabbi should leave the shul with his tail between his legs. Although beloved in the community, he didn't deserve the title of rabbi. He was a disgusting pervert. Hezekiah must warn the community! He would don his Superman cape, or better stated, a "Super-Jew" cape (but to be kosher, the cape must not combine linen and wool).

Hezekiah quickly called and texted his closest synagogue friends. Truth be told, he felt a little insecure about who was really a friend, since he was only acquainted with other Jews in Destiny County through the synagogue. They were not people he hung out with, nor did they visit each other's homes, they only saw each other in shul.

Hezekiah decided to text fellow congregants who came to services every Saturday morning, like he did, rain or shine. He liked them best because of their higher levels of observance.

Hezekiah took the time to describe, in detail, the text messages on Lacey's cell phone. They all took him seriously, given the gravity of the charges. They quickly agreed that the rabbi needed treatment, and that they should confront him and ask him to step down immediately. The key was getting Lacey's consent to share what was on her phone and to let others see it. Otherwise, the rabbi could deny the charges. They also wanted to see for themselves the damning evidence of the rabbi's improprieties, not that they believed Hezekiah would make up something like this.

Initially, Lacey did not want to share everything on her phone. Rachel convinced Lacey how important it was to meet with her and Hezekiah in person. Together, they convinced Lacey that she had to do the right thing. Hezekiah told Lacey that Rabbi Dreidel's texts showed "grooming" behavior. This was a term he gleaned from the internet. Perverts, he learned, engaged in bad behavior that almost always escalated.

"Lacey," Hezekiah said, "You have to share your information, because children are at risk. It is only a matter of time until he is going to molest the kids, including my kids, in Hebrew School or during bar or bat mitzvah lessons. He's a sexual pervert. That's what perverts do. His behavior is going to get worse. Action has to be taken!"

"Well, when you put it that way," said Lacey, still reluctant to share the text messages in their entirety. She feared that someone might also accuse her of impropriety. "Here, I'll forward the most disgusting emails and texts to you, but I don't want you to give them to anyone without my permission. You already heard the voicemails."

That was all Hezekiah needed. She said not to give them to anyone, but she didn't say he couldn't show them. He showed them to his three closest synagogue friends that very night, passing his phone to them around his kitchen table. The written words, excerpted from the strings of emails and texts between Lacey and Rabbi Dreidel, looked even worse standing alone. These were his friends' reactions:

"Disgusting."

"Horrible."

"Oh my God."

"Rabbi Dreidel is sick."

The group decided to call Marshall Goldman. They respected Marshall, who was a highly observant, regularly attending congregant. He was a recently retired investment manager, rumored to be wealthy, and viewed as the biggest financial contributor to Rabbi Dreidel and the synagogue.

Rabbi Dreidel always called Marshall up to the Torah for the most important *aliyahs*, the prayers before the Torah readings. Hezekiah and his confidants decided that Marshall's support would be crucial in getting the rabbi to leave. If Rabbi Dreidel heard the demand that he step down directly from Marshall, one of his closest and most important contributors, he would realize the jig was up.

Perhaps, Hezekiah and his small group speculated, Marshall could lead a temporary takeover of the synagogue mortgage payments, or maybe he'd do it himself, until a new rabbi was selected. Hezekiah also worried out loud about how Marshall would react, given his longstanding, close friendship with the rabbi.

They needn't have worried. Marshall was a black and white kind of guy. The texts and emails were all he needed to see.

"I don't need to hear the voicemails," Marshall barked when Hezekiah asked if he wanted more proof of the rabbi's transgressions.

"The rabbi has betrayed all of us!" he exclaimed, thinking sadly about the hundreds of thousands of dollars he'd contributed to a dishonored man.

The little group debated how best to go about getting rid of the rabbi. They decided the fairest approach was to confront him personally. They would demand he resign immediately and check into a facility for treatment of sexual deviancy and addiction. They also decided to write a letter to the Beis Din, the Jewish Court in San Francisco, asking for the rabbi's removal. They wouldn't send the letter, yet. They would hand the letter in person to Rabbi Dreidel as a threat to force him to resign.

The group decided to keep things to themselves. But when a fire starts, it spreads as soon as the wind begins to blow even a little.

Hezekiah, his wife, and Marshall's wife started telephoning other women congregants to see if any of them had been sexually harassed by the rabbi. A phone call between Marshall's wife and Sarah Shofar led to a blast of emails and phone calls that swirled among the three couples.

Elmer tried to shield Sarah from all the calls she started getting. But soon, she felt the pressure and called Hezekiah. Sarah wanted to hear all the details about Lacey's allegations against the rabbi. Hezekiah filled her in. From Sarah's questions, Hezekiah figured out that Sarah also was one of the rabbi's victims. Sarah, while not admitting it, didn't deny it either. Hezekiah wanted her to meet with him and his wife at a place and time of her choosing. He figured he could convince Sarah to tell him everything, if there was a sympathetic woman like his wife in the room.

Sarah didn't want to meet. She definitely wanted to stay out of it. Sarah and her family had already ceased contact with the Jewish Center of Destiny County and made alternate bar mitzvah plans. She didn't see an upside for herself or her family from being involved in a scandal. She didn't see a need to get involved, either, since Hezekiah and Marshall Goldman had all they needed from the rabbi's communications with Lacey.

While the fire spread by telephone and email, those in the know decided that Hezekiah and Marshall would attend the next Wednesday evening study group and meet with the rabbi afterwards. Marshall would be their spokesperson.

And so, that Wednesday night, after the rest of the class left the community hall where the class was held, Hezekiah and Marshall remained. As the rabbi gathered books from the tables where his students had been sitting, the two men approached him.

"Please sit down, Rabbi," Marshall said. "We have an extremely serious matter to discuss."

"What's this about?" asked the rabbi, initially all smiles and happy to attend to his congregants.

Marshall handed him the letter.

Rabbi Dreidel started to hyperventilate as he read. Here is what the letter said:

To the Honorable Beis Din of San Francisco:
And to Rabbi Mishegas Dreidel:

We, the following members of the Jewish Center of Destiny County, undersigned below, representing all members of our community privy to information and evidence indicating that

Rabbi Mishegas Dreidel has engaged in behavior disqualifying him to serve as Rabbi, respectfully request the Beis Din of San Francisco investigates fully the sexual deviancy of Rabbi Mishegas Dreidel, determine how to prevent further harm by Rabbi Dreidel to other members of the community, and monitor his compliance with inpatient treatment. Our demands for temporary relief as follows, pending the Beis Din's investigation, are non-negotiable. We also ask for the direction and assistance of the Beis Din in providing us with a new Rabbi for our shul on both a temporary and permanent basis.

1.   Rabbi Mishegas Dreidel shall immediately enter inpatient treatment for sexual deviancy at the Goldberg Residential Treatment Center of Los Angeles, California. The Center shall provide the Beis Din and a committee of congregants of the Jewish Center of Destiny County with monthly progress reports confirming attendance and compliance with treatment. Until released in writing by the Goldberg Residential Treatment Center, the Rabbi shall not have any unsupervised contacts, either in person or on the phone, with women or children.

2.   Rabbi Mishegas Dreidel shall cease and desist from any and all further contact with the Jewish Center of Destiny County and shall resign his position immediately. He shall not serve as a pulpit Rabbi for any other organization. He shall publicly announce on social media that he is taking an immediate leave of absence from his current duties as Rabbi for the County of Destiny. He need not announce the reasons for his leave of absence to minimize embarrassment to himself and to his family. If Rabbi Mishegas Dreidel fails to comply with the conditions herein, we shall sever all financial support to the Jewish Center of Destiny County and inform the other members of the community of what has occurred.

3.   If the Beis Din acts quickly and summarily as outlined above, pending its investigation, we agree to assist in helping our synagogue remain open to all its congregants while a transition takes place. We agree to continue our financial support as long as the records of the Jewish Center of Destiny County are subject to an independent audit by a CPA approved by the undersigned and any new Rabbi is hereafter supervised by a Board of Directors selected by our community.

Rabbi Dreidel looked up from the letter, hands shaking, and stared angrily at Hezekiah. "You are behind all of this aren't you?" he hissed, sounding highly un-rabbinical.

"Rabbi, let's stay on point and not make this about personalities, okay?" Marshall demanded calmly but firmly. "What do you intend to do? You really have no choice. You need to go into treatment immediately. We haven't sent this to the Beis Din yet. We are willing to spare you that shame and handle this quietly."

"What are you talking about? Resigning? I'd sooner jump off the roof! I'm not resigning. This is all Hezekiah's doing, isn't it?"

"No, Rabbi," Marshall responded. "We all agree this has to happen. I have seen the text messages with Lacey. We are trying to keep this quiet. Only a small number of us have seen the text messages and heard the voicemails. You need treatment."

"Those were private messages about my marriage. Why are you reading my private messages? When a rabbi and a person speak privately, those talks are privileged and not for you to see.

"Oh my God! You are reading my private messages! You hacked my phone!"

"No one hacked your phone," Marshall said. "Lacey showed us all your disgusting messages. You need help."

The rabbi got up and started pacing, crying, yelling, and accusing Hezekiah of seeking his ruination. Hezekiah stood up, towering over the shorter man. Marshall remained seated. Hezekiah crowded the rabbi as he paced. He told him that he was following Jewish law and to calm down.

"Get away from me!" the rabbi screamed at Hezekiah. "You guys can't do this to me. I already know I am going to get counseling. I admit I might have some problems. But you are not taking over my shul!"

Everyone started shouting at once. Nothing was resolved, and emotions rose to a notch above hysterical.

Finally, Abigail walked into the community hall to see why her husband hadn't come home. She was shocked by what she saw.

Her husband was pacing about, mumbling, yelling, and repeating himself. He looked like he'd been crying.

"What's going on?" she asked, wide-eyed.

"They are trying to take over the shul!" Rabbi Dreidel handed her the letter to the Beis Din. "They think they can kick us out because I have been having some personal problems."

Abigail looked at the letter. She looked at Marshall. "And you are part of this? I don't understand."

She saw Marshall as one of the rabbi's best friends and their number one financial supporter. How could he be part of this without talking to them first?

"I suggest we all calm down," she said. "I can't stay here. I have all the kids at the house with no one supervising. I have to get back." She turned to the rabbi, "Mishy, please come home soon, so we can talk about this."

Abigail left.

This discussion between Hezekiah and Rabbi Dreidel followed:

Hezekiah: "What you are saying is stupid."

Rabbi: "You are an idiot."

Hezekiah: "You are sick."

Rabbi: "I'm not sick. You're insane."

Hezekiah: "You are the sick one. You are a pervert."

Rabbi: "I am not going to listen to this. I am going to jump off the roof. Will that make you happy, if I jump off the roof of the synagogue?"

Hezekiah stepped out of the room and called 911. He gave the address to the police dispatcher. He reported a person was threatening suicide and should be taken to a mental hospital.

Whether Hezekiah really believed the rabbi intended to commit suicide or just wanted to upset him further by involving the police became a subject of serious debate in the months that followed.

Marshall, seeing that nothing was going to be resolved, left before the cops came. Hezekiah also called another TUCAS rabbi who lived in a town nearby, and he arrived soon after the cops and helped calm down Rabbi Dreidel. The police left, confused but convinced nobody was going to die.

In the meantime, Abigail waited anxiously at home for Mishy. She called her mother, even though it was the middle of the night back east, where she lived. She also called an older sister and woke her up.

By the time her husband came through the door, she was upset, exhausted, and still in shock.

The following questions pierced her heart: *What happened? What did they say Mishy did? What did Mishy do? Who said what? What's going on?*

MANSPLAINING

The rabbi didn't sleep all night. He spent the night "mansplaining" to Abigail. He rationalized how all of his intentions were good. Everything he did was for a spiritual purpose— to reach a higher and holier relationship with Abigail. He freely admitted his texting with Lacey, but he explained that these were privileged texts between a woman Navy counselor and a rabbi; that absolutely no touching and nothing improper had occurred. His intention was clearly misinterpreted by the person in question. Hezekiah twisted the messages and took them out of context. He did not go into the juicy details of his texts with Lacey. The rabbi talked and talked, and Abigail listened.

Some things he didn't want to talk to her about, he explained, because he didn't want to make her uncomfortable. That's why he talked to Lacey. If his needs had been met better, the rabbi explained, none of this would have happened.

He swore that the only time he even met Lacey was when

she came that one time to pick up her kosher meat, and Abigail was there. He never had any other in-person contact with her. Abigail saw with her own eyes how innocent that one contact with Lacey had been. Absolutely nothing happened. That showed how Hezekiah and Marshall were blowing this up. He cried and sobbed.

Once the rabbi's crying jag ran its course, Mishy railed on to Abigail that the text messages never should have been shown to anyone. He was sorry he couldn't show them to Abigail. He deleted all the messages and voicemails as soon as Lacey didn't want to message or talk to him anymore. He respected her wishes. He respected her confidentiality. There must be something vicious about her to share confidential messages and conspire with Hezekiah.

The real problem was Hezekiah. He knew it. Mishy told Abigail that he knew Hezekiah never would be happy in their community. Hezekiah belonged in a frum community, where everyone was strictly orthodox, instead of how people were here in Destiny County—culturally Jewish but not observant. In a frum community, Hezekiah wouldn't be criticizing the level of observance like he did here. Hezekiah always had a complaint, but he never paid his family's fair share.

"You told me not to worry about him, remember?" Mishy accused Abigail. "A converted, born-again Christian! What a mistake that was.

"A laborer know-it-all with his half-witted kids. He and Marshall want to take over the synagogue. Does he think he is going to lead services?"

The rabbi paused to cry some more. He felt like a worm named Hezekiah was in his head eating his brain. He felt like a bug named Hezekiah was in his ears buzzing around, as loud as a fire alarm. He couldn't believe a *schlemiel*, a know-nothing like Hezekiah, created this crisis.

"This is our shul," he blurted between tears. "We started here with nothing. This is a two-million-dollar synagogue. No one believed we could accomplish this much. We sacrificed and gave everything to build things up. What has Hezekiah ever done?" he moaned, clenching his fists.

Abigail looked at the clock. It was 3:00 a.m. The baby would be up in an hour or two.

"Mishy, keep your voice down. I have to lie down now. The baby will be up soon."

"I can't understand Marshall," continued Mishy. "How could such a close friend, who supported us from the beginning, turn on us like that?

"He guaranteed the mortgage, bought our second Torah, and donated so much every year.

"He always was such a *mensch*. I called and left three voicemails after everyone finally left last night. He won't answer."

And so it went, later and later, until night became morning.

While the birds outside started chirping, and the daily routines of the people of Destiny County began, the stresses of the previous night weighed on the participants. The hangover soured everyone's breath and turned everyone's stomach.

After Hezekiah filled in Marshall over the phone about what had happened after he left last night, they strategized about their next steps. It was simple. They would keep the pressure on. They would call the top financial contributors to the synagogue to let them know what was going on.

They divided a short list of people to call. In the meantime, Marshall went online and stopped his automatic, monthly contributions to the Jewish Center of Destiny County. He was not going to talk to Rabbi Dreidel, no matter how many times he called or emailed.

Marshall called Lenny Spiegleman first. Lenny was another

secular Jew with a family living and working away in the diaspora, in this case, the County of Destiny. Like Marshall, he also ponied up real *gelt* to support the Jewish Center. He and his wife were among Rabbi Mishy's earliest and most loyal supporters and contributors. Rabbi Dreidel charmed them with his youth, enthusiasm for Judaism, and deep Jewish knowledge and scholarship. Rabbi Dreidel, they felt, was a holy man, the real deal, a *Tzaddik*, a truly righteous man. They particularly admired how hard the rabbi worked and how inclusive he was, reaching out to every Jew in the area without hesitation or judgment.

Rabbi Dreidel gave Lenny the honor of reciting an *aliyah* practically every time he came to morning services for the Sabbath or Holidays. He, like a core handful of congregants, celebrated the new synagogue's dedication, many Jewish holidays he hadn't before, and Sabbath dinners on Friday nights. He also attended each *Bris*, the male ritual circumcisions, for each of the Dreidel sons. Lenny met and socialized with Rabbi Dreidel's and Abigail's extended families over the years—all rabbis or wives of rabbis. Many times, Rabbi Dreidel and his family came to Lenny's house on a summer day to have a picnic on their lawn, a short walk above a small lake that had a beach. The older children went kayaking, and the toddlers played on the beach.

In sum, Lenny felt that Rabbi Dreidel was an old and dear friend, although he was still a young man and Lenny was not. Lenny thought maybe they were even best friends, despite the age difference.

Marshall Goldman's relationship with Lenny went back to when Rabbi Dreidel first arrived in Destiny County and brought them together. Years ago, Marshall and Lenny attended Rabbi Dreidel's first Talmud class in Destiny County, which he taught at Lenny's kitchen table. Marshall became devout, koshering his kitchen, attending every Saturday morning and holiday service, and every Wednesday evening adult class. Lenny attended less frequently, but he put real *gelt* into the *pushke*.

Lenny was surprised to get an early morning phone call from Marshall.

"Lenny, Marshall here, is it okay to call you this early?"

"Marshall, everything okay?"

"I'm fine. I want to let you know some terrible news, though. I want you to keep it confidential. It's something you should know, and you can tell your wife, but we want to keep it quiet."

"Okay. What's up?"

"Will you keep it confidential?" Marshall asked.

"Sure. I promise to keep it confidential. What's going on?"

"Rabbi Dreidel has engaged in some disgusting behavior. We asked him to resign and to immediately begin treatment for sexual deviancy.

"I know this comes as a shock, but I wanted you to know. He should not be around kids or women without supervision. He certainly should not be acting as our rabbi. He is sick and needs to get help."

"I don't understand."

"I can tell you, Lenny," said Marshall, "that I have personally talked to one of the women he has harassed, and I have seen the rabbi's disgusting texts from his phone number."

"I don't know what to think," stuttered Lenny. "I don't have any reason to doubt you, but I guess I'd like to see the evidence myself."

"I am respecting the wishes of the victim, here, so I am not at liberty to tell you her name or more details. But I can tell you that I personally saw text messages and emails that are clearly from the rabbi. I wish I could tell you more.

"This all comes as a horrible shock, but Rabbi Dreidel needs to resign. We had a meeting last night, after the adult class, and confronted him. We gave him a letter asking him to do just that.

"He was distraught, reacted hysterically, and threatened suicide. I'm told he remained pretty crazy until the police arrived to calm things down."

"What do you mean he threatened suicide?" Lenny exclaimed.

"Is he okay? I don't know what to say. Unbelievable. I am in shock."

Lenny's wife, Hannah, was in the room during the call and knew something was wrong. After she asked her husband several times to repeat everything Marshall had said, they both felt like their insides had turned upside down. They didn't know what to think. Marshall was a serious person. He was a credible person. They couldn't discount anything Marshall said, and he said he saw the evidence personally. But they loved the rabbi.

"Drop everything, and go see Rabbi Dreidel," Hannah said. "Just go."

"Right now?"

"Right now," Hannah said, adding, "You go, and I'll call Adam and Anna to see what they know. If I get them and learn anything, I'll call you right back."

Adam and Anna Habbibi were their close friends. They had socialized for years, even before Rabbi Dreidel came to Destiny County. They were strictly orthodox, attended all the services, kept kosher at home, and focused on Judaism and their affinity for Israel.

Anna, in particular, was always at the shul helping Abigail. She volunteered in the preschool and helped with all the holidays. She saw first-hand how hard the rabbi worked. Like the Spieglemans, the Habbibis loved the rabbi.

Lenny put on his shoes and grabbed the car keys. He didn't know what had happened, but his instinct was to protect and help. His rabbi was in trouble.

RABBINICAL SUPERVISION

J ewish law tells the Jews to obey secular laws. Lenny knew it was illegal to talk on a cell phone while driving, but Lenny called Rabbi Dreidel while speeding down the road.

Lenny drove fast, feeling panicked, oblivious to the speed limit. He got the rabbi's voicemail with its cheerful recording, "Shalom, this is Rabbi Dreidel from the Jewish Center. Please feel free to leave a message."

The happy voice contrasted with the dread Lenny felt at the pit of his stomach. He felt enormous fear for Rabbi Dreidel. His own sense of balance and well-being were on tilt.

Within seconds, the rabbi texted Lenny back, "I'll be in the shul."

Lenny next called Adam Habbibi, who had already heard from Anna that someone else had said that something bad happened after class last night.

Lenny told Adam that he was going to meet Rabbi Dreidel at the shul. Adam said he'd come too.

As soon as Lenny walked into the sanctuary, Rabbi Dreidel hugged him tightly, crying. His eyes were red and bloodshot. He was a wreck—miserable and shaky.

"You can't believe what's going on," the rabbi said tearfully as they both sat down at a table at the back of the sanctuary.

"What is going on?" asked Lenny.

"I asked the attorney, Harold Bernard, to come also. You know Harold, right?"

"Sure. I just talked to Adam Habbibi, and he is coming too.

"What's going on?"

"What happened is … well. Look, I was having some intimacy issues with Abigail. It isn't easy to talk about." The rabbi teared up and rubbed his eyes. "I was having performance issues with my wife. This never happened before. I was worried about it, as you can imagine.

"Lenny, this is strictly confidential. I can tell you. You are such a close friend, but you can't repeat anything.

"I started talking confidentially with this woman named Lacey, because I wanted to hear from a woman's perspective. I thought everything we said was private. She's a lay counselor on the Navy base. Our communications are supposed to be confidential. That is what we agreed.

"She violated the confidentiality and showed some text messages and emails to Hezekiah and Marshall. Now they are out to get me."

"I got a call from Marshall saying you should resign," Lenny said.

"I can't believe that they'd gang up on me like this at the end of a class, especially Marshall," the rabbi said. "That hurts so much. I never trusted that Hezekiah, but Marshall …"

"Marshall talked about a letter of some kind," Lenny said.

"That's what I'm talking about. Here," said the rabbi, handing Lenny the letter. "Here's their manifesto threatening to take me to the Beis Din in San Francisco if I don't resign immediately.

"They want me to check into inpatient treatment for sexual deviancy, God forbid, in Southern California. So ridiculous. They sprung this on me at the end of class. Hezekiah even called the cops on me claiming I was unstable and suicidal.

"All lies. What I said was, 'Do you want me to jump off the roof, would that make you happy? Sure, I'll go jump off the roof.'

"Hezekiah used that to call the cops on me. I would never jump off the roof. I was just venting because of what they were doing to me."

Lenny began to read the letter to the Beis Din. Rabbi Dreidel started to whimper and moan as the attorney, Harold Bernard, walked into the shul.

The rabbi got up and hugged Harold tightly, like he had hugged Lenny, and they sat down at the table as Lenny continued reading. Adam arrived.

"Thank you all for coming," he said, crying again.

"Rabbi, calm down. It will be all right," Harold said.

"Harold, we need to litigate immediately against this woman who violated confidentiality."

"Let's slow down and take things step-by-step," said Harold. "What are the allegations?"

"That's it. This woman, Lacey, I only met her one time. Abigail was there when it happened. She came to pick up kosher meat after a delivery to the house. I never saw her in person another time. That's it, the only time we met.

"She is involved down at the base, unhappy that Rabbi Hazzarai wasn't listening to her about wanting her husband to convert. I introduced her to Hezekiah and his wife, because they had been through the conversion process. Hezekiah and Lacey took my emails and texts out of context. They want to take me down."

"Let's start there," the lawyer said, "I want to see the texts and emails."

"I deleted them all when she said she didn't want to talk about anything and claimed I was harassing her. I said fine, I'll stop. I completely respected her wishes. So I deleted everything to protect her privacy. I don't have them."

"What were they about?" Harold asked.

"Look, I am very embarrassed about this," the rabbi replied. "I was having some intimacy problems with Abigail. You can never talk about this with anyone else. I told Lenny. I'll tell you all. These were very private issues. These were things Abigail would never talk about.

"That I am even talking about any of this, even in a general sense, is a violation of the sacred things in a marriage. Abigail would be mortified."

"Lacey was having some issues with her husband as well," the rabbi continued, "so we agreed to compare notes to help each other out. What bothers me the most is that I violated Abigail's trust by talking about these things with another person. But I couldn't talk about them with Abigail, so what was I supposed to do? *Oy vey iz mir,* (woe is me)!"

Rabbi Dreidel wailed and sobbed, cupping his hands over his face.

"So, you aren't accused of assaulting anyone or some sexual impropriety?" asked Harold Bernard.

"Assaulting? Are you kidding me? Not even touching! Never. Nothing like that," the rabbi answered.

"Maybe I crossed a line talking to her like I did. I admit that. I haven't been right with certain issues. I admit that. TUCAS has online counseling that I tried, but it wasn't helpful. I have been thinking about going to a counselor for a while. I'll do whatever anyone wants me to do. I'll go on an indefinite leave, whatever I need to do ..." and the Rabbi started sobbing again.

"*Oy vey iz mir.*"

He put his head down on his arms, which were folded on the table, and cried.

He bobbed up between tears to say, "I feel like Joseph being sold into slavery and then falsely imprisoned when he wouldn't be seduced.

"I don't know what Lacey wanted from me. What does anyone want from me?" he pleaded. He lowered his head and continued crying.

Lenny, Adam, and Harold couldn't look at one another. They felt embarrassed. They had never seen the rabbi in even a negative frame of mind, much less a meltdown.

"I know a very good clinical psychologist," Harold said. "He's Jewish, too. I am pretty sure he isn't orthodox, but I doubt there are any orthodox psychologists or counselors in this area. He would know if there were. I can make a referral."

"Let's check in with Rabbi Yitzak Yosef," Lenny suggested. "Isn't he the head honcho of the TUCAS rabbis out here?" He remembered the senior rabbi from a speech he gave when the synagogue was inaugurated.

"Anna and I have known him for years," Adam said. "He's a good man. He should know what's going on. Let's call him now."

"He already called me," Rabbi Dreidel said, poking his head up again. "I have his voicemail from this morning.

"I haven't called him back yet. Hezekiah must have called Rabbi Cohnman in Salem. I have a voicemail from him, too. My phone is blowing up like you wouldn't believe. I don't know who to call back first."

"Well, the first thing is to get you to a psychologist so we can get you evaluated. The evaluation is probably key," opined Harold. "We can figure out what is needed. An evaluation can prove Hezekiah and Marshall both wrong, that you aren't a danger to anyone, and whether you need any counseling, that type of thing. This fellow I am thinking of is very, very good. And Jewish."

"I agree that's got to happen," added Lenny. "Also, I think you should authorize the psychologist to share the report with Rabbi Yitzak Yosef, your wife, and with Harold, if he is your attorney."

"Harold," cried the rabbi, "Please help me and be my attorney, please!"

"I will, Rabbi. Don't worry. We'll get through this together."

The rabbi's cell phone rang.

"It's Rabbi Yitzak Yosef. I'll put it on speaker."

As Rabbi Dreidel said hello, he started crying again.

"Rabbi Yitzak," Adam said into the cell phone, "I am very glad you called. The rabbi is very upset. We need your advice."

"Rabbi," gulped Rabbi Dreidel, "I am sorry I didn't get back to you sooner. You don't know what I'm going through.

"I crossed a line with some text messages and emails. I admit that. My actions were probably wrong, although my intentions were good. I am sorry.

"They are now going after me to take over the shul. They confronted me with so much disrespect last night. It was disgusting, demanding I resign and leave the state.

"This Hezekiah, who is frum, he converted with Rabbi Cohnman in Salem; he is clearly out to get me."

"Hold on," interrupted Rabbi Yitzak Yosef, "Let's slow down. Who else is there? I just talked to Abigail on the phone for the second time this morning. She told me you are not alone."

"Rabbi Yosef, Harold Bernard here, remember me? I'm here with Rabbi Dreidel, Adam Habbibi, and Lenny Spiegleman from the congregation."

"Yes, I remember you, Harold, and Lenny, too. Of course I know Adam.

"Thank you all for being there. Look, tell me how the rabbi is," Rabbi Yosef continued. "I got some calls, and I couldn't reach Rabbi Dreidel, so I talked to Abigail. She is concerned about him."

"Rabbi Yosef, Harold here. Rabbi Dreidel is upset. We think the first thing that we should do is get Rabbi Dreidel in to see a psychologist. I have someone in mind, a Dr. David Plotznik. Do you know him? His office is in Portland."

"No, I don't know him, but I agree the first thing to do is to take care of Rabbi Dreidel. If you know someone good, that's fine with me. I don't need to approve your selection. I trust your judgment," the senior rabbi said.

"In the meantime, I will meet with Rabbi Dreidel, Abigail, of course, and I will ask Rabbi Finklestein and maybe Rabbi Schvitzerman to attend the meeting as well.

"Rabbi Dreidel, are you listening?" Rabbi Yosef asked. "I want to see both you and Abigail tomorrow. I also will talk to the other senior rabbis in TUCAS to assess the situation.

"But the first thing, Rabbi Dreidel, is for you, listen to me now, to understand something. We are going to proceed rationally, and your health is our number one priority. Your health means your physical health, your mental health, and your spiritual health. That's number one.

"I will also need to hear from the community at some point soon," the senior rabbi said. "This is going to be a process."

"I will do whatever you want me to do," Rabbi Dreidel agreed. "I want to do counseling. I've said that."

"And as part of the evaluation," chimed in Lenny Spiegleman, "this Dr. Plotznik, the psychologist, should have the actual texts, emails, and voicemails."

"That's right," said Rabbi Yosef, "the psychologist should do a complete and thorough job with all the information. In the meantime, I have a young couple who can come down and stay with Rabbi Dreidel for Shabbos to lead services and give him a little time off.

"This young rabbi is staying with one of my colleagues. He's looking around the area to see if he wants to move here. This is a temporary situation, until we figure out how we want to proceed."

After the phone call, Lenny, Adam, Harold, and the rabbi talked about how to get the deleted messages and voice mails from his phone.

Adam telephoned Hezekiah and asked for a copy of the messages. Hezekiah said he would provide them, but only when he received confirmation that the rabbi had resigned.

Harold took Adam Habbibi's phone and explained that Rabbi Dreidel was undergoing an evaluation and was now under the supervision of Rabbi Yitzak Yosef. He told Hezekiah that the rabbi was on indefinite leave and would be meeting with at least two or more senior rabbis tomorrow. A student rabbi would be leading services for Shabbos. Therefore, he had every reason to turn over the materials.

That did not satisfy Hezekiah. But he said he would check with the victim and the community members who had seen the evidence.

He said that, once the rabbi resigned, he was confident the victim would turn over the messages to the proper person. But she was not going to facilitate some kind of whitewashing of the rabbi's problems.

"The rabbi should resign, or the entire mess must be turned over to the Beis Din," Hezekiah said.

"See what I am dealing with?" shouted Rabbi Dreidel, after

Harold hung up. "Hezekiah is out to ruin me and my family. There is no talking to him."

"We'll work on getting the materials, don't worry," said Harold. "Let's go caucus in your office. I want you to tell me everything you know about this woman, Lacey, and everything that has happened."

"Before you go," Adam Habbibi interjected, "please let me ask one question, Rabbi. Are there other women who are going to come forward?"

"No, of course not," cried the rabbi. "This is it. I haven't touched anyone or committed any crimes.

"I have sinned horribly against Abigail by sharing things about our relationship that I shouldn't have. I will never forgive myself for that."

Rabbi Dreidel put his head down on the table, again, and sobbed.

THE EVIL
TONGUE

What similarities did those who attended the Jewish Center of Destiny County share? Not everyone knew everyone else. Not everyone attended regularly. Most lived in different neighborhoods. No one's background or Jewish heritage was alike. There might be some details common to the stories of the children of immigrants, but after a generation or two, assimilation dissolved them.

True, they were all Jews. But what else did they have in common?

The only unifying factor for every Jew connected to the Jewish Center of Destiny County was Rabbi Mishegas Dreidel. He was the linchpin. He knew everyone. He reached out and recruited everyone. His kind invitations and gentle nudging roped everyone in.

The rabbi believed God created the world for the Jewish

people, including the great Jewish Patriarchs, and creation was ongoing, including the world created for Rabbi Mishegas Dreidel in Destiny County. His belief in the one true God was constant, unshakable, and unbreakable. Just as God's Great Hand directed the cosmic forces of the universe, the force of Rabbi Mishegas Dreidel's personality pulled the Jews of Destiny County into orbit around him.

Rabbi Dreidel, and he alone, possessed everyone's phone numbers, email, and street addresses. He, and he alone, solicited the contributions. He knew what everyone contributed, exactly how much, and how often. He paid all the bills. He hired the paid help.

Rabbi Dreidel ran a one-man show. He decided the schedule. He led the services. He planned the holiday programs down to the smallest detail. No one worked harder on the arrangements and the decorations. He sent out the announcements to his mailing list and his email list. He followed up with personal phone calls. He knew that if he didn't, hardly anyone would show up. He gave every sermon. He decided who got an *aliyah*. The Jewish Center of Destiny County ran on a single, turbo engine.

What happens to the orchestra when the conductor can't attend because he caught the flu? In the absence of a conductor, the members of the orchestra murmur and talk, some in hushed tones and others quite loudly, depending on their personalities. Soon, even those who talked in muted tones are forced to raise their voices to be heard above the cacophony. Who is going to grab the baton? Does the music stop, or do the musicians keep playing, however discordantly?

And what happens when you lose your close friend? That friendly smile is nowhere to be seen. Didn't the rabbi love you unconditionally, simply because you were a Jew? Did you ever know a rabbi who was also such a close friend?

How does it feel to lose your spiritual leader, your teacher, your religious anchor, and with it, your equilibrium? Even if you were not very involved with the Jewish Center, how do you feel when the man who rekindled your Jewish spirit falls into the gutter?

Your heart breaks. Your stomach turns. Should you call the rabbi now? He reached out to you. Isn't it time to reach out to him? Is it okay? You used to call the rabbi without thinking; now, doubt and worry rule the day. Is it okay to call again if he hasn't returned your other voicemails? Everyone is so worried about him. The rumor is that he threatened to jump off the shul's roof. Is he okay? How is Abigail? How are the kids?

Your friend, the rabbi, is no longer available. You cannot leave a message. His voicemail is full. The rabbi has entered a drama in which the actors suddenly change roles. The once towering David or saintly Moses is now Cain or Abimelech. Our beloved rabbi, the most learned and pious Jew in the County of Destiny, is under attack and suspicion, incommunicado and in desperate trouble. You can't think of anything else. You can't talk about anything else.

And what's it like for the subject of the controversy, whose ears are constantly burning? He knows everyone is talking about him. How can a holy rabbi function when he feels shame and embarrassment? What would the Grand Rabbi of blessed memory want him to do?

He must fight! Like every Jew ever wrongly accused, besmirched, and defamed, he must fight for his very survival against those out to get him. He must fight for his family! He telephoned Harold Bernard, his lawyer. He telephoned his close and extended family, his closest supporters in Destiny County, and even his oldest friends from yeshiva.

The rabbi's father told him on the phone, "Look, you were a bad boy. But you didn't carry it too far. Nothing happened, physically, with another woman. Not to minimize, but you didn't have sexual intercourse with anyone who wasn't your wife.

"Yes, your thinking went astray, but you can remedy that with trust in God. Now you've learned your lesson. It won't happen again."

His entire family shared his father's attitude. They minimized and denied the extent of the rabbi's psychological problems. To be fair, they relied on Rabbi Dreidel's version of events, and he limited the story to Lacey's involvement. Like the rabbi's local supporters, they never saw the texts or emails.

When Rabbi Dreidel huddled with attorney Harold Bernard it wasn't a short consult. The rabbi went on and on, never fully disclosing his peccadillos. He was a master of beating around the bush with generalities. Harold postponed his other appointments and court appearances. Rabbi Dreidel dominated Harold's time emoting, scheming, worrying, and grasping for an elusive legal solution to his problems.

The rabbi demanded that Harold sue Lacey for invasion of privacy, defamation, infliction of emotional distress, and ruining his professional reputation. Harold discussed the elements of each of these claims, pointing out where they lacked evidence to make even a colorable case. The rabbi argued that there must be vulnerabilities in Lacey's past. Perhaps they could show that she was a scarlet woman who was disdainful of rabbis and other men in positions of authority. Harold brainstormed with the rabbi and took notes about how to obtain background information to impeach Lacey's character and destroy her credibility.

Ultimately, he decided—and politely explained to his distraught client—that their best option was to seek a restraining order to stop Lacey from disseminating the rabbi's private communications. He would draft the documents and get an interim order. However, Harold explained, the court would set a show-cause hearing in two weeks to determine the conditions, including the length of the restraining order, which could last only up to a year. Lacey would have a chance to hire her own lawyer and file a response.

"You don't know what her papers might say," Harold warned. "She also could appear at the hearing, and you don't know what she might say or what witnesses she might call."

Rabbi Dreidel said the risk was worth it. They had to stop her from ruining him. He was certain she was "out to get him." They had to fight, and if they showed strength, he argued, she would fold.

They strategized about how to go on the offensive.

Acting on their discussion, Rabbi Dreidel called his colleague, Rabbi Hazzarai, to see if he could influence Lacey to stop embarrassing him, or, better yet, withdraw her allegations and publicly apologize. He asked if Rabbi Hazzarai had any dirt on Lacey they could leverage against her.

"We have to shut her down!" Rabbi Dreidel exclaimed. "For God's sake, she worked as a bikini barista. Something must have happened in her past that we can use!"

Rabbi Hazzarai said he would help any way he could.

Rabbi Dreidel also called Rabbi Cohnman, who sponsored Hezekiah Miller's conversion before he moved to Destiny County. He asked Rabbi Cohnman to tell Hezekiah to back off.

Rabbi Cohnman agreed to call his old congregant, but privately he was disgusted by his fellow rabbi.

Marshall, Rabbi Dreidel's other nemesis, was a mystery, given their close relationship, his history of generous contributions, and his loyalty and dedication to the rabbi over the years. The rabbi asked Lenny and Rabbi Yitzak Yosef to call Marshall.

That was the plan of attack—discredit Lacey, pressure Hezekiah, and calm Marshall down. All hands on deck!

The problem was that the "other side" also had a plan of attack. Only the rabbi's full and complete admission of wrongdoing and his stepping down permanently would satisfy Hezekiah and Marshall. The rabbi was *trayf*, as un-kosher as a rotten pig. He was unfit and he had to go. There was no alternative.

Marshall and Hezekiah's wives continued to call other women in the congregation to see if there were more victims. Some of the women seemed hostile, true believers in and defenders of the rabbi. In fact, they blamed Lacey, a woman they didn't know, for the fallout. Others wanted more details. Some wanted all the details. Hyperbole, descriptions, and condemnations flew this way and that; imaginations filled in the details and raised the levels of disgust and distrust. As the proverb said, "The words of a gossip are choice morsels."

The phone lines lit up like everyone's Chanukah Menorah on the eighth night. The Dreidel loyalists commiserated with each other. The detractors commended each other for their righteousness. Each side criticized the other. Everyone believed his or her understanding was correct. How could anyone think differently? What was wrong with the people on the other side?

Some of the detractors had their own stories to share about being harassed, though not by this rabbi. Because of their experiences, they didn't doubt a single allegation, even when they didn't know the allegations. Some wondered if the rabbi lingered a little too long when talking to good-looking, younger women at services or holiday events. Others discussed his secrecy about donations. They repeated one elderly woman's story about feeling pressured for a large donation. She had complained that the rabbi had the *chutzpah* to suggest she leave her entire estate to the Jewish Center. He even offered to pay for a lawyer to change her will.

A few of the rabbi's doubters also asked each other how much it cost to fly all his children back and forth to New York and elsewhere several times a year, why the Jewish Center never had a financial committee, and why the finances were kept secret. They even discussed how much the rabbi spent on his sons' bar mitzvahs. They wondered if Abigail had known her husband betrayed her.

The conversations were not limited to discussions of the rabbi and his family. Many just wanted to express their feelings of anger or grief. Some were upfront attackers of the Dreidels or other members of the congregation, others were behind-the-back attackers. The source of any particular, juicy statement was often unknown, but it spread from one Jew to the next like a virus.

Marshall started researching past TUCAS rabbis, including Rabbi Yitzak Yosef. A simple computer search turned up a checkered past for him! Thirty years ago, he pled guilty to acting as an accomplice in a money-laundering scheme and spent two weeks in jail. Anyone could pull up the YouTube video of the old television news report. Marshall was flabbergasted. He felt like he was peeking behind the curtain, like Toto in the Wizard of Oz.

Marshall asked himself why he gave all that money. Why was he so naïve and trusting? He started researching other rabbis accused of crimes or misdeeds, including sexual abuse. He found articles about rabbis who had fled to Israel to escape consequences. He found other instances where claims of sexual assault were swept under the rug.

Look, thought Marshall, *how they closed ranks and protected their own.* He was certain that is what they'd try to do with Rabbi Dreidel—reinstate him after a few months. They had already announced a student rabbi would substitute for Rabbi Dreidel at the shul during his "leave of absence." *Why hadn't Dreidel resigned yet? Why wasn't he fired?* If they were not going to summarily dismiss Rabbi Dreidel, Marshall was done with the Jewish Center of Destiny County and TUCAS.

The rabbi's supporters felt emotions that ranged from outrage to hurt, to "wait a minute," to "what's going on?"

Many thought, "Where there's smoke there's fire."

"Maybe the rabbi did something not exactly kosher," they said to one another, "but what's the big deal? No one's perfect. Perhaps he was under too much pressure because there never was enough money?"

Still, imaginations created the worst possible scenarios in many minds. Dread entered many hearts.

While the anger, dismay, and confusion spread, Rabbi Dreidel and Harold Bernard scoured the internet to track Lacey's electronic footprints, and they put her social media posts under a microscope. They cold-called people from her past. They constructed a narrative about Lacey the Troublemaker. Their story claimed that she fought with employers and failed to hold a job for any significant length of time. The tale suggested that her family background was dysfunctional. The rabbi and his lawyer looked for witnesses to support their claims.

They also burned up the phone lines with Rabbi Hazzarai at the Navy base. The chaplain shared everything he knew about Lacey, including every confidence and secret, her emails to him, and his best recollections of her various confessions. She had confided to Rabbi Hazzarai in great detail about her past, her parents, her childhood, and even the relationship with her Navy husband. This was preliminary to discussing her husband's possible conversion to Judaism. In the process, Rabbi Hazzarai learned about her psyche, her vulnerabilities, and her insecurities.

Rabbi Hazzarai's fellow Rabbi, Mishegas Dreidel, was under attack. He must help him! He was a TUCAS rabbi. His loyalties were clear. Congregants may come and go, and they always had their little problems. But a rabbi was a rabbi!

Rabbi Hazzarai met with Lacey privately and told her that she had made a grave mistake in attacking Rabbi Driedel. When Lacey tried to tell her chaplain what really happened, he didn't want to hear the story. He explained that, whatever she and the rabbi had discussed, even if it had crossed a line, was not relevant. What was important was that she had engaged in gossip. In Judaism, gossip was a grave sin. She had endangered her very soul.

Under Jewish law, the rabbi said, gossiping about Rabbi Dreidel was the equivalent of committing murder. She should remedy her sins by recanting. If not, Rabbi Hazzarai told her, she no longer would be welcome at his shul. Otherwise, he would be condoning her sinful behavior. He was sorry, but he had to act in accordance with Jewish law and his own conscience.

Lacey could not believe Rabbi Hazzarai would speak to her this way. She wasn't gossiping; she was reporting sexual harassment. In her mind, Rabbi Hazzarai was in cahoots with Rabbi Dreidel. Now, because she had done the right thing, she was being excluded from the shul on the base. To eighty-six a drunk from a bar was one thing, but to eighty-six a military spouse from a Navy chapel? Lacey filed a formal complaint. The Navy investigative office took her complaint against Rabbi Hazzarai seriously and assigned an investigator.

When Rabbi Dreidel followed up with another call to Rabbi Cohnman, Rabbi Cohnman patiently listened to all of his hysterical criticisms of Hezekiah. He told Rabbi Dreidel that he would talk to Hezekiah again. Privately, he thought Rabbi Dreidel was a broken person, no longer a *mensch*. He felt sorry about the situation, but without telling Rabbi Dreidel, he largely agreed with his convert's view that the rabbi should step down and get serious help.

When Rabbi Cohnman next spoke to Hezekiah, he told him that calling the cops the night he and Marshall confronted Rabbi Dreidel probably saved a life.

"Who knows," he said, "maybe Rabbi Dreidel would have jumped off the roof like he screamed he was going to?"

He recommended that Hezekiah allow the head TUCAS rabbis and God Himself to take care of the situation.

Meanwhile, Rabbi Yitzak Yosef's phone wouldn't stop ringing. Rabbi Dreidel, Harold Bernard, Lenny, Abigail, Rabbi Cohnman, Adam, and Anna Habbibi—and soon, all of Rabbi Dreidel's relatives—

were calling. Rumors saturated the old neighborhood in New York.

Rabbi Yitzak Yosef soon heard from his superiors, including two very senior and respected rabbis from the TUCAS national organization. They wanted to know what was going on. More than anything, they wanted Rabbi Yitzak to keep the scandal quiet. They related that several senior TUCAS rabbis at a weekly leadership meeting had advocated for Rabbi Dreidel's immediate firing. Rabbi Yitzak took every phone call, although he cut most of them short to take other calls.

He wanted to hear directly from Rabbi Dreidel and Abigail. Would Rabbi Dreidel admit his fault? Was Abigail standing behind him? That was key. If so, maybe he could work with them. All was not lost, but he had to be able to trust them. Rabbi Dreidel had to come clean. Rabbi Yitzak wanted to look him in the eyes. He was confident he could judge his sincerity.

The old rabbi decided he wouldn't meet with the couple alone. He drafted his oldest colleague in the region, Rabbi Finklestein, and a contemporary and friend of Rabbi Dreidel's, Rabbi Schvitzerman, to attend with him. Two sets of trusted ears could confirm what was said if there were questions in the future.

As Rabbi Yitzak saw it, he had two choices. He could fire Rabbi Dreidel now and nip the scandal in the bud, or he could take things step-by-step and not make any decisions precipitously. He considered Rabbi Dreidel a real star among the younger rabbis in the region. His shul was amazing, and now he was already planning to build a mikvah, a ritual bathhouse.

Rabbi Yitzak Yosef asked his wife what she thought he should do.

"Go slow," she advised. "Mishy has been such a wonderful young man. It doesn't make sense!

"And Abigail is so beautiful, and the *kinder*, think of those little children! Take your time to figure it all out."

The old rabbi agreed that the situation made no sense, given his protégé's accomplishments.

"Mishy has so much support," Rabbi Yosef said, "and from such fine people, like Adam and Anna Habbibi and Lenny Spiegleman and even Harold Bernard, the lawyer.

"I must take that into account, no matter what terrible things the others say."

Rabbi Yosef told his wife that he wouldn't decide anything without consulting Rabbi Finklestein, Rabbi Schvitzerman, and her.

"Nothing is going to happen overnight," he declared. "Everyone needs to calm down."

COME TO JESUS

The Jews do not have an expression about a "Come to Jesus Moment," when a person realizes that he is on a mistaken path and acknowledges he has done wrong and must change. Rabbis are not expected to do wrong, God forbid, and rabbis would never have a "Come to *Jesus* Moment" because they are Jews.

In Rabbi Mishegas Dreidel's case, pride caused him to distinguish between his identity and his actions. He fully identified as a holy person chosen by God. He was the son of a rabbi and the grandchild of a kosher butcher who, back in the day, provided kosher meat for Passover to the Grand Rabbi in New York, a great and holy honor.

Rabbi Dreidel was born and raised to be a rabbi. He fully embraced his mission leading the unaffiliated, wandering Jews of Destiny County out of the desert to the promised land of Judaism and the eventual coming of the Messiah. This was his calling. That was who he was. He was certain of it. No one would accomplish more than he would. He worked harder than anyone without complaint and with joy.

His actions, while at the root of the scandal and admittedly wrong, were, in Rabbi Dreidel's own mind, motivated by good intentions. As stated in the ancient proverb, "A good person falls seven times, a wicked person only once."

In other words, he rationalized that he was allowed a few mistakes; he was only human. He was under attack by toxic enemies who sought his downfall. Didn't they realize that rabbis were human too? He was deeply offended by Hezekiah's and Marshall's criticisms. How could they be so offensive and disrespectful to him, a rabbi? How dare they, especially after all he had done for them and the community over so many years? What a betrayal!

These thoughts bounced around and around in the mind of Rabbi Mishegas Dreidel as he drove the family van from home to his "Come to Jesus" meeting with the three TUCAS rabbis in Portland. Rabbi Dreidel's inner rage turned the family van into a Maserati. He zipped in and out of the morning traffic, passing on the right as well as the left, tailgating the slowpokes and lookee-loos, and accelerating whenever he saw a little gap in the lines of traffic.

Abigail sat in the passenger seat silent, exhausted, and tense. She had called Gloria Epstein at the last minute to babysit. Gloria jumped at the chance to spend time with the children. This was the first time in months that Abigail was going somewhere without any of her kids in tow.

Finally, irritated and stressed, she spoke these words in a low voice:

"Mishy, please slow down."

"I can't help it," he complained, "look at these fools on the road."

But he slowed down a little while his thoughts and emotions kept racing.

The night before their trip, Rabbi Dreidel had rehearsed and strategized with Abigail about what to say. He love-bombed her to death, telling her how important she was, how much he loved her, how much he needed her, and how he trusted her. He insisted that he had worked so hard only to provide for her and the kids. He confessed that violating her privacy is what hurt him the most.

This made him tear up again and again.

"Can you ever forgive me?" he asked through the night.

Abigail was fully aware of the crisis they were facing. She knew her husband wasn't himself right now, but she was going to stand by him. Her job was to support her husband. Wasn't that the job of the rabbi's wife? What else could she do? They had nine kids. Separating from Mishy was unthinkable. Where would she go? Who would want a woman with nine kids?

She didn't need to cross-examine him. She could see his misery. Someone had to be there for him, she thought. She would do what was necessary to preserve her marriage and her family.

Rabbi Dreidel and Abigail were still lost in their separate thoughts as they pulled into the parking lot behind the TUCAS Center in Portland. Abigail's legs felt rubbery as she followed her husband into the building, with its brown-brick facade designed to look like an old shul back east.

Rabbi Dreidel felt his blood heating up as he got closer to the library conference room. They walked in after knocking at the door and Rabbi Yitzak Yosef saying, "Please come in."

The room was lined with bookcases that overflowed with centuries of Jewish scholarship. Rabbi Dreidel's three colleagues were sitting on one side of a conference table in the middle of the room. Rabbi Yosef gestured to two chairs on the other side. Rabbi Dreidel wondered how long they had been there, and what they had said about him before his arrival with Abigail.

Rabbi Yitzak Yosef, the elderly Rabbi Finklestein, and Mishy's contemporary, Rabbi Schvitzerman, were an imposing troika—two long gray and white beards next to a long, full, black one. Rabbi Yosef's paunch of a stomach abutted the table. Rabbi Schvitzerman peered through his thick glasses. Rabbi Finklestein, thin as a leaf, perhaps emaciated by his years of holy study, sat silently. They were all dressed in black, as were Rabbi Dreidel and Abigail, who faced them across the table.

"Let's start," Rabbi Yosef said. "We want to know what's happening."

Rabbi Dreidel cleared his throat. He placed his delicate hands on top of the conference table. His voice was calm and respectful, yet emotionally charged. He thought it was very important to set the right tone.

Rabbi Dreidel said, "Thank you for being here. I am obviously sorry to meet under these circumstances. You know how much I appreciate each of you. Anything you want me to do, I will do.

"I know I need psychological counseling. I am going to do it. I already tried some counseling online with a TUCAS counselor. I have an appointment with a psychologist recommended by my lawyer, a Dr. Marvin Plotzky. I talked to him briefly on the phone. He will see me initially, but he also wants to see Abigail during the process. Abigail has been very supportive.

"I want each of you to know," he continued, pausing to look directly in the eyes of each of his fellow rabbis, and settling his gaze on Rabbi Yitzak Yosef, "that I have confessed everything to Abigail."

He failed to mention that his confession to Abigail skipped the details, but to be fair, she never asked for them.

"Yes, I crossed a line, but I am taking responsibility for that. I have done nothing illegal, nothing criminal, and everything has been blown out of proportion.

"Look," said Rabbi Dreidel, clicking his tongue, "all this *tsuris* stems from one real troublemaker, a former born-again-Christian, a know-it-all construction worker named Hezekiah Miller. I always knew there was something wrong with this Hezekiah from the very beginning. He belonged in a frum community. Abigail can tell you, I thought he was trouble from the very start, but she said Hezekiah was as entitled to come to shul as anyone else."

Rabbi Dreidel did not repeat all the dirty names he had called Hezekiah since the attempted coup. That would not sound rabbinical.

He told the other rabbis that his attorney, Harold Bernard, had discovered information about Lacey Johnson, the lay counselor with whom he had shared his private feelings.

"She's not a credible person. Rabbi Hazzarai met with her to ask her to stop talking about me and delete the emails and text messages. She won't do it. Hezekiah worked her all up. She is being completely unreasonable. What can I tell you? Rabbi Hazzarai was forced to ban her from the chapel at the Navy base."

Rabbi Dreidel also neglected to say that his attorney was preparing a petition for a restraining order. He didn't want to risk the rabbis telling him to avoid court. Instead, he told them about Lacey's background as a barista who wore skimpy clothes and said Rabbi Hazzarai knew some shocking things about her past. He repeated that everything he and Lacey discussed was supposed to be confidential, and, as a lay counselor, she should have kept them private.

"I am ashamed," he told the rabbis. "I have ruined my reputation and violated my wife's sacred privacy.

"I don't know if I can ever forgive myself."

This triggered tears which, Rabbi Dreidel figured, would underscore his sincerity and remorse. Indeed, he felt enormous guilt towards Abigail when he wasn't blaming her for his misfortune.

The rabbis were moved. They had never seen Rabbi Dreidel cry before.

The tearful performance notwithstanding, Rabbi Schvitzerman said that he had some questions.

He began by describing the close brotherhood he felt for Rabbi Dreidel, who he called Mishy, and proclaimed his respect and admiration for all his colleague had accomplished in Destiny County.

Still, he understood there were some sinful voicemails, texts, and emails, and not just unrecorded phone calls. In other words, this wasn't a "he said, she said" situation. He didn't need to know every detail, but he thought the rabbis should know more than just the generalities. They particularly should know what words were recorded on someone's cell phone.

"Ah, this is exactly my predicament," Rabbi Dreidel responded. "After a while, the woman didn't want to talk anymore and asked that I leave her alone. I deleted every communication we had from my phone.

"That's what's so unfair. She agreed everything was confidential. I complied with that by deleting things, and then she violated the very agreement she insisted upon."

Rabbi Yosef didn't want to know the details of the messages, especially with Abigail sitting there.

"Okay, you made mistakes," said the senior rabbi. "You admitted that. You will go through intensive counseling to get to the root of what happened.

"I am asking you to dig deep, very deep with the psychologist. You have to work as hard on this as anything you have ever done.

"In the meantime, your marriage and your family are intact. We will let things calm down a little and then have a community meeting. You will not participate in the synagogue until we tell you otherwise. You cannot step foot in there. It wouldn't look right. That will be how it is for a matter of some months; I can't say how long.

"You both understand that, right?" Rabbi Yosef asked, as he shifted his gaze to Abigail, who nodded her understanding.

"We can't have this look like we are sweeping things under the rug. We are not. We will deal with this head-on.

"Mishy and Abigail, are we all on the same wavelength?"

Both nodded.

"Okay. I need to ask you what I consider the most important question. I absolutely need to know this. And I am not even asking Abigail to leave the room when I ask. She needs to know this too, Mishy.

"We love you. You are surrounded by people right now, Rabbis Finkelstein and Schvitzerman and myself, who love you. This is all confidential. We care about you and Abigail and your family. You know that.

"Whatever your answer is to this question, we can deal with it, but we need to know the truth. I need to know," Rabbi Yosef declared. "Are there other women involved?"

Rabbi Dreidel raised his eyebrows and hands, palms up, and looked at the other rabbis. "Rabbi Yosef, there aren't. There isn't anyone else."

"This is very important," Rabbi Yitzak Yosef repeated. "We needed to ask you that to go forward."

"There is no one else," Rabbi Dreidel repeated, raising his shoulders and again gesturing with his hands. Although she didn't think the rabbis noticed, Abigail saw her husband's face redden ever so slightly. She felt faint, knowing in her *kishkas* that her husband was lying to save his neck.

"And here's another thing," Rabbi Yosef added, "There is no guarantee this is going to stay quiet. We could be sued for something. I don't know what exactly, but it happens.

"Your name could end up in the newspaper. I want you to think about whether you want to resign and relocate. You have that option. You and Abigail should discuss this together. I can use my influence to get you an administrative job back in New York.

"In other words," Rabbi Yosef explained, "it might be best to avoid more problems by leaving the area. Think about your children reading articles in the newspaper about this.

"Once something gets in the newspaper and on the internet, it is there forever. It's a stain that won't go away, true or not."

"We are not moving anywhere," Rabbi Dreidel said.

"Are you sure of that? It is an option you can think about and discuss on your own," the old rabbi repeated, looking intently at Rabbi Dreidel and then Abigail.

"Abigail, you have sat here very patiently. I want to hear from you, too," Rabbi Yosef said.

"Rabbi," Abigail said, "we've put so much into the shul and the Destiny area. I'm not telling you anything you don't already know.

"I can't answer for Mishy's sins. I can only say that I support him, and I will do whatever is needed to get my husband reinstated and our family back to normal.

"This is our life. This is our home. To pack up nine kids and move somewhere doesn't make sense. It's not what I want to do.

"I haven't done anything wrong," Abigail added, "and our kids shouldn't be punished either. Destiny County is their home."

"Thank you, Abigail," Rabbi Yosef replied. "You bring up a very good point. You and the kids obviously are as much victims here as anyone. I hear you loud and clear. We are here for you. You are free to call me with anything you need at any time."

"Now," Rabbi Yitzak Yosef said to Abigail, "we are asking you to please step out of the room so we can talk to Mishy a little more."

Once Abigail stepped out, Rabbi Yosef cross-examined Rabbi Mishegas about other women. "Look," he said, "search your mind. Even if another woman misinterpreted something you said, took it the wrong way, thought you looked at her funny, *whatever it may be,* you need to tell us *now.* We need to know."

"There's nothing," Rabbi Dreidel insisted once again.

Rabbi Finklestein, who had been silent, brought up the patriarch Joseph, who refused intimacy with Potiphar's wife in Egypt, leading to his imprisonment. Rabbi Finklestein wanted Rabbi Dreidel to feel that his road to reinstatement was much less severe than what Joseph faced, nor was he as innocent as Joseph.

Rabbi Finklestein then discussed the famous parable from the Talmud in which Rabbi Eliezer taught his disciples to repent before the day of one's death. His disciples asked, "How can we know when that will be?"

"That is why we must repent today," Rabbi Eliezer told them, "because we could die tomorrow."

That led Rabbi Schvitzerman to talk about the rules of repentance codified by Maimonides. The elements included regretting and acknowledging the behavior; never repeating the sin; remaining conscious of the sin going forward; acting with renewed humility; acting with more decorum than ever before, regardless of the level of lasciviousness exhibited in the past; refraining from other sins, no matter how small; praying for atonement; seeking forgiveness; pursuing other good deeds; and teaching others not to sin. Rabbi Schvitzerman said all of the elements applied to the current situation.

The rabbis realized that their colleague already knew everything they had said, but they felt obligated to say it anyway.

"All right," added Rabbi Yitzak Yosef, "we will meet at least once a month. We will plan on a community meeting in several weeks, and we will meet with you prior to that."

At the conclusion of the meeting, Rabbi Dreidel didn't know whether he should hug or shake hands with the other rabbis. It felt so awkward. He felt insulted. It wasn't fair that he could not attend the very synagogue he built.

Okay, he thought, *I can see how you don't want me on the pulpit for the time being, but where am I supposed to pray?*

He left without shaking hands or hugging anybody, and he and Abigail were silent all the way home.

A COMMUNITY
MEETING

Six weeks into the crisis, nothing was resolved, but the lines were drawn. Hezekiah and Marshall had only collected a handful of resolute, righteous supporters in favor of the immediate dismissal of Rabbi Dreidel. Destiny's frum Jews, the ultra-orthodox true believers, were in the minority. Phone calls had not turned up more victims other than Sarah Shofar—yet.

The rabbi commenced professional counseling with Dr. Plotzky. Abigail kept a close and constant watch on the rabbi's whereabouts by cellphone, frequently calling him and demanding to know his comings and goings.

Word of the scandal extended beyond Abigail's and Mishy's large families to old yeshiva friends and acquaintances in the old neighborhood. Family members—rabbis or wives of rabbis—flew out to stay with the Dreidels in a steady stream to provide emotional support and stability.

Rabbi Dreidel's family considered him the golden child. His parents always held him out as such a mensch of a *boychik*, so talented, full of charm, and a constant source of great *naches* (Jewish and parental pride). They extolled his every Jewish achievement.

So, his parents, siblings, and in-laws were utterly shocked when they learned Mishy was in the midst of a scandal. They wanted to believe he was the victim of a crazy *shiksa*, a troublemaker who had stirred up a hornet's nest, and everything would soon blow over.

Rabbi Dreidel and Harold Bernard, with Harold working for free, got their restraining order prohibiting Lacey Johnson from disparaging the rabbi or disseminating his private communications. A process server rang Lacey's doorbell and handed her the documents, stating, "You have been served."

Lacey's hands shook as she read the papers. She was not going to be told to shut up by anyone. How dare the rabbi! What a slime! He was trying to bully her. This was the same person who pleaded with her to text him "good morning" and "good night" every day without fail because of their "special connection."

Now, he was suing her. She could not believe the lies she read about herself in the legal papers. The source of some of the twisted information was undoubtedly Rabbi Hazzarai. That was the only way Rabbi Dreidel could have learned about some of the things in her past that she wasn't proud of. The rabbis were in cahoots. They twisted her most private and sensitive information to make her sound like a nutcake. As far as she was concerned, they were rotten, evil *bastards*.

Lacey immediately phoned Hezekiah, blasting into the phone her feelings about the injustice, the unfairness, the *chutzpah*, and—on the verge of tears—her lack of funds to hire a lawyer.

Lacey was not easily mollified. She started to calm down only after Hezekiah and Marshall promised to arrange a free consultation with a lawyer for her that they would all attend. That way, they could freely discuss the restraining order. Lacey agreed to photograph and email the legal documents to Hezekiah so that he and Marshall could send them to the lawyer.

The court action, which was public, led to more rounds of phone calls among the rabbi's detractors and supporters.

"You won't believe this!" was the tenor of most calls. "The rabbi actually sued this Lacey person, the lady making the allegations!"

Clearly, the rabbi's attempt to quiet Lacey and save his reputation had backfired. As they say, you cannot un-ring a bell. He and Harold only managed to ring it louder.

When it comes to local scandals, there are fires and then there are *fires*. This fire wasn't going out any time soon. It was on everyone's mind, and the evil tongues were going to *kibitz*, offering their own opinions and advice.

The Jews of Destiny County talked about what they heard and from whom and when they heard it, embellishing a detail here and there and then asking whether to believe it. The Jews from the Reformed Synagogue caught wind of the conflagration. Why shouldn't they chime in with their two cents? They were able to say, "I told you so!" and "I always wondered about him!"

Marshall was disgusted. They still hadn't fired Rabbi Dreidel. True, the rabbi wasn't attending shul since they confronted him. But Marshall didn't see why he should bring himself and his family to shul, either. It was uncomfortable to even think about going there, even though his checkbook, as much as anyone's, had built the damn place.

His faith in Judaism was steadfast, but his faith in TUCAS was destroyed. Marshall's principles and values were severely violated. He debated with himself and his wife about whether to even attend a community meeting called by Rabbi Yitzak Yosef for next week. He doubted things were moving in the right direction. He already was exhausted and burned out by the entire affair.

Judaism, he thought, was a beautiful religion. But, as the saying went, even in the best apple, you sometimes found a worm.

Marshall ultimately decided to attend the meeting. He felt an obligation to see things through.

He wrote a well-organized statement in preparation for the meeting about (1) the need for transparency in the selection of a new rabbi, (2) the creation of a democratically elected board of directors with oversight authority, and (3) other measures that would help guard against future abuses. He rewrote it to make it shorter. When he was happy with it, he put the statement in the pocket of the sports coat he planned to wear to the meeting so he wouldn't forget it.

The Jews of Destiny County packed into the Jewish Center's synagogue the night of the community meeting like the overflow attendance on Yom Kippur. Their greetings were muted as they filled in the benches under the gracefully arched ceiling and soaring, stained glass windows. It was so crowded that some congregants had to stand at the back and sides of the chapel.

The three rabbis, Yitzak Yosef, Finklestein, and Schvitzerman, sat upon the stage in front of the brightly polished, cherry-wood ark that held the holy Torah scrolls. A podium and microphone sat in the middle of the stage and another stood at floor level in front of the chapel for speakers from the audience. The *mechitzah* had been pushed to the back of the synagogue, but women and men sat on separate sides of the expansive room, as usual.

Rabbi Dreidel and Abigail, along with their children, were nowhere to be seen.

Rabbi Yitzak Yosef began by thanking everyone for coming. He said every single member of the congregation was important to him, and, he added, the community's input was essential for resolving its problems.

"Everyone who has something to say will have every opportunity to say it," the senior rabbi declared.

"If someone doesn't want to speak publicly, call me or one of my colleagues here at any time," he continued. "Everyone will be listened to with love and concern."

Rabbi Yosef went on to explain that the decision to suspend Rabbi Dreidel was his and, ultimately, his alone. But it was important to go through a process to sort things out, giving due consideration to everyone involved.

He confirmed that Rabbi Dreidel would be undergoing an evaluation and counseling, and that he and the other two rabbis would be monitoring the process. Rabbi Yitzak Yosef also said Shabbos services would continue under the temporary leadership of rabbis he would send to Destiny County, and he promised to regularly convene community meetings to keep everyone informed.

He then called on Rabbi Finklestein, the most eloquent of the three rabbis, to share some remarks.

"*Teshuvah*, atoning for sins and returning to God, is the bedrock of Judaism," the old rabbi said, his voice initially frail but gaining strength as he went on. "All the sin and guilt offerings commanded in the Torah are about Teshuvah," he explained. "After the Holy Temple was destroyed, the sacrifices were replaced by prayer."

Rabbi Finklestein spent some time explaining the root meaning of the Hebrew verb, *lashuv*, to turn, and how it became a noun, *teshuvah*, to turn back to God.

"Now," he said, "it is prayer that can turn, or reconnect, sinners to God. And the community must accept those who stray from righteousness if their prayers are sincere. This tenet of Judaism applies to absolutely everyone. The lessons of the Torah apply to congregants and rabbis alike."

Rabbi Finklestein completed his spiel and Rabbi Yitzak Yosef thanked him, commented on the importance of *teshuvah* and forgiveness in Judaism, and then asked who wanted to speak.

No one jumped up.

Finally, one mentally disabled lady rose and walked up to the microphone set up in front of the chapel. She pointlessly told Rabbi Yitzak Yosef how much she enjoyed the student rabbi who was substituting for Rabbi Dreidel and then walked back to her seat.

The next speaker from the audience was a middle-aged lady who sporadically attended the shul. She held several typewritten pages.

"First," she began, sounding as if she might break into tears, "may it be the will of God that Rabbi Dreidel fully regain his physical and mental well-being as soon as possible. He is such a talented and wonderfully giving person. God knows that whatever the rabbi may have done, it is outweighed many, many thousands of times over by all the good.

"Rabbi Dreidel," she said, her voice now strong and clear, "is the most outstanding Torah scholar to ever live in Destiny County. He has shared his knowledge and wisdom and taught classes in our dining rooms, living rooms, and offices—in the evenings and at lunches, week in and week out, not to mention all of the beautiful classes at shul and all of the beautiful sermons, Shabbos after Shabbos, holiday after holiday, year after year.

"Rabbi Dreidel was always so generous with his time, whether helping someone put a *mezuzah* on their doorway at home or office, getting a *minyan* for a *yartzeit,* or helping organize a bris or bar or bat mitzvah. He has always been exemplary and acted beyond anyone's expectations.

"He has done all this with great charm and kindness, always with humility, with great feeling, sincerity, good humor, and consistently helped Jews feel pride about their identity and spirituality.

"It is worth remembering that he arrived with very little financial support and miraculously put together an amazing effort to build a beautiful synagogue, purchase our own Torah scrolls, and sponsor many programs, all while growing a family of nine kids with Abigail, all of whom we have enjoyed watching grow up, as they are beautiful, smart and fun."

Looking up from her speech toward the rabbis on the stage, she said, "I hope that all of the mitzvahs and wonderful achievements of Rabbi Driedel and Abigail are fully taken into consideration by all the people here tonight. I hope Rabbi Yitzak Yosef, Rabbi Finklestein, and Rabbi Schvitzerman all have the experience and skills to help heal this situation so that we can go forward in health and wellness, and allow Rabbi Dreidel to recover fully with all the support and love that he and his family need.

"As Rabbi Dreidel has lifted up this community over and over again, I hope this community can reciprocate with kindness, understanding, and compassion."

As the lady sat down, the audience burst into loud, heartfelt applause.

Marshall, who held his typewritten speech in his hands, refolded it and put it back into the pocket of his sports coat. This group, he thought, was lost, and nothing he said was going to change anyone's mind. Rabbi Dreidel was their cult leader, and they had swallowed the Kool-Aid.

The lady's spiel broke the ice. Several others stood to endorse her statement and say what the rabbi meant to them. One talked about how he was there for her when her mother was dying. Another, how the rabbi taught him how to pray. Two men, one right after the other, said they wanted him back as soon as possible.

These statements resonated with the rabbis up on the stage. They did not want to fire their fellow rabbi, although others in TUCAS had suggested they cut their losses. They knew that Rabbi Dreidel had suffered a significant mental and spiritual disturbance, but they believed he could rehabilitate himself quickly and that he was motivated to do so. The support from the congregation meant he might very well weather the storm.

Rabbi Yitzak Yosef, in particular, was gratified by the expressions of support. He considered Rabbi Dreidel a star, the synagogue to be a real gem, and Rabbi Dreidel and Abigail a tremendous success story. It was clear why Rabbi Dreidel and Abigail didn't want to move away. People in Destiny County loved them.

A lone voice broke the flood of goodwill.

Walking to the microphone, Rachel, Hezekiah's wife, said, "I want to know why the person who suffered the misbehavior is being ignored and no one is speaking up for her?"

Rabbi Yitzak Yosef rose from his chair and slowly walked back to the podium.

"Please, I certainly want to hear from you. Thank you for speaking up. I value what you are saying. That you spoke up for someone else means that you have a big heart and the courage to go with it," the white-haired rabbi said. "I have love and consideration for everyone involved in this matter, including the lady you are speaking about. I haven't met her, but her experience is not being ignored at all, and I would be happy to meet with her and you.

"I decided the rabbi needs to go through a process here," Rabbi Yosef said, "I suspended him. This is an extremely serious matter, and you can rest assured, I am taking it seriously.

"Suspending the rabbi may not have been the popular thing to do, but I felt it had to be done, and I did it.

"My decisions about his future will be based entirely on my best judgment and, whenever possible, consultations with the congregation, my fellow rabbis, and the psychologist who is now involved.

"I promise you," Rabbi Yosef concluded, "my door is open to

absolutely everyone. But at the end of the day, I make the decisions."

And that was that. Marshall never rose to speak. Hezekiah never rose to speak.

Marshall and Hezekiah rushed out the door after Rabbi Yitzak Yosef finished. But it wasn't over. Hezekiah knew there had to be other victims. At the very least, he thought, he had to get Sarah Shofar to come forward.

IMBROGLIO

Gloria Epstein attended the community meeting with her husband, who didn't want to go. She *schlepped* him along, anyway. He sat on the men's side of the syna-gogue, while she sat on the women's. She felt nervous.

The rabbis' spiels flooded Gloria with ill feelings. In her mind, they were unsupportive of the woman who had been abused, and they failed to condemn the rabbi's misbehavior. Instead, they had categorized it as a mental health issue, like he had a bad cold or flu, and he was now going to rest and take some over-the-counter cough medicine to get better.

These rabbis, she thought, didn't have a clue. She didn't see a way that anything would be resolved. She knew, in her gut, that there were other victims that the rabbis hadn't even heard about. She was one of them. The supervising rabbis didn't seem interested in digging out the truth.

"They are going to protect their own," she told her husband

on the ride home. "I can't stop feeling terrible for Abigail. I couldn't care less about Rabbi Dreidal. He can go to hell."

Her husband, Benjamin, agreed.

"What bothers me," he said, "is that we still don't know what the rabbi did or didn't do. While people are getting up and singing his praises, nobody knows what he did. Nobody talked about that."

"I know what he did," replied Gloria.

"How do you know?"

"Well, he did it to me."

"What?" Benjamin exclaimed.

"I haven't wanted to tell anyone. It wasn't that big a deal. I could tell he wasn't himself. I dealt with it. Any time I went over there, I made sure one of the kids was with me in the same room. He only strikes when he gets you all alone. I didn't want to tell you. I didn't see how that would help anything; it would only make you mad.

"I feel so bad for Abigail and those kids," Gloria continued. "You know how much I love the kids. The devil can take Rabbi Dreidel. The way this is going, I don't think he will get better, not if they whitewash what he did."

"What in the hell did he do to you?"

"He started asking me for hugs. He said he was depressed. He hugged me."

"Where? How did that happen?" Benjamin asked, almost shouting in surprise.

"Usually in the social hall or in the kitchen setting up for holiday events or cleaning up after lunch on Shabbos.

"It was a pattern. He'd ask to talk to me," Gloria explained. "His *shtick* was, could he ask me some questions, some personal questions? He'd say that I was so close to Abigail, could he confide in me, would I keep it secret, not tell Abigail, not tell you either? And foolishly, I haven't told you. I didn't want to upset you."

"What the hell! We are never going to that place again!" her husband roared.

"That's how I knew you'd react. I want to see the kids and Abigail. I understand how you feel, but nothing really happened. He's off his rocker."

"So what happened other than hugging?" he asked.

"He kissed me once. It was on the lips. It was so weird. I was in shock. I told him not to. He immediately apologized. But the sensuality could not be mistaken.

"I decided I would never be left alone with him again. After that, I always brought one of the Dreidel kids to the kitchen or social hall with me if Abigail wasn't there.

"I was so embarrassed when it happened," Gloria continued.

"Before that, I thought he saw me as another grandmother to his kids. I'm an old lady, for crying out loud. I thought he just wanted a hug, that he felt overwhelmed and confused. I felt sorry for him. He seemed lost.

"Obviously, he isn't supposed to touch another woman, let alone hug someone. That was so far afield from his rules as a rabbi that I knew he wasn't right in his head. That sympathy went away when he kissed me on the lips. Poof. That was too much. That was something else entirely."

"Are you going to tell anyone?" Benjamin asked.

"You don't know how much I have thought about that. I really don't want to tell anyone. Now that the cat's out of the bag with whatever happened with this Lacey woman, I don't really see the need. I would prefer to keep it quiet.

"Abigail always thought the world of him. She always thought she had a great marriage," Gloria said. "She was so proud of him, the Jewish Center of Destiny County, the kids, everything they've done. They did it all as a couple. Now, she is devastated. How can you blame her?"

"What a lie. What a mess!" Benjamin said. "Well, we should pull our monthly credit card contributions."

"What are they supposed to live on? They have nine kids, for *chrissake*. He won't be able to fundraise or put on programs while he's suspended. How are they going to pay the big mortgage for the shul?"

As she walked through the door at home, Gloria's phone was already ringing. Her friend Peggy Cohen wanted to know what happened at the meeting. She also wanted to tell her favorite friend from the Jewish Center of Destiny County what her daughter said the rabbi did to her. After she gave Peggy a rundown of the meeting, Gloria expressed her concern for the Dreidel family and her love for the kids. Then the subject finally came up, like sewage backing up from the drain when it has nowhere else to go.

"I know for a fact that there was more than one victim," Peggy told Gloria.

Gloria's pulse quickened. What was this? She hadn't told anyone other than her husband just minutes ago.

"Okay, tell me, what do you know?"

"Remember when my brother was still in the hospital in New York? The hospital wasn't far from where my Miriam goes to college. She visited her uncle regularly.

"So, when the rabbi was going to his annual convention in New York, I asked him to visit my brother. He ran into Miriam there at the hospital."

"Okay."

"Well, to make a long story short, he hugged and kissed Miriam and then must have texted her a hundred times asking to see her again. Miriam was mortified. She would be upset if she knew I was telling you this, so please don't tell anyone."

"When did you find out?" Gloria asked.

"Right after it happened. Miriam freaked out. Of course, she called me. You know how close we are. She didn't know what to do, so naturally, she reached out to me.

"I thought about it a lot, really stewed on it. Boy, was I mad. I finally called the rabbi," Peggy said. "He didn't deny anything. He apologized and apologized. I got him to agree to never contact Miriam again, ever. Miriam wanted it kept quiet, and he wanted it just between us, but I had to tell you."

Gloria decided she would return the favor.

"Peggy, you won't believe this. Well, actually you will. What happened to your daughter? Well, it happened to me, too."

"No!" exclaimed Peggy.

"Oh, yes!" replied Gloria.

The ladies hung up the phone only after discussing, in excruciating detail, what happened to Gloria and what happened to Miriam, the apologies to Gloria, and the apologies to Peggy. Then they discussed several familiar subjects all over again—the community meeting, the rabbi's suspension, their love and concern, especially for Gloria, for Abigail, and the rabbi's nine children. But neither wanted to go public, and they wondered what would happen next.

Gloria and Peggy's conversation about the community meeting wasn't the only one that night.

An anxious Lacey Johnson waited to hear from Hezekiah and Marshall. The more Lacey finally heard, the angrier she got. They told her that no one had mentioned the lawsuit filed against her or talked about what the rabbi had done to her at the meeting.

"Well," Lacey concluded, "it sounds like a charade to me. It is good if he is seeing a psychologist. Maybe he'll finally get some help. If not, he won't be back on the pulpit any time soon. He's one sick puppy."

She was aghast at their reports of the depth of community support expressed for the rabbi. That made her feel lonelier, more isolated, and angrier. She also felt more determined to stand up for herself against Rabbi Dreidel and Rabbi Hazzarai.

Dorothy Braun did not attend the meeting, either, but her mother did. Selma reported to Dorothy that the rabbi and Abigail did not attend the meeting and that she had been calling the rabbi's voicemail to find out if her granddaughter should keep her tutoring schedule with him despite his "leave of absence." The girl's bat mitzvah was coming up fast. Invitations had already gone out. The rabbi hadn't called back. Selma asked Dorothy to call the rabbi and to leave a voicemail.

Dorothy didn't want to call Rabbi Mishegas Dreidel given his questions about sex, female arousal, and the selfie photo bomb he had texted her. Instead, Dorothy called Sarah Shofar. Sarah's bar mitzvah-aged son had a birthday following her daughter's by a couple of months.

Sarah, she learned, had not attended the meeting, either. Sarah deflected the question of one-on-one study with the rabbi and told Dorothy that they had decided to celebrate her son's bar mitzvah with a family vacation in Israel instead of a ceremony at the shul.

Sarah didn't comment on the imbroglio and the rabbi's suspension, other than to say she hoped he would address his issues. She did not sound like she supported the rabbi. Dorothy wondered if Sarah also had some sort of ugly experience with him.

It sure as hell wouldn't surprise me, she thought.

Sarah called a few women friends from shul to get their take on the community meeting. She got the vibe that they supported the rabbi. This confirmed her decision to keep things to herself.

However, that started to change when she listened to the voicemails at her office the next day.

First was a voicemail from Harold Bernard, who, she knew, was a lawyer in the area. She was introduced to him once at a Jewish Center of Destiny event, but only to say hello. In the voicemail, Bernard said he was representing Rabbi Dreidel and that a Hezekiah Miller had been talking about her. Could she please call him back?

The second voicemail was from Peggy Cohen, who said that Sarah didn't know her, but she wanted to share confidential information about her daughter, Miriam, and another victim of the rabbi's.

In the last message on her phone, Hezekiah Miller declared that she had a duty to the community to disclose that she was a victim of sexual harassment by the rabbi.

Sarah's breathing quickened; the blood rushed to her head. Who could possibly have said anything about her? There was only one suspect—her husband and office partner, Elmer.

He was dropping off the kids at school when he answered his cell phone.

"Who did you talk to about me and the rabbi?" Sarah hissed into the phone.

Elmer immediately realized his mistake. He had made some calls to find out what happened at the meeting, and he was shocked that the two people he telephoned were bemoaning the rabbi's suspension and advocating for his immediate reinstatement. He also had learned that Marshall Goldman was one of the original shul members who asked the rabbi to resign. Elmer called Marshall.

They didn't know each other well, but they had seen one another often at the synagogue. Marshall had a favorable impression of Elmer and his wife. They were both accountants and dressed nicely. Elmer thought of Marshall as a benevolent elder of the Jewish community, and he knew that Marshall donated substantially to the Jewish Center.

Marshall told Elmer that he was "done" with the Jewish Center. He explained that he thought the suspension was superficial and that the rabbis intended to reinstate Rabbi Dreidel as soon as they could get away with it.

He said that he personally had met with Lacey and read

the rabbi's disgusting texts and emails to her. He told Elmer he was frustrated that the rabbi had not resigned and the other rabbis were supporting him. Elmer felt that he had the ear of a sympathetic friend, someone who not only was leveling with him but was sharing his innermost feelings. He agreed with everything Marshall said.

When Marshall added that he strongly suspected there were other victims who had not yet come forward, Elmer spilled the beans about his wife.

"After Rabbi Dreidel harassed her, she couldn't get away from him quickly enough. She was upset, literally, for days on end," Elmer told Marshall. "I feel so stupid and guilty about trying to resolve the situation.

"We met with the rabbi, he apologized up and down, said it would never, ever, happen again.

"I was seduced by his apologies and position as a rabbi," Elmer went on. "My son, my little bar mitzvah boy, idolized him, even tried to dress like him.

"When I finally saw his texts to Sarah and realized how increasingly personal and weird they became, I didn't want to believe this was a wider problem.

"Honestly," Elmer explained, "I thought he had a teenager's crush on Sarah. I thought that was all it was. He admitted that he felt romantic feelings towards her. I took him at his word.

"He begged us not to tell anyone, especially his wife. He seemed genuinely sorry. I thought he was sincere and that it was a crazy blip in behavior.

"Sarah and I decided we would distance ourselves from him, but considered the matter closed, and we decided to turn our kid's bar mitzvah into a family trip to Israel.

"Then, after a while, he started up again, trying to talk to Sarah, saying how he missed her, how lonely he was, that they had a special connection.

"He commented on her beauty, her clothes, her hairstyle, and her legs.

"That was it," Elmer said. "We blocked his phone number on both of our phones. We canceled our landline at home. I specifically emailed him and told him to stop communicating with Sarah in any manner. We knew we were right to cancel the bar mitzvah plans here and hold it in Israel instead."

Marshall repeatedly expressed sympathy with Elmer and told him that the messaging to Lacey Johnson was surprisingly similar to what Elmer described. Sharing notes only underscored Marshall's decision to sever ties with Rabbi Dreidel and the greater TUCAS organization. He complimented Elmer on shifting gears and coming up with a different bar mitzvah plan.

Elmer felt unburdened, cleansed, and relieved after spilling the beans. He imagined this was how a Catholic who had just gone to confession and said ten Hail Marys might feel.

Marshall suggested that Sarah tell what happened to her to someone else who would really listen, someone who had been completely ignored and disrespected by the community—Lacey Johnson. The toll of the rabbi's behavior on Sarah might ease if she shared her story. It certainly would help Lacey feel better, Marshall said.

Sarah, to Elmer's relief, didn't get mad when he explained why everyone was calling her. He repeated his entire conversation with Marshall, leaving nothing out. She understood that sometimes a person must open the window to get the smell of rotten fish out of the room.

To the ever-practical and business-minded Sarah, the question, now, was how to deal with all the phone calls. She and Elmer agreed that he would call everyone back, sheltering her from the storm and sharing her stress.

SCHMOOZING

Schmoozing, talking with a relaxed intimacy, especially when the *schmoozers* enjoy a special connection and common history, feels comfortable and fulfilling. Is there anything better than talking to someone who is really listening and understands you?

Gloria Epstein, the only regular at the shul with a special connection to Peggy Cohen, was an extraordinary telephone *schmoozer*. She could always count on Peggy for a very animated conversation. Gloria was accustomed to hearing about Peggy's favorite subject, Peggy's daughter Miriam.

Ordinarily, Gloria understood that what Peggy said about Miriam was infused with a certain emotionality that might color a description or slightly bend a fact. After all, Peggy's version was based on her love for her daughter and her interpretation of what she said.

In this instance, however, Gloria found Peggy's second-hand account of the rabbi's encounter with Miriam entirely credible, and it dramatically increased their *schmoozing* frequency and intensity.

The surprising, mutual disclosures from the night of the community meeting created a bond between Gloria and Peggy as strong as iron.

Gloria no longer considered Peggy just a shul friend who sat with her during Passover at the community Seder. Now, they were important characters in an ongoing drama. They each regarded the other as the best person with whom to discuss the heavy burdens that neither wished to trumpet to the rest of the Jewish community. Their secrets, now disclosed to each other, did not stay secret for long.

With the floodgates officially opened wide by the community meeting and the public suspension of the rabbi, the ladies no longer felt constrained about what they *schmoozed* with others.

What are the odds that conscientious, ethical, and decent Jewish women who had promised—with all the sincerity of a *Sh'ma Yisrael* on Yom Kippur—to keep the rabbi's "intimacy issues" confidential would let a little info slip out here and there? The odds are one hundred percent!

No one can be held to a vow of confidentiality when that promise was conditioned upon being the only person involved. The rabbi's *shtick* about each lady being the only person that he could confide in was clearly a whopper. Sure, he could rely on their word, but as they say, a half-truth is still a whole lie.

Put another way, Rabbi Dreidel baked promises of confidentiality like they were bagels, and no one bakes one bagel at a time. He had subjected others to his same *shtick*, including Lacey Johnson, and who knew whom else?

Gloria knew that Peggy's professional work included training businesses on issues of sexual harassment in the workplace. Gloria considered Peggy a cutting-edge expert on the subject. This case, involving her own daughter and her telephone *schmoozing* friend, fell right into Peggy's wheelhouse. Peggy told her that, based on her training and experience, there must be other victims. Gloria didn't doubt it for an instance.

Gloria Epstein felt an awful dread. She had a front-row seat to the entire melodrama, due to her deep emotional connection to Abigail and the kids.

Gloria's telephone *schmoozing* with Abigail increased dramatically. They had loved *schmoozing* on the phone well before the scandal. Their telephone time now increased in proportion to their lack of in-person contact due to the rabbi's suspension.

The suspension meant that Gloria rarely watched the kids and no longer helped Abigail set up for Shabbos luncheons or other events. The events went by the wayside. Gloria's love for the Dreidel kids did not. If anything, she loved them all the more.

She worried that the kids missed the extra attention Gloria loved to give them. She was like an extra *nana*, an extra *bubbela*, a fun old lady who the kids knew loved them. That love didn't go away because the rabbi was suspended. Gloria's heart ached for the kids.

The more dread she felt about what Abigail didn't know, the more pessimistic she felt about the rabbi's future, and the more her heart broke. The hole they each felt from the absence of frequent in-person contact was partially filled by telephone schmoozing.

Neither woman saw the situation as black or white, but neither could really level with the other. There was no way, Gloria decided, that she was ever going to tell Abigail that the rabbi kissed her on the lips. But she did let on to Abigail that the rabbi had hugged her, though she left out the number of times. She couldn't mention Peggy's daughter. Why pile on? Why hit a sore spot with another hammer blow?

All Abigail could do was try to insulate the kids from what was happening and keep her family together. Her survival instincts kicked in. She had to support Mishy. He wasn't himself, but he was contrite and would get better. Time would pass, and things would get back to normal.

In the meantime, Rabbi Yitzak Yosef was scratching his head and pulling his beard. The calls kept coming in from his superiors in New York, from Mishy's and Abigail's parents, even from people Rabbi Yosef didn't know.

Jews from Destiny clamored for their beloved rabbi's reinstatement. Anna Habbibi wrote Rabbi Yitzak Yosef's wife a long letter criticizing the rabbi for not supporting Mishy and Abigail.

A couple of callers wanted to know why he hadn't fired Rabbi Dreidel. Fire the rabbi? He really didn't want to do that. Rabbi Dreidel was a star. He had built a beautiful shul and established a real community in Destiny County. Others said it couldn't be done, but Rabbi Dreidel did it.

Rabbi Yitzak wanted a complete psychological evaluation of his star rabbi. He wasn't going to put the cart before the horse. Everyone needed to relax, take a breath, and let things settle down.

He wasn't initiating calls to anyone, except for Marshall Goldman, who, he knew, had a long relationship with Rabbi Dreidel and who had contributed so much *gelt*.

The old rabbi didn't understand why Marshall had joined Hezekiah in bushwhacking Rabbi Dreidel with a letter full of such harsh demands. This was not the Jewish way to go about things. This was not a kind and compassionate approach. This was not a respectful way to address a rabbi regardless of the problem.

Marshall was not surprised to get a call from Rabbi Yitzak Yosef. He immediately figured that the rabbi wanted to preserve Marshall's financial support—a cynical but perhaps accurate assessment.

Hoping for a friendly schmooze with Marshall, Rabbi Yosef said, after some pleasant preliminaries, "I can't make heads or tails out of what happened with Rabbi Dreidel.

"It's all so out-of-character," he went on. "It must be some psychological condition."

"I've read the messages," Marshall responded. "They are

disgusting. It goes beyond some kind of temporary breakdown."

"Can't we slow down, a little?" Rabbi Yosef pled. "Let's try to withhold judgment until the psychologist can tell us something. Let's try *rachmones* (mercy)."

The normally calm and soft-spoken Marshall lost his self-control. "To text and say what he did, Rabbi Dreidel must be sick and rotten to the core.

"He has to go immediately, or I will have nothing to do with the Jewish Center of Destiny County," Marshall insisted. "You can't put a black hat on a pig and call him a rabbi!" he spat out. "He's got to go. I don't want him near my wife or kids."

Oy, thought Rabbi Yitzak after the call ended, *it's hard to be a Jew, but harder still to be a rabbi. I don't understand these people.*

Hezekiah, unlike Marshall, wasn't going to withdraw from the field of battle. He obsessed over the situation. He wanted to *schmooze*, but he quickly ran out of people to talk to.

At the community meeting, he identified those who were sympathetic to the rabbi and wanted him back. He would have nothing to do with anyone who was aiding and abetting the joke of "rehabilitating and reinstating" a corrupt rabbi.

With whom, then, could Hezekiah *schmooze*? Marshall took his calls and told him about his conversation with Elmer. But Marshall wanted to drop out rather than fight. Certainly, he could commiserate with Lacey, who Hezekiah now encouraged to counter-sue Rabbi Dreidel for sexual harassment. He regularly spoke to a small handful of other frum Jews, but that was it. That was like preaching to the choir.

Hezekiah wanted to fight. It wasn't enough to expose the corruption and then just lie down and die. To whom could Hezekiah trumpet the injustice, corruption, and offending behavior? To his social media contacts on the internet, that's who!

Thus began a series of posts decrying the rabbi's behavior. They escalated from vague complaints, put forward in the form of questions, to detailed specifics. These included references to "The Jewish Offenders List," an online listing of prominent Jews accused and convicted of sex crimes. He asked his social media followers if Rabbi Dreidel belonged on the list. He asked everyone to, "Wake up, already!" He quoted famous Jews from the time of the Holocaust who said the world would be destroyed by those who watch others do evil without doing anything.

"Did you see what Hezekiah just posted?" one Jew asked another.

When Hezekiah blocked Rabbi Dreidel from his social media, the rabbi asked others to text him the posts. He obsessed over them. He spoke to Harold Bernard multiple times a day strategizing, kvetching, wringing his hands, and lashing out at his detractors, especially Hezekiah. He wanted to sue Hezekiah. Wasn't Hezekiah breaking the law when his posts were based on what Lacey was now temporarily restrained from disseminating? Harold wrote Hezekiah a strong letter threatening legal action.

Meanwhile, Harold decided to ask the rabbi again about other victims. Was there anything to the rumors he was hearing through the grapevine about Sarah Shofar? The rabbi told his lawyer that there was a slight issue, a true misunderstanding with Sarah Shofar, but that he had met with Sarah and her husband, and all was resolved.

This did not fully satisfy Harold. Sarah had not returned Harold's phone messages, but finally, Elmer did. Elmer and Harold danced around the question of whose side Sarah was on in the only way two learned professionals could, with veiled threats against each other.

Ironically, they wanted the same thing—to keep Sarah's name out of the whole mess.

Lacey started talking too, to a Navy investigator, about how Rabbi Hazzarai violated her confidences and banned her from attending services at the Jewish chapel on the base. Hezekiah started talking to a cub reporter from the *Destiny Dispatch*, the local newspaper. The reporter called Lacey, telling her she got her name from someone named Hezekiah Miller. The reporter had spoken to him and to another gentleman named Marshall Goldman. Would she be willing to meet?

INDIGESTION

Harold Bernard, Lenny Spiegleman, and Adam and Anna Habbibi, among others, wouldn't stop pestering Rabbi Yitzak Yosef about Rabbi Dreidel's reinstatement. The rabbi adeptly handled the phone calls and was afforded great respect due to his seniority, but he sensed desperation in many of the calls.

All his years as a rabbi taught him how to flatter, deflect, inquire and confide—techniques that made it easy to beat around the bush. He wasn't going to get into arguments with these longtime TUCAS supporters, the very people whose repeated and significant donations built the beautiful synagogue in Destiny County. Sure, it would not have happened without Rabbi Dreidel's inspired leadership, unbounded energy, vision, and hard work. But these people were the bedrock of the Jewish community.

Rabbi Yitzak Yosef felt that what they said mattered. He wanted them to confide in him. He wanted to keep them close to

TUCAS. He knew that they were hurting without a rabbi, and he knew that these people had become the rabbi's best friends. He needed to hear them out and not misinterpret their anxious calls for the rabbi's reinstatement as criticism of how he was handling things.

Lenny Spiegleman, for example, consistently *nudged* Rabbi Yitzak Yosef about three things. First, he wanted him to get Rabbi Cohnman, the rabbi with whom Hezekiah converted, to tell Hezekiah to knock it off with the social media. The posts made people angry and sent Rabbi Dreidel into the crazy-sphere.

Couldn't they sit Hezekiah down and explain that Jews do not publicly criticize other Jews, especially a rabbi, and that his actions offended Jewish law?

Second, why hadn't they turned over copies of Rabbi Dreidel's messages with Lacey to Dr. Plotzky, his psychologist? How was the psychologist supposed to fairly diagnose and treat the problem without seeing the offending material?

Third, why hadn't Rabbi Dreidel undergone a full psychological evaluation, with all the bells and whistles, to put to rest these rumors of sexual deviancy or bipolar disorder or who knows what else? Wouldn't it be helpful if they could tell everyone Rabbi Dreidel went off the rails because of some highly treatable anxiety- or stress-related infirmity and posed no threat to anyone?

Adam Habbibi wrote Rabbi Yitzak Yosef an emotional letter claiming that TUCAS had ignored the Jewish community of Destiny County before Rabbi Dreidel came to town. He sang Rabbi Dreidel's praises and underscored the depth of his suffering. He wrote that he was worried about the toxic effects Rabbi Dreidel's suspension was having on the rabbi's children.

"TUCAS is handing the Hezekiahs of the world a victory every day Rabbi Dreidel continues to be humiliated," his letter concluded.

Rabbi Yitzak Yosef rubbed the bags under his eyes. He found

the letter highly offensive. He decided he wouldn't respond, at least for the time being.

Harold Bernard was on the phone almost daily feeding Rabbi Yitzak Yosef the latest spin on newly uncovered gossip about Lacey Johnson. The senior rabbi caught wind from Rabbi Hazzarai about a Navy investigation involving Lacey. He asked Harold to explore what was happening there. Harold made it sound like the Navy was investigating Lacey's misconduct, not that of Rabbis Hazzarai and Dreidel. Rabbi Yitzak Yosef stressed that Harold should keep everything out of the newspapers.

The elderly rabbi called another meeting with Rabbi Dreidel and Rabbis Finklestein and Schvitzerman. When they all got together again, Rabbi Yosef let Rabbi Dreidel go first, because he wanted to gauge his demeanor and mental state.

Rabbi Dreidel sounded contrite and spoke softly, but he arrogantly demanded his own reinstatement.

"My banishment from shul feels like an eternity," Rabbi Dreidel said. "There is no chance I will repeat my mistakes," he declared, adding that his congregants missed him horribly. "Worst of all, I can't fundraise.

"Without an unsolicited, ten thousand dollar check from the Spieglemans," he told the rabbis, "the shul would be in default on its mortgage, and I wouldn't be able to take care of my family."

Rabbi Dreidel went on to say that he was doing his counseling, which also cost a fortune. "Why stretch things out? Isn't the punishment exceeding the crime?"

"Slow down," Rabbi Yitzak Yosef said. "I have to know how the counseling is going. When can I talk to your psychologist?"

Rabbi Dreidel told the rabbis questioning him that his therapy involved marital confidences and other private information that could not be divulged. To do so would chill the therapy and invade not just his privacy but Abigail's.

151

"With all due respect, our marital issues are nobody's business. Surely, you can understand that?" Rabbi Dreidel said, adding that the psychologist had assured him and Abigail that he didn't have a psycho-sexual deviancy issue.

"We had to borrow money from our families to pay for the counseling, and I don't know how I'm ever going to pay it back," he said.

"Dr. Plotzky says adding to my financial stress will just make things worse."

He told the rabbis, again, that he had erased the offending messages from his phone at the request of the woman causing all the problems. And the other side, meaning Hezekiah and Lacey, wouldn't turn the messages over unless he resigned.

"Lacey won't cooperate—she's controlled by Hezekiah," he told them, "and Hezekiah has it in for me. You have no idea what this guy is like! Have you seen his posts criticizing Rabbi Yitzak and TUCAS?"

Rabbi Yitzak Yosef said he wasn't a psychologist and didn't know what testing was required. "But I need to talk to your psychologist, and I need a written report! I will keep it confidential."

This intensified the back and forth between Rabbi Dreidel and his boss.

How do rabbis argue? Eventually, they yell and insult each other, just like anyone else.

Rabbi Yitzak Yosef raised his voice to state the obvious, that all of their current problems were of Rabbi Dreidel's creation. Therefore, he was going to bear the costs, whether he could afford it or not, if he wanted to be reinstated. "You will not dictate this process," he shouted at Rabbi Dreidel.

Rabbi Dreidel screwed his face up, aghast at the effrontery. *I am ten times the rabbi you ever were*, he thought to himself. Lashing out, he brought up Rabbi Yosef's old money-laundering case. "At least I wasn't involved in anything criminal. Didn't the Great Rabbi support you through your *tsuris*?" he taunted.

Rabbi Yosef's blood pressure skyrocketed, and he felt faint, while Rabbi Dreidel hyperventilated, panting like a dog.

Only by divine intervention did they avoid coming to blows.

The other two rabbis, who, by this time, were also highly agitated, started putting in their two cents, with everybody speaking at once. The cacophony drowned out their final *farkakte* remarks, words chosen to shit upon the other.

Finally, as the air was sucked out of the room, Rabbi Finklestein reminded everyone that they all wanted the same thing— and what were they really arguing about, the difference between a month or two until the reinstatement?

After going 'round and 'round, the learned rabbis settled on a plan. The psychologist would write a letter giving the rabbi a clean bill of health. Once the psychologist committed in writing that Rabbi Dreidel was fit to serve again, the other three rabbis would "consider" his reinstatement.

Rabbi Dreidel would provide a limited release to his psychologist allowing him to have a follow-up conference call with Rabbi Yosef and the others. Rabbi Dreidel would address the congregation at the next community meeting to offer a heartfelt apology and reassure everyone that "the behavior" would not be repeated.

Only then would Rabbi Yosef announce Rabbi Dreidel's reinstatement, assuring everyone the rabbi was still under his supervision. The reinstatement meeting could not occur for at least six months after Rabbi Dreidel's suspension. Rabbi Yitzak Yosef insisted upon that; otherwise, he said, they would be accused of a whitewash.

Rabbi Yosef felt shaken after the meeting. He had not expected his shining star, who he could have fired right off the bat, but for whom he had stuck his neck out, to be so hostile. He was so ungrateful, whiny, and prideful when he should have been humble, contrite, and quiet. It started to feel, in his *kishkas*, that he and his fellow rabbis were never going to discover Rabbi Dreidel's problem. The younger rabbi was not going to repeat his sins, that much was certain. But the question remained—had he gained sufficient insight into his own character? Frankly, Rabbi Dreidel seemed more than a little *meshugganah*, a little nuts. His craziness made everyone else start to feel crazy, too.

Rabbi Yosef suffered so much indigestion the rest of the day and later that night that he hardly ate dinner, even though his wife made a potato kugel that he always enjoyed. Later, after saying his prayers upon retiring for the night, he beseeched God to give him the strength to see things through with wisdom. Every bone in his body ached, but he fell right to sleep.

It was around three in the morning when he awoke, feeling clammy, uneasy, and with pain in his chest. He'd suffered a horrible dream. A *dybbuk*, a malevolent, wandering spirit who looked a bit like his grandfather, had rattled on and on about *a schande far di goyim*, a disgrace in front of the gentiles.

He woke up moaning and feeling utterly *famischt*, completely disoriented, grasping his chest and waking his wife up.

She turned on the light, took one look at her husband, and shuddered. "Oh my God, is it your heart?"

"No, I think it's just the same indigestion I had all day," Rabbi Yosef replied, getting some of his composure back.

She could see that he was in real pain, holding his chest and grimacing.

"We have to call the ambulance!" she exclaimed.

The rabbi told her to calm down. But the pain didn't subside, so he agreed to go to the hospital, but not by ambulance.

With his wife's help, the old rabbi threw on some clothes,

and she drove them to the emergency room. There, he received a full work-up and was diagnosed with a heart attack that had done little damage.

He wasn't discharged until almost noon the next day with directions to follow-up with his own doctor who should adjust his blood pressure medication and refer him to a cardiologist. The ER doctor also ordered a week off work. Rabbi Yitzak Yosef took off two days, but the telephone never stopped buzzing. Things were always happening.

During his time off, Rabbi Yosef let go of the anger, and his heart ached for Rabbi Dreidel. Maybe anyone who was embarrassed and suspended, especially someone with so much energy and spirit, would go a little *meshugganah* sitting around. That had to be the case here.

Rabbi Yitzak Yosef had spent a lifetime listening to and reading people, including many rabbis. His star rabbi had lost his luster, but Rabbi Dreidel still had that burning desire to resume his mission. That counted for a lot.

Rabbi Yitzak Yosef told himself that he also had to think of the rabbi's wife and kids. If he got a good letter from the psychologist, he and the other rabbis should reinstate Rabbi Dreidel. Rabbi Yitzak Yosef was certain he wouldn't misbehave again. Whatever it was that he had done, he had been punished. Abigail also would watch him closely.

The people of Destiny County, other than a few detractors, like Marshall and Hezekiah, wanted him back. Rabbi Yosef couldn't thwart the community. He was going to reinstate Rabbi Dreidel. What choice did he have?

CARRYING ON

Rabbi Mishegas, despite the lack of money in the *pushke*, paid the month's bills as best he could. He then took his family to visit cousins in *Eretz Yisrael*, the holy land of Israel.

If they weren't going to let him set foot in the synagogue, *his* synagogue, the rabbi thought, the synagogue that wouldn't even exist if it weren't for him, *fine*, they'd take a trip and get away. They deserved a vacation, a grand tour of the Holy Land. So, they closed up their house, bundled up all the kids, and took off for three weeks. A sympathetic congregant donated a ton of airline miles to dent the cost.

Rabbi Dreidel's petulance was such that he would not allow the student rabbi to stay at his house while the family was in Israel. The student rabbi had nowhere else kosher enough to stay. He couldn't stay with the few frum Jews like Hezekiah who were opposed to Rabbi Dreidel's reinstatement. He stopped leading services at the synagogue in Destiny County. No one really missed him. He was not a star in the making. He was, as rabbis go, especially when compared to Rabbi Dreidel, a little "bleh," a bit of a *nebbish*, nice enough, but nothing to write home about.

While the Master of the Universe loves all the Jewish people, and the Jewish people heartily embrace their rabbis, not every rabbi is a star.

* * *

In the absence of a substitute rabbi, Adam and Anna Habbibi, who owned a jewelry store in a strip mall, stepped up to try and fill the void, even if it meant closing the store early. They did everything they could to keep the shul running. They attended like clockwork. They knew all the prayers. Adam, a tall, muscular man with a ready smile, happily led the services even though his singing resembled that of a frog. He tried to copy the rabbi's inflections in the songs with only limited success, but the handful of congregants who showed up did their best to keep the tunes on track.

In the absence of the rabbi, the Habbibis texted the men whose phone numbers they knew to get a *minyan*, ten men, to come to each service so that they could recite the *kaddish,* the mourning prayer. Usually, they succeeded, although just barely.

Adam Habbibi also selected a male congregant to give the *D'var Torah*, a sermon on that week's section of the Torah. Most of the guest *spielers* surprised everyone with excellent sermons. At the conclusion of each lay sermon, the *spieler* was greeted with applause and handshakes by the few other congregants on the men's side.

Anna, who was as tall as Adam and often outran him on their daily, four-mile runs, went beyond the call of duty, getting everything ready for the after-service luncheons. Still, those who continued to attend missed Rabbi Dreidel and Abigail terribly.

Adam and Anna also reached out to the two most prominent members who no longer attended, Marshall and Hezekiah. Marshall wouldn't return their phone calls. Hezekiah couldn't be convinced to attend services, but he agreed to meet the Habbibis at their home for a heart-to-heart.

At the kitchen table one Sunday night, Anna put out cookies while Adam made tea. They made short shrift of the small talk and Adam got down to brass tacks.

"Listen," he said plaintively, "our community needs to stick together. I don't care if you are orthodox or reformed, we're all Jews, right? We need to stay united. We have a wonderful rabbi. He went off the deep end. He's not himself. He needs time to get better, don't you agree? Shouldn't everyone get a second chance?"

He may well have asked Hezekiah to roll around in pig manure.

"He forfeited all rights to call himself a rabbi," said Hezekiah.

"Wait a minute, hold on," said Adam, frowning. "You haven't lived here very long. Anna and I were here from the very beginning. We saw what the rabbi built up from scratch, from absolutely nothing. He went from person to person creating a community and building a beautiful synagogue. Look at all the support he has …"

"Adam," interrupted Hezekiah, "you can't make a prayer shawl out of a pig's tail."

"What does that mean?" demanded Adam.

"You never saw the texts or heard the voicemails. Rabbi Dreidel knew exactly what he was doing. Instead of getting the intensive help he needs, he is spending his time suing Lacey. He can never be a rabbi again."

Anna couldn't stand it. She *shried* and jabbed her index finger in the air at Hezekiah, "Can't you at least stop posting such mean stuff on social media? Don't Jews have enough enemies in this world?

Listen to Adam, we have to stick together. Jews should not publicly assail other Jews."

"Let me ask you a question," replied Hezekiah. "I know you are good people and mean well. I admire your standing in the community. But I want to know why you are supporting a sexual deviant. Can you answer me that?

"No one at TUCAS investigated anything," he continued. "Rabbi Dreidel disgraced himself, his family, and Judaism itself. He knows what he did is disgusting. That's why he threatened suicide the night we confronted him. He didn't deny anything. He knew how sick he was the whole time."

"You have to give the rabbi a chance," yelled Adam. "You don't kick a guy when he's down."

"You don't know what's going on," said Hezekiah. "Here's a letter from his lawyer threatening me," he said unfolding a letter from his jacket pocket. "Do you want to see it for yourself? He sent one to Lacey, too.

"I will not be intimidated," Hezekiah said through gritted teeth as he pounded his fist on the Habbibi's kitchen table.

"Can't you at least think about Abigail and the kids?" blurted Anna.

"You either need to get on board with the rabbi's reinstatement," yelled a trembling and angry Adam, "or find another synagogue!"

Hezekiah, in contrast to the Habbibis' meltdown, kept his voice calm.

Adam and Anna became more and more *vershimmelt*, rattled and frustrated, and the conversation grew as bitter as horseradish. Soon, there was nothing more to discuss.

Hezekiah left the meeting reinvigorated, sure of his convictions and confident that the rabbi's loyal followers, like Adam and Anna, had no clue about what really happened.

Three weeks later, when Rabbi Dreidel and his family returned to Destiny County, the rabbi also was reinvigorated. He immediately checked in with Harold Bernard and his most loyal supporters about how to keep pressuring Rabbi Yitzak Yosef to reinstate him. He complained to anyone who would listen that he was unable to fundraise due to his suspension, and he told them Rabbi Yitzak Yosef had done nothing to make up for the financial shortfall. Counseling was putting him and his family in hock. It cost a fortune, and he knew he had to do it, but how was he ever going to pay for it? He neglected to mention the cost of his trip to *Eretz Yisrael*. After all, most of the plane fare was donated.

Rabbi Yitzak Yosef heard Rabbi Dreidel's criticisms loud and clear through the grapevine. Each time, he felt his chest tighten. Obviously, business was business, and he understood that Rabbi Dreidel would feel awkward trying to raise money while suspended. He thought he and the other rabbis could take a stab at reaching Destiny County's donors.

He called Rabbi Dreidel and asked him to provide a list of his top-twenty contributors. He would ask other TUCAS rabbis to help reach them. He also suggested that Rabbi Dreidel recommend three congregants to form a committee to review the synagogue's finances and start a fundraising campaign so the bills, especially the mortgage, could be paid.

Rabbi Dreidel told Rabbi Yitzak Yosef that he would get back to him. He didn't like anything he was hearing. The requests struck Rabbi Dreidel as another affront to his dignity. There was no way he would ever turn over the donor list. He had built it person-by-person, year-by-year.

He justified his refusal to turn it over the same way he denied the rabbis a full release to talk to his psychologist. First, he told himself that the list was completely confidential. Second, it was entirely his. They could keep their mitts off it. He wasn't going to let any of the other TUCAS rabbis form a cozy relationship with *his* donors and pilfer money from them that rightly belonged to him.

A finance committee also was a big problem. He didn't want anyone poking around in his expenditures and second-guessing what he spent on this or that. He'd already heard the whispers questioning how he could afford to fly his family back and forth from New York or pay the out-of-state yeshiva tuition for his older kids. *A finance committee to raise funds? What a joke. No layperson could raise funds as he had. They had no idea how hard it was to raise money in this community. You couldn't just cold call a Jew in Destiny County and get a donation. That wasn't how it worked.*

The Board of the Jewish Center of Destiny County consisted of himself, his wife, and his father. If push came to shove, he could tell Rabbi Yitzak Yosef that his board did not agree to the disclosure of the donor list unless each person on it consented. In the meantime, he would stall all these requests. All he needed to do was stall long enough to get reinstated.

On the other hand, thought Rabbi Dreidel, *I better protect myself, too. We put the house in the name of the Jewish Center of Destiny County to avoid property taxes. This is our house, and the Jewish Center owns it in name only.*

I'll have a board meeting with Abigail and my father and transfer it back to me and Abigail, just in case. I'll copy what the lawyer did back then, but in reverse. I can do it myself, he thought. *Nobody needs to be the wiser.*

The house has jumped in value, just like the surrounding homes. It's our house, our equity, and our money.

REINSTATEMENT

Harold Bernard was nervous. A lawyer he knew as contentious and argumentative had approached him in the courthouse. The lawyer said he was likely to be hired by Lacey Johnson. He asked for an extension on the *Rabbi Mishegas Dreidel vs. Lacey Johnson* hearing.

"By the way," he told Harold, "you don't have a case."

Harold immediately reported to Rabbi Dreidel. That Lacey had hired an attorney sent shockwaves through the rabbi. He had thought she would fold without a fight.

The rabbi wanted Harold to rush to the courthouse to jam the case through before Lacey's lawyer officially appeared. Harold said he couldn't do that and asked the rabbi to please calm down. He recommended a mutually agreed order, restraining each party from disparaging the other, rather than going to a hearing. Harold hadn't obtained the offending communications. He imagined their surfacing was not in his client's interests. They should avoid a hearing at all costs. He hoped Lacey also wanted the materials kept secret.

The problem, now, was that an opportunity that had existed when Lacey wasn't represented had passed. Harold could not ethically contact Lacey directly if she was represented by an attorney. Her attorney had not formally appeared, which required the filing of a formal Notice of Appearance. If Harold proceeded to a court hearing to try and jam something through before Lacey's lawyer officially appeared in the case, Harold could hardly deny he had received verbal notice. Anything the court ordered would be rescinded once Lacey's lawyer appeared and screamed bloody murder about the verbal notice. Worse, Harold could get in trouble for failing to disclose it. If he disclosed the verbal notice, Lacey would get a continuance anyway.

In the meantime, Harold and Rabbi Yitzak Yosef spoke frequently to negotiate the terms of Rabbi Dreidel's reinstatement. Rabbi Yosef wanted continued verification of counseling and oversight—in essence, an extended probationary period. Rabbi Yosef also demanded that they dismiss the lawsuit against Lacey because the committee of three rabbis feared litigation and publicity.

Harold found himself in the middle of a burgeoning abyss between the troika of rabbis and his stressed-out client. He used his best powers of reason and persuasion with all of them, but to no avail.

Rabbi Dreidel opposed every one of Rabbi Yitzak Yosef's demands. Neither rabbi wanted to negotiate, nor would one speak directly to the other.

Rabbi Yitzak Yosef's excuse was that he had to run everything by Rabbis Finklestein and Schvitzerman. Rabbi Dreidel's excuses were "as numerous as the stars of heaven and the sands of the seashore." Rabbi Dreidel and Rabbi Yitzak Yosef liked Harold acting as the intermediary so they didn't have to talk to each other. The mere mention of one rabbi's name or proposal to the other served as a lightning rod for complaints.

Harold listened to Rabbi Dreidel disparage Rabbi Yitzak

Yosef, characterizing him as old and out of touch. He was a timid, mental midget who couldn't act without Rabbis Finklestein and Schvitzerman giving him the green light. Those rabbis didn't escape criticism, either. They were simply yes-men to whatever Rabbi Yitzak Yosef wanted, Rabbi Dreidel declared.

After a while, Harold gave up trying to change the subject or rein in Rabbi Dreidel's comments. The lawyer's only goal was to get the rabbi reinstated. He loved the rabbi, but just as importantly, he wanted his law practice back. Everything was always a crisis with Rabbi Dreidel! He was the most unusual and demanding client of Harold's decades-long career.

Rabbi Dreidel was in a lather. He had successfully stalled Rabbi Yitzak Yosef about the donor list, coming up with one excuse after another. He was certain that he was about to be reinstated if his psychologist, Dr. Plotzky, and the three rabbis just played ball. He was that close. It was almost six months since he was ambushed by Marshall and Hezekiah. Everyone wanted him back, and Rabbi Yitzak Yosef knew that.

Mishegas wrote a reinstatement spiel for himself and a separate one for Abigail. He showed his speech to Lenny Spiegleman, Harold Bernard, and a brother-in-law who was a rabbi in Canada. He wanted to say he was sorry, thank everyone for their support, and promise a bright future. The sorry part was tricky. He wanted to apologize without admitting that he had done anything wrong. He didn't want to say anything that could be used against him by Lacey or Hezekiah. He wanted Harold, in particular, to carefully check the speech.

He also wanted Harold to talk to his psychologist to make sure that Dr. Plotzky would reveal as little as possible to the three rabbis during their conference call. The rabbi had insisted to his psychologist that their counseling sessions were private, including all discussions of sex and his relationship with Abigail. The other rabbis didn't need to know the details.

Rabbi Dreidel also wanted Harold to nudge the psychologist to write a letter certifying he was fit for work. He knew Rabbi Yitzak Yosef would never okay his reinstatement without some paper to hide behind.

Harold called the psychologist, but he found out that his client had not given Dr. Plotzky permission to talk to him. Getting Rabbi Dreidel to sign a release was worse than pulling teeth. They had to go over each and every word in the release to restrict how much detail the psychologist could talk about while still assuring the other rabbis he could return to work. In other words, he wanted his matzah balls and to eat them, too.

Harold started to feel that he was being tested like Job. He quietly asked himself what he had done to deserve a hyper-vigilant, contradictory client who was never satisfied. After much coaxing, Rabbi Dreidel agreed to sign off, and Harold faxed the psychologist a limited release.

Dr. Plotzky spoke to Harold later that day. The psychologist told Harold that he didn't have a problem writing a letter recommending Rabbi Dreidel's return to work, but he could not guarantee the rabbi would never have problems of the same nature in the future. He understood Harold wanted him to say that, but no one could ever say that. In fact, no definitive treatment or medication would address Rabbi Dreidel's specific issues long-term. He recommended extended counseling.

Rabbi Dreidel had tied his hands about how much he could actually disclose, the psychologist continued, and it wasn't therapeutically indicated to provide a detailed report of their counseling sessions. Rabbi Dreidel, in his present frame of mind, thought you were either for him or against him. Thus, it was vitally important that he, as Rabbi Dreidel's psychologist, having gained a necessary measure of trust, not violate that confidence.

He could reassure the rabbis on the conference call that, in his opinion, a full-blown psycho-sexual evaluation was a waste of money. He also could state that it was clear Rabbi Dreidel had learned a lot from their counseling sessions. Most importantly, he could tell the rabbis that the likelihood of repeat, inappropriate behavior was minimal, especially given the consequences to the rabbi. He could also tell the rabbis how utterly traumatic and humiliating Rabbi Dreidel's suspension had been for him. The pain the rabbi felt was very real. Dr. Plotzky believed that suffering from the suspension had led to situational depression and anxiety that would lessen with a return to work.

Harold asked, "Is there some way, subject to the limited release, perhaps invoking a joint attorney-client and psychologist-client confidentiality, that you can tell me the diagnosis?"

"I can tell you the following only in the strictest confidence," the psychologist said.

"Again, I don't want to jeopardize the therapeutic relationship.

"What we are working on, specifically," the psychologist said, "are boundary issues caused by overconfidence, recognizing manipulative behavior to achieve one's personal needs, and learning to put one's personal needs in perspective.

"This likely is a lifetime challenge for the rabbi," Dr. Plotzky said. "He has trouble seeing how he got himself into this mess. He has trouble seeing his need for therapy, other than jumping through the hoops necessary to get his position back. He has trouble minimizing his own needs.

"His religiosity and ability to charm others are complicating factors. One of the reasons he has been successful as a rabbi is his inflated sense of self, which he justifies because it is intermingled with his religious mission.

"He also achieved tons of gratification as a rabbi," the psychologist continued, "from being admired and being the center of attention. This feeling of righteousness and his inflated sense of self have snowballed. They motivate him to encourage others to attend, to participate, and financially support the synagogue. He sees the synagogue, his services, and programs as spectacular achievements for which he deserves credit."

Harold thanked the psychologist for his insight and all his support. He felt the psychologist was on his patient's side and would emphasize what Rabbi Dreidel wanted him to say to help satisfy the rabbis during their conference call. Dr. Plotzky wanted Rabbi Dreidel back to work to aid his therapy.

As soon as the phone call concluded, Harold typed the phrase, "narcissistic personality disorder" into his search engine. His eyes got big. The descriptions he saw and the articles he read described the rabbi. There was no medication or cure, nor was the condition well understood. Often, the narcissist had suffered some kind of childhood trauma. Harold wondered whether the rabbi was sexually abused in the yeshiva, or if one of his parents was a narcissist.

The word "narcissist" never came up in Dr. Plotzky's conference call with the rabbis. The psychologist sounded all the right notes, reassuring the rabbis about their greatest concern—that Rabbi Dreidel would not repeat the offending behavior. He recommended that Rabbi Dreidel be allowed to return to the pulpit.

The rabbis heard what they needed to hear—that Rabbi Dreidel had undergone counseling as directed, sincerely participated, and gained a lot in the process. He sounded committed to continuing the counseling. The psychologist would get a letter out to Harold Bernard that the lawyer would forward to Rabbi Yitzak Yosef.

Rabbi Yosef summoned Rabbi Dreidel to meet with the rabbis one more time. He told Harold that he wanted to look Rabbi Dreidel in the eye to gauge his commitment to continue the counseling. He wanted Rabbi Dreidel to show humility and contrition. He also wanted the lawsuit against the woman dismissed, and he wanted Rabbi Dreidel to sign an indemnification agreement taking responsibility for any judgments against the TUCAS organization arising from his conduct. TUCAS lawyers at the headquarters in New York said the indemnification was mandatory and non-negotiable.

Rabbi Yitzak Yosef compromised on learning more about the counseling out of respect for Abigail's privacy, and he gave up on a full-blown sexual deviancy evaluation due to its great cost. In his *kishkas*, he still felt it was too early to reinstate Rabbi Dreidel, but he was willing to do it. He was leaning over backward to compromise and resolve the situation. But Rabbi Dreidel would have to show him and the others humility and contrition, and he would have to agree to all the other conditions.

Harold held an early afternoon meeting with Rabbi Dreidel that stretched well into the evening. They reviewed the indemnification agreement word-by-word. Ultimately, Rabbi Dreidel signed off after Harold's repeated promises that the shul's insurance policy would cover any claims, should, God forbid, anyone sue.

The biggest problem was convincing Rabbi Dreidel to drop the lawsuit against Lacey. He didn't want to. He felt that was a sign of weakness. He didn't want to give Hezekiah, that *mamzer*, that bastard, any sort of victory.

Harold repeatedly pointed out that, if he were reinstated, that was the end of the story. He could lose a small battle, so to speak, to win the war.

Rabbi Dreidel *kvetched* and whined that no one understood how much he had suffered. He *kvetched* that, although he knew he did wrong, the punishment far exceeded any sin.

What did he actually do that was so horrible? His reputation was ruined. Even when he was on vacation in Israel, people he met there had heard about the whole *schmeer*, and he had to take the time to set them straight. How was he going to make up the financial shortfalls of the last six months? He was so close to getting a grant to build a beautiful *mikvah*, and despite all the *tsuris*, nothing was going to stop that from happening.

Harold let him rant and vent. He carefully counseled him about how to respond in his final meeting with the rabbis, how to show contrition and humility, and how he better not blow his chance at reinstatement. And he had to behave himself.

READ ALL
ABOUT IT!

The rabbi's reinstatement went off without a hitch.

A late rumor, that Lacey Johnson planned to attend the community meeting or protest with picket signs in front of the synagogue, caused real consternation. It may have been the product of Rabbi Dreidel's supercharged state of anxiety.

Whatever the source, Rabbi Dreidel called upon his most ardent male supporters for panicked "security" discussions. They planned how they would station themselves at the entrance to bar Lacey from entering the building and disrupting the meeting. The forces of evil never slept, and vigilance was necessary. Lacey must not mar the rabbi's reinstatement.

The security plans evaporated when Lacey didn't show up, and those responsible for suppressing any disruption abandoned their posts in less than ten minutes to join the meeting.

The synagogue's pews were filling up, with men on the right side and women on the left. All anxiously awaited the big announcement; yet the mood was subdued. The solemnity of the occasion did not stop Adam Habbibi from greeting all the men with friendly handshakes, slaps on the back, bro-hugs, and laughs as everyone found a place to sit.

Hezekiah sat in a corner with his little clique of frum supporters, sitting upright and looking straight ahead, trying to look as pious as possible. He didn't say a word. He avoided all eye contact with Rabbi Dreidel and his most vocal supporters. They wondered how Hezekiah had the *chutzpah* to show up where he wasn't wanted. So much for "loving your fellow Jew."

Rabbi Yitzak Yosef led the community meeting. The podium hid his paunch, the product of decades of heaping helpings of cholent, a traditional Jewish stew, served after services.

"I know this has been a difficult period," he told the seated audience while stroking his long white beard and adjusting his yarmulke. "I appreciate, and I mean this from the bottom of my heart, everyone's input. Your patience, and frankly, the outpouring of love and concern, have really touched me.

"Ultimately, the decision I am announcing tonight is my decision and mine alone. Input from the community has been very important. I also prayed constantly about what was best for the community and for all concerned."

In a deliberate, restrained tone, the old rabbi continued, "I am following the recommendations of one of the most respected psychologists in the region after his extensive counseling of your rabbi, and I am reinstating Rabbi Mishegas Dreidel immediately."

The announcement, although completely anticipated, was met with loud applause.

After the clapping, Rabbi Yitzak said, "Rabbi Dreidel has

successfully completed the first and most important part of an ongoing *process* that will include continued counseling and supervision."

Rabbi Dreidel, sitting with Abigail in the first row on the women's side of the synagogue, silently bristled when Rabbi Yosef mentioned ongoing supervision. He thought to himself, *Haven't I been humiliated enough already?*

Even though ongoing counseling was part of the deal he struck to win back his position, was it really necessary to tell everyone? He tabled his feelings so he could pay attention to the next speaker, his lawyer.

"I am now calling upon Harold Bernard," concluded Rabbi Yosef, "whose counsel and advice have been helpful and appreciated throughout this process." He left the podium without taking any questions.

Harold Bernard spoke at length, calling upon the Jews of Destiny County to unite against the enemies of the Jewish people. He invoked his own family history, including his grandmother's experience during the Holocaust. With his voice cracking, and stopping twice to wipe away tears, the lawyer extolled his client's virtues. He reminded the congregation how Rabbi Dreidel had lit a spark and kept the flame of Judaism alive in Destiny County. He told everyone that the rabbi's reinstatement was the only reasonable resolution of the situation.

"We are so lucky to have Rabbi Dreidel and his beautiful family in Destiny County," the lawyer concluded. His spiel also garnered applause.

Then it was Abigail's turn. She read a heartfelt speech thanking everyone for all their support. "Everyone here," she said with her voice cracking, "all of you, are like family. You welcomed us. You opened your homes to us. We have enjoyed so many holidays and meals together. You have helped raise our children. I am forever in your debt. You mean the world to us."

Even though her commitment to the couple's mission in Destiny County had been severely tested, she continued, "The rabbi and I aren't going anywhere. I guess," she smiled, "you are stuck with us forever."

She also received hearty applause. Many of the women sitting on the women's side of the synagogue hugged her when she stepped down from the stage.

Rabbi Dreidel's big moment came next. He had spent days preparing. Notwithstanding years of experience delivering sermons and leading classes—thousands of them—he had practiced this speech over and over. He wanted his voice to sound strong, but contrite, sensitive, yet masculine, sure, but still humble.

After a long pause for dramatic effect, Rabbi Dreidel took a deep, shaky breath and began his spiel. For five minutes he described how sorry he was. He knew, he said, that he had let everyone down, but he had learned painfully from the experience.

Pausing again, he said, "Most of all, I want to thank Abigail, my rock, my best friend, and my soulmate—someone who has always been there for me. Her forgiveness has been a tremendous blessing."

Then, looking down from the stage at Abigail in the first row, he declared, "I love her with all my heart."

Turning back to the audience, he said, "I appreciate the forgiveness and support so many have shown, which means the world to me. I also want to thank," he said, starting to sound like he was accepting an award, "the learned rabbis, and especially Rabbi Yitzak Yosef for his leadership in this crisis. Thank you, Rabbis Yosef, Finklestein, and Schvitzerman.

"I always considered the Jews of Destiny County one big family," the rabbi went on.

"Despite everything, I still feel that way," he said, "and I will continue to love every Jew I meet here."

The rabbi went on to say he was not giving up on those who had not forgiven him yet, and he wanted everyone to know that. He realized that, for some, it might take time to put this matter in the rear-view mirror, but he would give them as much time as they needed. He was sorry he had breached everyone's trust and would do everything in his power to regain it.

"I promise, from the bottom of my heart, that I will never let anyone down ever again," the rabbi said.

"The most important thing is just how much is left to accomplish and how ready I am for the challenge."

And that was it. The spiel was over without any mention of Lacey Johnson or any other victim, what he did, or why he did it.

But the congregants applauded, and he was back in the saddle; he wasn't ever going to go away again. He stood basking in the warmth of his supporters in his beautiful synagogue. He was endorsed by the rabbis and was glowing in the kind words of his esteemed lawyer. The Jewish Center of Destiny County had its rabbi back.

As they mingled after the meeting saying their goodbyes, everyone breathed a big sigh of relief. Adam Habbibi shook hands again with all the men (except Hezekiah), laughing joyfully and slapping everyone on the back. Lenny Spiegleman schmoozed with the visiting rabbis. Harold Bernard accepted congratulations for his speech and apologized for tearing up.

Just when you think you've turned the corner, with the butterflies flying, the birds chirping, the sun shining, and the rabbis davening their prayers of thanks, look out. As Jews often say, "Man plans, God laughs."

The very next week, the Navy's report on Rabbi Hazzarai came out, and Lacey couldn't wait to email her copy to Hezekiah, who couldn't wait to email his copy to everyone he could think of. Most of all, he couldn't wait to give it to a cub reporter from the local newspaper, the *Destiny Dispatch*.

The Navy report supported Lacey's claim that she was shunned by Rabbi Hazzarai on base. It also stated that the Navy rabbi had colluded with a civilian rabbi who had sexually harassed Lacey, a Navy wife. The Navy rabbi wrongfully covered for the civilian rabbi's very questionable behavior.

The report went on to say that, although the Navy rabbi did not officially bar Lacey and the Johnson family from attending services, he made it uncomfortable and uninviting. That was contrary to his designated role and in violation of regulations governing chaplains. The report concluded that Rabbi Hazzarai should be investigated further to determine whether he had violated the confidentiality requirements of a Navy chaplain, and whether he had made false statements in the course of the investigation.

The cub reporter called the Navy and Rabbi Hazzarai for comment, but they would not comment on an ongoing investigation. The Navy also would not allow Rabbi Hazzarai to speak to the reporter.

The young reporter put a little twist on the Navy report, focusing on the civilian rabbi's misbehavior rather than the Navy chaplain's. The reporter saw the story as extremely timely; it fell smack dab into the wheelhouse of the Me Too movement. Here was a military wife who suffered sexual harassment from a rabbi, a man in a position of power. When she sought relief on base from a different rabbi, an actual Navy chaplain, that man ostracized her. He was a buddy-boy of the rabbi who harassed her.

The cub reporter's editor loved the story and decided to play it across the top of the front page. The editor felt that his reporter had nailed the story. A rabbi, a beautiful woman, the military, and sexual harassment—here was a real local scandal and a sexy story! Sex sells.

When the reporter told the editor that Lacey was very attractive, he immediately ordered a staff photographer to take pictures of her. He wanted the article to feature a serious picture of Lacey juxtaposed to photos of the offending rabbis.

She and her editor felt confident going after the rabbis after seeing some of Rabbi Dreidel's text messages. The reporter didn't quote them in the article because she was never able to obtain all of them. She made sure the *Destiny Dispatch* article stated that the paper was not provided access to all the texts. However, she saw enough of them to conclude that the rabbi had sent highly inappropriate messages of a sexual nature.

The editor and his staff spent twenty minutes coming up with a headline, finally settling on, "NAVY WIFE SEXUALLY HARRASSED BY RABBI."

Rabbi Dreidel referred the reporter's phone calls to his lawyer, Harold Bernard. Harold spoke to the reporter several times, denying that his client harassed anyone. He admitted that the rabbi and Lacey Johnson had "troubled communications," but he denied that the rabbi said anything of a sexual nature.

Unfortunately for Harold Bernard, he hadn't seen the text messages or heard any of the voicemails, but the reporter had. Harold advanced the view that the rabbi discussed private relationship issues with Lacey because she held herself out as a lay chaplain who could counsel him from a woman's perspective. Their conversations, claimed Harold, should not be considered sexual in nature.

Harold Bernard simply adopted his client's version of events. The reporter, however, had seen text messages and heard voice mails that made Harold's claims ridiculous. So, she quoted him just that way—sounding like a real *schlemiel*, incompetent and untrustworthy.

Meanwhile, Rabbi Dreidel called his father and his brothers, his favorite brother-in-law, all his rabbinical friends, and his local supporters, including Adam and Anna Habbibi and Lenny Spiegleman. He complained that Rabbi Yitzak Yosef, who also had been called by the reporter and declined comment, had ordered him to avoid talking to the reporter under all circumstances. Rabbi Dreidel felt this was surely his call to make, not Rabbi Yitzak Yosef's.

The senior rabbi's admonition only served to stir up Rabbi Dreidel's desire to clear his name. He felt that his reputation was horribly and unfairly besmirched and that Lacey was telling lies about him. If he could just sit down with the reporter, she would see there was nothing to the allegations.

Rabbi Dreidel went 'round and 'round with everyone he talked to on the phone. The more he talked, the more he convinced himself he absolutely needed to talk to the reporter. He discussed the issue at length with his attorney. Every time Harold got another call from the reporter, he gave his client a play-by-play of their discussion to throw cold water on the idea of the rabbi talking to her. The more Harold argued, the more his client convinced himself of the need to clear his name.

Rabbi Dreidel was confident he could match wits against anyone. He was smarter than Lacey. He was smarter than the reporter. He could charm anyone and explain everything. He hadn't committed a crime. His only mistake was to be overly trusting of someone in whom he naively believed he could confide.

Surely, the reporter would see that. The reporter hadn't realized that Lacey was out to get him, that it was all a setup. It was irrational to destroy a good person's reputation and all the good work he had done simply because someone twisted his words out of context. Lacey had it all wrong. She was put up to this by her friend Hezekiah, may he grow like an onion with his head in the ground. Hezekiah's excessive and misguided self-righteousness was obvious for all to see. He was so pigheaded, a real *chazzer*!

The reporter, however, understood Lacey's story. It was easy to recount. Lacey innocently signed up for a kosher food service, and then the texts started coming. They increased quickly, becoming weirder and more graphic and obviously sexual in nature. Worse, they became more and more intimate. The rabbi wouldn't stop texting, sending messages at all hours of the night. He asked to meet her in person. He even suggested she drop off her kids with his wife, Abigail, so they could be alone together. Even though Lacey eventually blocked his number, Rabbi Dreidel found other ways to contact her.

The reporter interviewed the rabbi for more than two hours in Harold Bernard's conference room. When the reporter confronted Rabbi Dreidel with one text message about genital hair, Rabbi Dreidel claimed he was talking about women's wigs, not pubic hair. When the reporter asked about his texts about "pleasing a woman," he claimed they were taken out of context. He denied that he asked Lacey for nude pictures. He insisted that he thought she was talking to him confidentially. These conversations were about personal and private matters that he couldn't comment on, claimed Rabbi Dreidel, because of the ethical constraints of his position.

The reporter let Rabbi Dreidel talk to his heart's content and took copious notes, not believing a single word of what he said. Meanwhile, Harold tried to interrupt the interview to mitigate the damage he was sure the rabbi was inflicting upon himself by blabbing on and on. Harold imagined great trouble on the horizon, which tempered the relief he felt when the interview mercifully ended. The two hours seemed like two days to him.

The same day, the reporter interviewed Hezekiah's wife. She told the reporter that the text messages she had read and the voicemails from the rabbi to Lacey that she had heard were shocking and disgusting. In the newspaper article, which ran the next day, she was quoted but not identified because, the reporter wrote, "she feared retribution against her family."

The reporter also gave Rabbi Hazzarai "the business." She quoted the Navy report, which said Rabbi Hazzarai appeared to provide confidential information to Rabbi Dreidel about Lacey Johnson. According to the report, Rabbi Dreidel then used the confidential information to harass Lacey and ostracize her from the local Jewish community.

The reporter relied on Hezekiah and his wife to state that Rabbi Dreidel "allegedly" began to spread malicious information about Lacey and her husband to his congregants. Another friend of the Johnsons confirmed that Rabbi Hazzarai started to give Lacey's family the cold shoulder at religious services. It was uncomfortable, the friend related, to the point that the Johnsons stopped attending services. At a holiday party, Rabbi Hazzarai appeared to pull Lacey and her husband aside and looked like he was yelling at them. The Johnsons collected their son and left the party, the source said.

Another source complained that Rabbi Hazzarai regularly ignored LGBTQ people at his services. In fact, this confidential source related that on one occasion he offered a lesbian woman a yarmulke, worn only by men in orthodox settings, because he mistook her for a male. This factoid also made it into the article.

Hezekiah also was prominently featured in the article, finally getting his chance to spout, belch, and burp the criticisms that had smoldered in his throat long enough to form prickly lumps. He related how his family had moved to the area and immediately noticed offensive behavior by the rabbi, who was dictatorial, needy, and demanded adulation by the community.

Hezekiah complained that he and his wife had remained quiet because of social pressure to do so. But when the allegations of sexual harassment came to light, he and other community leaders finally confronted Rabbi Dreidel. The rabbi never denied anything; to the contrary, he admitted to Hezekiah and another leader, Marshall Goldman, that he knew he had a problem. The two quietly asked him to step down and seek counseling. But Rabbi Dreidel refused and became hysterical, ranting about legal action one minute and threatening suicide the next. So, they knew he would not leave voluntarily.

The reporter contacted Marshall, who confirmed Hezekiah's version of events.

The reporter also was able to obtain the police report from the night of the confrontation. It said the rabbi was upset because he had been asked to resign due to sexual misconduct. The police report also stated that Rabbi Dreidel reassured the officers he was not suicidal.

Hezekiah also was quoted saying the rabbis of TUCAS suspended Rabbi Dreidel but never investigated what he had done. Harold Bernard confirmed the suspension, but he explained that it was only a voluntary leave of absence.

At the end of the article came the big matzah ball in the soup, the bombshell, the real coup de grace. Hezekiah related, and Marshall Goldman confirmed, that Lacey Johnson wasn't the only victim. There was another victim the rabbi had hugged and *kissed*.

The article said the kissing victim, who refused to comment when contacted, had related this experience to several persons the reporter was able to track down. In confirming this part of the story, the reporter mixed up various rumors about Gloria Epstein, Sarah Shofar, and Peggy Cohen's daughter, Miriam.

When confronted by the reporter, Rabbi Dreidel told her that he hadn't kissed anyone, bizarrely adding that there was a difference between kissing someone on the side of the face and on the lips. He admitted that he had told someone that he "needed a hug" from time to time, and the person had consented. The rabbi said he was merely expressing emotions. He also said that he had met with the woman in question and her husband in his office and all had been forgiven.

The reporter wrote that touching non-family members was strictly forbidden for a TUCAS rabbi, citing the FAQ page of the TUCAS organization. The article stated that the allegation of kissing was confirmed by several congregants.

The end of the article included quotes from Harold Bernard saying that the TUCAS organization had completely cleared Rabbi Dreidel of any wrongdoing. The reporter also quoted Lacey Johnson saying no one from TUCAS ever contacted her, and it said the head rabbi for TUCAS in the region had declined to comment. It concluded by stating that the Office of the Inspector General of the Navy would not comment on its ongoing investigation.

THE KUGEL
HITS THE FAN

Harold Bernard sat in his bedroom at home with the door closed, ignoring his wife and kids, not feeling well enough to eat dinner. His cell phone kept buzzing, but he didn't want to answer it. He just wanted his pounding headache to go away. He kept looking at his glass of bourbon but not drinking it. That's how badly his head hurt.

When the article came out earlier that day, the reporter emailed it to him. He had trouble reading it. It was so long! Look at the pictures of Lacey! He had to force himself to read it and steady his hands from shaking, even though he wasn't holding anything other than the mouse for his office computer.

Harold could not believe how badly he came across—like a fool, an honest-to-God idiot. The rabbi came across as a liar who was guilty of harassment. Lacey and Hezekiah were the stars of the story. Harold's stomach turned over. His bowels acted up.

Dutifully, he emailed the article to his client. Harold knew he was in for a very long day: Rabbi Dreidel would vacillate between acting furious, hysterical, pleading, and demanding—and he would have to listen to the rabbi's *shries* and *geshreys*, gut-wrenching expressions of misery. No doubt, the rabbi would view the article as a hit piece and focus on the injustice of it all, like it was the end of the world.

Harold had repeatedly advised his client to avoid all reporters, that no good would come from speaking to the press, but Rabbi Dreidel hadn't listened. Bitterly, Harold thought, it served him right, although Harold focused more on his own foolish portrayal in print than on how his client looked. In his *kishkas*, he felt that he deserved what he got for making statements on behalf of his client that were so easily contradicted.

When he summoned the courage, Harold also called Rabbi Yitzak Yosef to warn him about the article. Rabbi Yosef listened to the news with intense concern, interrupting to ask questions. He then asked Harold to set up a conference call with him, Finklestein, and Schvitzerman for later that day to discuss what to do next, especially if a lawsuit was coming.

"Listen," complained Rabbi Yosef, "didn't I tell Rabbi Dreidel, in no uncertain terms, not to talk to the press? What didn't he understand about that?"

"I know, I know, I told him, too," responded Harold.

"This is exactly what I predicted," Rabbi Yosef continued. "I told him to think about the stain on his character. I told him this could happen."

"I know, I know," Harold repeated.

"But no, he thinks he knows better than everyone," lamented the old rabbi.

By the time Rabbi Yitzak Yosef said goodbye, Rabbi Dreidel

was waiting on hold for Harold. All the lawyer could do, in response to the shrill *kvetching*, was to remind his beloved rabbi that he was reinstated and that a nasty newspaper article wasn't the end of the world. Yes, the article was devastating; yes, the article was bad, but he couldn't dwell on it for the love of God and for the sake of his own sanity.

"Who even reads the *Destiny Dispatch* anymore?" Harold asked his client.

Unfortunately, while they were on the phone call, they had their computers on. They saw the article go viral, with versions appearing in online publications across the country and even in Jewish publications in New York and Israel. The headline in one of Israel's leading newspapers read, "KISSING RABBI ACCUSED OF HARRASSING NAVY WIFE."

Their cell phones wouldn't stop vibrating with calls. Rabbi Mishegas decided to take the other calls. Most of Harold's new calls were from other reporters. The paper with the largest print circulation in Portland was on the line. They wanted to know if Rabbi Dreidel would agree to another interview. They also were planning a story and a likely editorial. Would the rabbi and Harold care to comment on the story in the *Destiny Dispatch*?

Hezekiah, Marshall, and Lacey celebrated on social media, reposting the article, claiming vindication, and spitting in the eye of the TUCAS organization. They publicly called for Rabbi Dreidel's immediate resignation. Hezekiah went one step further, calling out Rabbi Yitzak Yosef, who he accused of a cover-up, and even posting the senior rabbi's phone number.

Hezekiah didn't get much response to his posts, but Lacey got a lot of, "You go, girl!" comments in addition to praise for her courage and sympathy for suffering sexual harassment.

* * *

Sarah Shofar was mad. When she read the article, Lacey's allegations resonated. She was certain everything Lacey said was true, and she was furious about the rabbi's denials. She did not appreciate a newspaper article in which the rabbi said she and her husband met in his office and all was forgiven. Even though she and Elmer were not identified by name, she knew that part of the article referred to them. Rabbi Dreidel's quotes in the article were outright lies. She didn't know about the kissing, but she imagined he would have tried the same monkey business with her if he thought he could get away with it.

Sarah told her husband, Elmer, that they should tell their side of the story to get the truth out. Otherwise, the rumors arising from the article and what Rabbi Dreidel had already said about them would only get worse.

Elmer agreed. He'd heard comments about Sarah before the article came out—how she wasn't really a victim because nothing had happened to her, and how she had entirely forgiven the rabbi for any "misunderstanding." These were all lies. There wasn't any misunderstanding about what Rabbi Dreidel did to Sarah. He admitted what he did when they confronted him. Why was he lying about it now? They had withdrawn from the synagogue, hardly evidence of forgiveness. They knew Rabbi Dreidel was the source of the false statements.

* * *

Gloria Epstein was not going on the record. She told anyone who asked that she couldn't care less about Rabbi Dreidel, but that she was heartbroken for Abigail. She felt only pity and deep *rachmones,* compassion, for Abigail and the kids. What had they done to deserve this? As soon as she saw the story on the internet about "The Kissing Rabbi," even before she read the article, she dialed Abigail's cell. Abigail sounded weak, extremely tired, and horribly hurt. Her voice was almost a whisper.

"To tell you the truth," Abigail told Gloria, "I haven't read more than the beginning of it. I know I'll read it at some point, but I'm not ready yet. I am beyond devastated.

"Please call me back later," Abigail asked. "My phone hasn't stopped ringing. I am going to have to call my mother. She's called three times already, not to mention my father and brother and sisters. It's horrible."

With a sigh, she added, "The internet is calling him 'The Kissing Rabbi.' Did you see that?"

* * *

Peggy Cohen wasn't talking to the newspaper, either. Despite her anger at the rabbi for hugging and kissing her daughter, Miriam, she didn't feel comfortable publicly criticizing a fellow Jew, let alone a rabbi. Wasn't there enough anti-Semitism in the world? Why give the haters more fodder?

I won't go public, but I won't let things pass, either, she thought.

Mishy had a screw loose, clearly, but she wasn't going to forgive him for attacking Lacey's character. She couldn't believe his or his lawyer's quotes in the paper. She felt they should be absolutely ashamed of themselves for attacking the victim, especially now that Rabbi Dreidel had been reinstated.

She dialed Rabbi Yitzak Yosef's office number. The rabbi's secretary asked to take a message. Peggy said she was the mother of another victim of Rabbi Dreidel and wanted to talk to Rabbi Yosef.

He called back in less than two minutes.

"I want to hear everything you have to say," Rabbi Yosef

assured her, "but given the subject of your message, I'd also like to get my wife on the call. Is that all right? As a Rebbetzin, she probably is more experienced than I am in asking the right questions."

Peggy agreed.

There weren't a lot of questions for Rabbi Yosef or his wife to ask. Peggy didn't hold back. She provided ample details of everything that happened with her daughter, including the unwanted touching, the texting, and the apology to Peggy after the fact.

Rabbi Yosef asked her to state exactly when all of this happened, clearly wanting to get the chronology right. Peggy also named Gloria Epstein as another victim, relating that the rabbi also had hugged and kissed her, despite the age difference.

"Wait a minute, wait a minute," said Rabbi Yosef, shaken by the double whammy of two new victims. "Who is Gloria? Can you describe her? I think I met her when we dedicated the synagogue. When did these things happen? Tell me everything you can, please."

Rabbi Yosef called Gloria Epstein. She also agreed to talk on the phone with him and the Rebbetzin. They had to wade through Gloria's reluctance to say anything for fear of damaging Abigail and the kids anymore.

Rabbi Yosef and his wife thanked Gloria for her *rachmones*, but they stressed the importance of knowing what she knew. Rabbi Yosef promised that what he learned would be kept in partial confidence, but that he would have to discuss it with his two fellow rabbis. He told Gloria that he also loved Abigail and the children.

Gloria told the rabbi and his wife the whole story: the lead-up to the hugging, the sensual kiss on the lips, how much older she was than Rabbi Dreidel, and how uncomfortable everything had been. Rabbi Yitzak Yosef wanted to know how often these things had happened. Gloria estimated the hugs occurred more than ten times, the kiss just once.

When the call concluded, the rabbi and the rebbetzin looked at each other for several moments without talking. The Rebbetzin could see her husband replaying everything in his head.

"You gave him every chance," she said. "You told him to tell you everything."

"I told him again and again," said the old rabbi, feeling defeated, angry, and betrayed. "What we have now is someone I can't trust. This is an integrity issue. He betrayed us all. I told him we could deal with anything as long as he was straight with us.

"Didn't I do everything I could for Mishy? I could have fired him right off the bat. I really stuck my neck out and risked my own reputation in TUCAS," Rabbi Yitzak Yosef *shried* to his wife.

"You ruined your own health for him," she agreed. "Nu? What more could you have done?"

"Now," the rabbi said, "we're going to have to fire him if he doesn't resign—but," he added, "I will still give Mishy a chance to respond, even though I'm sure these women are telling the truth."

"Okay," said his wife, "stay calm and think it through, like you always do."

"I'm calm. I'm okay," the rabbi said, pausing again to consider the situation. "Alright," he said, "you should be there, too, when Mishy comes back to my office. You heard what these two women said. Abigail should also be there. You can support Abigail.

"I also want to meet with Harold and the other two rabbis in person before we meet with Mishy. We need to discuss how to protect the organization."

Rabbi Yitzak Yosef called Harold Bernard. He was no longer requesting a conference call.

"We have to meet in person with Finklestein and Schvitzerman," he told the lawyer. "What I have to say can't be discussed on the phone."

Next, he called Rabbi Dreidel. He got his voicemail.

THIN ICE

The three rabbis met that night with Harold Bernard. They crowded into Rabbi Finklestein's well-worn Portland office, piled high with books, the closest meeting place.

"Before we start," said Rabbi Schvitzerman, "I want to tell you about my dream. Last night I woke up crying. I woke my wife up with this dream. I gave her a real scare. She told me that I was thrashing around and moaning. Usually, I don't remember my dreams, but this one is plain as day.

"I was smack dab in the middle of a big boat packed with Jews. It was an old sailing ship, like a schooner, or a pirate ship from the old days. I was on deck in the middle of all these Yids, Jews packed in like sardines. We were in the ocean, bouncing up and down on the waves. There, two hundred yards from the boat, was Rabbi Dreidel on a little raft, bobbing up and down, at times out of view because of the waves. I couldn't see him for a while, but when I saw him again, his raft was on fire. He had drifted much farther away, but I could still make him out. I got excited, pointing out the little raft and the fire to the other Jews surrounding me.

"Nobody listened, they all looked away. The raft drifted more and more. I could hardly see Mishy. Then I just made him out. His raft was all ablaze. He was looking at me with his hands up, with an expression of *nu*? And he mouthed the words, 'Can you help me?'"

"Then I woke up. I had no idea that the newspaper article was going to come out later in the day. And look what happened."

"In the Talmudic days," said Rabbi Finklestein, "those who suffered a bad dream would fast to ward off evil effects. Unfortunately, your dream presaged our reality, which, with this newspaper article, is a catastrophe. That won't go away by fasting."

"Harold," Rabbi Yitzak Yosef said, sighing while rubbing his forehead, "today's article refers to two victims. You know we asked Rabbi Dreidel to fully disclose everything. You talked in detail with him. And you talked in-depth with the psychologist.

"To your knowledge, how many victims were there? How many more are going to come out of the woodwork? That was always my worst fear. This is why we asked him, over and over, to tell us everything."

"Rabbis," Harold replied, in a low and serious voice, "I think I can safely say that, given the psychological condition we are dealing with, I always imagined there would be more than one victim. Maybe we all did.

"The important thing is that Rabbi Dreidel has complied with his counseling and continues to undergo therapy. He is closely monitored by Abigail and yourselves, and I am totally confident that no new incidents have occurred. I also believe that no additional incidents will occur."

"Were there other victims?" demanded Rabbi Yitzak Yosef, knowing full well that there were, but not knowing how many.

"That, I can't tell you," replied Harold.

"Well, here's the problem. If Rabbi Dreidel wasn't straight with you and he wasn't straight with us, I don't know where we are going with this. I believe there were other victims, because I heard from two of them today, with my own ears, and with the Rebbetzin also on the phone."

"I heard some rumors, but this is news to me," Harold replied, feeling pummeled to bits. "Keep in mind that Hezekiah and this Lacey woman are clearly out to destroy Rabbi Dreidel and, apparently, Rabbi Hazzarai. I think that's clear from the article," he offered meekly, forever his client's advocate.

Rabbi Schvitzerman had heard enough. "You are not answering the rabbi's questions," he said. "Did you or did you not know about other victims?

"We stressed how important it was to know the full extent of the problem. He said we had nothing more than this one lady to worry about. You told us the same thing. You told us she was a person with lots of issues.

"As far as I can tell," Rabbi Schvitzerman continued, "nothing to discredit Lacey Johnson ever materialized, at least not in this newspaper article. The crisis is deepening, not blowing over.

"Frankly, you came across very poorly in the article. Mishy came across as a liar. It makes all of us look very bad.

"This casts a negative light on orthodox Jews and all of the TUCAS shuls like ours. Why in the world did you let him talk to the newspaper?"

Harold Bernard didn't know what to say. He had never seen Rabbi Schvitzerman so upset. He felt that his client was on extremely thin ice, and that even he, an experienced and respected Jewish attorney, had lost his credibility with the rabbis.

No one said anything for what, in a group of Jews, was an eternity.

"Okay," Rabbi Yosef finally declared, "here's another problem, Harold. I have called Rabbi Dreidel, and he won't take my calls.

"First, I got his voicemail, and I left a long message that we need to meet. We need to see him and Abigail, ASAP. I mean immediately.

"You tell him that he cannot avoid my calls. Please remind him that he is still on probation.

"In the meantime, Harold, what happens if we get sued? You drafted the papers that Rabbi Dreidel signed that indemnified us. You told us we had insurance coverage for anything he did."

Harold was relieved to see the subject shift to legal claims. "We are insured. I looked at our policy," he said. "It clearly covers any claims of sexual harassment or what the insurance companies call clergy misconduct. If we are sued, we simply tender the lawsuit to the insurance company. They will appear and defend the lawsuit. You are in the clear."

"Other than the bad publicity," added Rabbi Schvitzerman, still as hot as freshly grated horseradish.

As soon as Harold got in his fancy Lexus to drive home from the meeting, he speed-dialed Rabbi Dreidel.

"Rabbi, you are on extremely thin ice. You absolutely have to call back Rabbi Yosef as soon as possible."

"He is just reacting negatively to the newspaper article," Rabbi Dreidel said. "He needs to calm down. It's a nasty article. I am sure he is getting a lot of calls from New York about the article going viral. I am not calling him for a reason."

"And what's that?" asked Harold.

"I want them all to cool down for a few days. They are reacting emotionally, and I need them to act rationally."

"Not calling back, Mishy, is making them mad and thinking that you have something more to hide," Harold said.

"Hide? I am now known worldwide as the Kissing Rabbi, for God's sake, splashed all over the internet. Where am I supposed to hide?

"They should be supporting me, not calling me on the carpet for the newspaper article. I am not responsible for the newspaper article. I thought I got through to the reporter, but I guess it sells more newspapers to defame a rabbi."

"Please call them back," pleaded Harold. "They are not happy that we talked to the newspaper."

"Listen, I can guarantee you that it would have been much worse if we hadn't said anything," Rabbi Dreidel insisted.

"People know that what they read in the newspaper is fake news! That entire article was a hit piece, and people know that.

"My people continue to support me. You should see all the sympathetic emails and phone calls I got today. I just talked to Adam Habbibi. He and Anna are totally in my corner, no matter what."

"Okay," said Harold. "It's been a long day.

"At least think about what you are going to say to the rabbis about the other victim mentioned in the newspaper. Rabbi Yosef said he also has spoken to other victims."

"I'm ahead of you. He's talking about Sarah Shofar. I apologized to her and her husband, and all is forgiven. That's water under the bridge.

"I can call them or see if they want to meet," Rabbi Dreidel continued. "They haven't come to shul for some time. I think they want to stay out of it. I can't imagine they'll talk to anyone. Nothing happened with her—absolutely nothing!

"The only other person he might be talking about is a much older lady who telephoned Abigail earlier today and told her that Rabbi Yosef had called. I will talk to her. Maybe I hugged her, *nu*? I don't remember."

After two days, Rabbi Dreidel gave up trying to call Elmer. Gloria Epstein hadn't called back either. But he didn't have to talk to either of them. Not now, not after another article had come out and the chopped liver hit the fan once again.

The headline screamed, "PRESSURE GROWS FOR KISSING RABBI TO RESIGN WITH NEW ALLEGATION." The article told the story of Sarah Shofar, who suffered repeated and unwanted text messages from her rabbi, Rabbi Mishegas Dreidel of the Jewish Center of Destiny County. The text messages included intimate sexual suggestions, which were highly inappropriate, and caused Sarah and her husband to leave their synagogue and question their religious faith.

The headline's bold letters underscored a handsome picture of Sarah and Elmer dressed in their professional clothes and standing in front of shelves of thick accounting text and reference books.

The article detailed Sarah's history with the synagogue. It explained how the rabbi gradually ingratiated himself with her, talking about their "special connection," saying that he had no friends he could really talk to. That was the excuse he gave for contacting her.

He also repeatedly told her to keep their communications private. The rabbi referred her to the laws of privileged communications between an accountant and client and between a rabbi and congregant. He told her not to tell her husband or his wife about what they talked about.

In the article, she said that she became more and more concerned when the rabbi started to compliment her on her looks, her clothes, and how she wore her hair. He wanted to know whether she found him attractive. She felt that he was extremely needy and self-centered, that he was acting like an insecure teenager rather than a rabbi with nine kids.

The article went on to say that he insisted on speaking to her before she went to bed every night. He was demanding, telling her to text him when she got up. The texts from him felt obsessive. He texted her at all hours of the night. The article quoted a witness, a fellow accountant who attended a conference with Sarah, sitting next to her because they were old school friends. He saw a string of texts that wouldn't stop, to the point where he saw Sarah shut off her phone to avoid the incessant messages.

Finally, she and her husband wrote Rabbi Dreidel a letter, telling him that Elmer knew what he had been doing and to never text Sarah again. Rabbi Dreidel then emailed her, telling her to erase all his text messages as he had erased hers. Sarah didn't want to have anything more to do with Rabbi Dreidel. But Elmer insisted on talking to him in person, in part, because their kids idolized the rabbi. When Sarah and Elmer met with him in his office, he admitted that he had romantic feelings toward Sarah.

In his office, the article continued, the rabbi said his behavior "violated his oath as a rabbi." He begged Elmer and Sarah not to tell his wife or anyone else. He apologized profusely. Although they weren't comfortable with him anymore and wouldn't attend the synagogue ever again, they both felt sorry for Rabbi Dreidel. They believed that, eventually, they could forgive him.

That changed when another congregant prevailed on them to meet with Lacey Johnson. The meeting was revelatory. The rabbi had used the same modus operandi, telling each woman of their special bond, how he didn't have anyone to talk to. Both women were victims of the rabbi's obsessive texting and the inappropriate things he texted, including sexual comments about his wife.

Sarah and Elmer had met with Lacey for more than two hours, the women commiserating, feeling violated, crying together, and sympathizing with each other's plight.

Sarah learned that the rabbi had filed a restraining order

against Lacey. She felt angry at the rabbi and Harold Bernard, and she considered their lawsuit an abuse of legal process, an example of bullying.

The article addressed head-on what had pushed Sarah and Elmer to come forward. They realized they had to after reading the newspaper articles about the Kissing Rabbi. They believed the rabbi had lied about what happened with Lacey Johnson. Harold Bernard also lied.

It was a relief to finally come forward and tell the truth. No one from TUCAS ever spoke to Lacey Johnson or Sarah, they said in the newspaper article. Further, the rabbi never apologized to Lacey for his actions or for filing his lawsuit against her, and they found it incomprehensible that he was reinstated.

After reading the second article about him, Rabbi Dreidel searched his name under the news bar of his computer. Among the print and online publications carrying new articles about him were the *Oregonian, Portland Tribune, Portland Herald, Chronicle of Israel, Jewish Insight, Navy News, Jewish Updates,* and *Popular Seas.* He hadn't recovered, yet, from the first disastrous article, and now he was worldwide news again.

The morning after the second article appeared, he had a blow-up with Abigail. She called him the Kissing Rabbi.

He stormed out of the house and locked himself in his office. He angrily texted her that she had humiliated him in front of the kids, which was unforgivable, especially when the accusations were outright lies. He had issues, but she knew how hard he was working on them. He demanded that she apologize to him in front of the kids.

She texted back that sure, she had stepped out of bounds, but how could she help it after suffering humiliation after humiliation? His apologies, she texted him, could never make up for what he had done to her.

After that, Abigail didn't speak to her husband, other than to mumble as little as possible when the children were there. She still hadn't recovered from the shame of the first article. She hadn't even read it yet. What she knew about it came from her relatives' telephone calls.

Now she suffered the additional humiliation of being married to the Kissing Rabbi. This article was worse, because, unlike Lacey, who Abigail had only met once in passing, she knew Sarah Shofar quite well. She was a credible, good person.

As Rabbi Dreidel stewed in his office, he worried that Abigail would never allow him to have sex with her again.

He finally ventured out to visit his most loyal supporters, the Spieglemans and Habbibis.

Neither Adam nor Anna had read the new article, but not for lack of trying. They loved their rabbi so much and felt so connected to him and his family that their eyes couldn't follow the words. He obviously had mental health problems, they had told each other, but he had gone into treatment and done everything asked of him. What more could he do?

Rabbi Dreidel asked the Habbibis to call Rabbi Yosef to reiterate their support and that of the community. He was worried that Rabbi Yosef was going to fire him.

"Remember," Rabbi Dreidel said to his friends, "when Abigail and I first came to Destiny County, everyone used to ask how long we were going to stay?

"My answer was always the same—we're staying for life.

"That was my promise then, and I'm not going back on my word."

After leaving the Habbibis' house, he visited Lenny Spiegleman.

At the Formica table in Lenny's bright kitchen, the rabbi confided that another Me Too advocate, the author and women's libber, Peggy Cohen, had jumped on the bandwagon. He'd hugged Peggy's daughter one time and later talked to Peggy about it. It was a non-event, the rabbi said.

But Abigail heard from Gloria Epstein that Peggy had called Rabbi Yitzak Yosef.

"How can he make a big deal about not disclosing something, when it was such a little deal?" Rabbi Dreidel asked.

He explained that he'd forgotten about Peggy's daughter amidst all the Lacey Johnson *tsuris*.

Lenny was disappointed to hear about additional victims, but he found Rabbi Dreidel convincing. Like the Habbibis, he was so committed to the rabbi that he swallowed his whole *spiel*, hook, line, and sinker, like the whale swallowed Jonah.

"Lenny, please call Rabbi Yitzak Yosef and tell him that you support me!" the rabbi pleaded.

Rabbi Dreidel believed Rabbi Yosef would listen to Adam and Lenny, and indeed, he did. But what they said didn't help, it just raised the old rabbi's blood pressure.

Three days later, the meeting that couldn't be avoided any longer took place. Rabbi Mishegas Dreidel, accompanied by Abigail, sat across from three somber rabbis and one frowning Rebbetzin. No one wanted to be there.

EITHER OR

The rabbis understood stress. They attended to the sick and infirm, comforting those departing this world to the next. They sat on the Beis Din, the religious court, resolving business disputes between bitter partners. They heard congregants vent about their personal problems. They'd heard it all.

Still, they weren't prepared for this meeting with Rabbi Dreidel. Their pulses quickened; their breaths turned shallow; they were filled with dread.

As difficult as it was, all of the rabbis looked Rabbi Dreidel in the eyes and vice versa; after all, they were rabbis.

Rabbi Yitzak Yosef finally began. He told Rabbi Dreidel that he had spoken to Peggy Cohen about her daughter, Miriam, and to Gloria Epstein, who recounted a number of inappropriate instances. Just the day before, after the new article came out, he had spoken to Sarah Shofar to verify whether or not that article accurately reported her experiences. She said it did.

"I heard very serious allegations from all three women," Rabbi Yitzak Yosef said. "My Rebbetzin participated in all three interviews."

His wife solemnly nodded her head. He did not call Rabbi Dreidel "Mishegas" or "Mishy" as usual, but by the more formal, "Rabbi Dreidel." The change was noticed by everyone in the meeting.

"I was very taken aback by what the women told me," Rabbi Yosef continued.

"Months ago, sitting down face to face with you, with the very same people in the same room as today, we gave you, Rabbi Dreidel, every opportunity to disclose everything.

"I even personally offered to use all my influence within TUCAS to help you and your family relocate. I told you I could help find you another position, so you could still get whatever help you needed.

"We were all here. We had your best interests and that of your family foremost in our minds. I warned you that a newspaper article might come out and tarnish your reputation, and that your kids might see the article. It was possible to avoid all that has happened since.

"But you, Rabbi Dreidel, assured us there were no other victims and that you wanted to stay in Destiny County."

"'Please level with us,' I said. 'Please don't hold back.' We absolutely needed to know everything—we told you unequivocally.

"You said it was just this one person. We believed you. We took you at your word.

"*Nu*, we believed what you told us, but you did not disclose these other women."

Rabbi Yitzak Yosef wasn't finished, but Rabbi Dreidel jumped in. "Everyone agrees I went over the line," he said, "but I haven't done anything that could be even remotely construed as untoward to anyone in the last six months. Nothing.

"I am not having contact with any women without Abigail or

someone else in the room," he avowed. "I am not texting any women other than my wife.

"I had a problem, and I went to work on it. My behavior since then has been impeccable. I have suffered immeasurably.

"The psychologist approved my reinstatement, just as you wanted. He hasn't changed his mind because of newspaper articles. There was overwhelming community support for me.

"What's changed other than the newspaper articles? I agree they are horrible articles, but let's not give in to fake news! Let's not allow the punishment to outstrip the crime. I have been severely punished already."

"This is your opportunity," Rabbi Yitzak Yosef interrupted back, "to tell me, honestly, why these instances were not disclosed. We are way beyond your telling me what happened.

"Again," he said, his voice rising, "I talked to Peggy Cohen, Gloria Epstein, and Sarah Shofar. I heard it from them. I don't need to hear it from you.

"I'm not going to go through everything each one said, detail by detail, especially with your wife sitting here. I know enough. I don't need to hear your version at this point. I don't think any of them are exaggerating, but even if they were, you were aware of the issues with each one. You did not disclose. That's open and shut. But before I hear anything more from you, I want to hear from Abigail. I am very interested in hearing from Abigail."

Abigail sat frozen, stone-faced, and sullen. She knew the axe was about to fall. Still, for the sake of her family, she had to rally.

"I can't answer for my husband's sins, rabbis," she said, "but he has followed through with everything, absolutely everything, since this all came to light. He has suffered tremendously, like he says. I can attest to that.

"Nothing that happened will ever be repeated. I am asking

that you take into account my situation with all the kids. I have put years and years into our shul and the community in Destiny County. This is our home. I haven't done anything wrong, and my kids haven't done anything wrong. We should not be punished."

"Okay, thank you, Abigail. I appreciate what you said very much," Rabbi Yitzak Yosef replied. "Now," he began, turning back to Rabbi Dreidel, "what is your explanation for failing to come clean with us?"

"First of all," replied Rabbi Dreidel, "I did come clean. I told you everything about Lacey Johnson. That she had a different version of events, and that the reporter in the newspaper didn't accurately put down my version, doesn't mean I was dishonest with you.

"I thought everything was going to be confidential when I talked to Lacey Johnson. And it was just words. Nothing happened. These other incidents were so minor, and in each case, I apologized."

Rabbi Dreidel continued, sounding more and more exasperated, his words more rapid-fire.

"I talked to Sarah Shofar and Elmer in my office. Everything was forgiven and resolved. To this day, Gloria Epstein is over at our house helping Abigail with the kids. She bears me no ill will. She loves us. I had an isolated, emotional moment in a hospital setting with Peggy Cohen's daughter. I hugged her. I'm sorry I did it. I'm sorry I didn't say anything. I was embarrassed about it. Peggy and I discussed it at length, and it was a non-issue. I apologized. We resolved it.

"In the midst of everything going on with the restraining orders, seeing the psychologist, reassuring all the community members, who would have even thought of her? My wife and I had significant private issues to work on with the psychologist. I thought the thing with Peggy's daughter was resolved. It wasn't worth mentioning. The information wouldn't have meant anything. The truth is, it didn't even register.

"All this is a Me Too movement pile-on. That's all it is. There's nothing new here. Let me get back on my feet. I just resumed my duties. Let me show you what I can do."

"You know," Rabbi Yitzak Yosef said, "we went out on a limb for you. We relied on what you told us. What you are telling me now doesn't wash.

"The truth is, I can't trust you anymore. I am offering you the opportunity to resign. That's the best I can do for you.

"If you don't resign, I am going to have to fire you. Don't make me do that. Take the better way out."

Rabbi Schvitzerman was crying, and Rabbi Finklestein sat mute, his head bowed, but both agreed with their senior rabbi's decision. Neither could look Rabbi Dreidel in the eyes any longer. Abigail, numb, also stared at the floor.

"What do you mean?" cried Rabbi Dreidel. "This is absurd! Fire me? Have you lost your mind? Have some compassion!"

"Didn't the Grand Rabbi of TUCAS show compassion to you when you had legal problems? That was far worse. This is a Me Too pile-on. I haven't committed any crime.

"You are just reacting to the newspaper articles," Rabbi Dreidel insisted. "Don't cave in to pressure!"

"This is awful for all of us," Rabbi Yosef replied. "Don't make it worse than it already is.

"I can give you twenty-four hours to write a statement of resignation, if that's what you want to do. Otherwise, you are fired, effective today. You are not going on the pulpit for Shabbos."

"So, I am supposed to just hand you the keys to the synagogue?" Rabbi Dreidel shouted. "After all we built up, you just want to take it over for free? You think we are just going to give it to you and go away?

"That's not going to happen. No way. Are you insane?"

"Mishy," quietly interjected Abigail, "we better leave now. You've said enough."

"Yes, we better leave!" exclaimed Rabbi Dreidel, standing up and looking deranged, like he might strike the old rabbi. "You are a disgrace. You haven't heard the last of me," Rabbi Dreidel shouted at Rabbi Yitzak Yosef.

He stormed out of the room.

All Abigail could do was say, "I'm so sorry," and trail after her angry husband.

As soon as they returned to Destiny County, Rabbi Dreidel dropped off Abigail and proceeded to Harold Bernard's law office.

There, he broke down in tears.

"How much can one man suffer?" he asked the lawyer while looking heavenward. "What am I to do?"

"Legally," Harold said, "your board of directors consists of you, your wife, and your father. The synagogue is owned by the Jewish Center of Destiny County, not by TUCAS. I question whether Rabbi Yosef can really fire you. Legally, only your board of directors can do that."

"I can't go rogue," said Rabbi Dreidel. "I can't do it. Not in a community this small. My website is from TUCAS, my sermons, my entire support system. All my brothers and brothers-in-law are TUCAS rabbis, like my father and father-in-law. My sisters and sisters-in-law are married to TUCAS rabbis.

"I can't go against the organization. I must either resign or get fired. I have to resign. Shabbos is coming up tomorrow. I'll write a resignation letter. I'll see you tomorrow."

Rabbi Dreidel spent another sleepless night. After talking to his parents and favorite brothers and sisters, he sat alone with the door to his synagogue office locked. He was blind to his own missteps along the way. He felt the world conspired against him, not that his wounds were self-inflicted.

He decided it was really Gloria Epstein who was the final straw. He wondered what exactly she had said to Rabbi Yitzak Yosef that she really didn't need to say. He knew Gloria Epstein loved Abigail and the kids. How ironic, he thought, that she would also knife him in the back.

The next morning and throughout the day, Rabbi Dreidel emailed Harold multiple drafts of a resignation statement. They abandoned a lengthy statement in favor of a short one. They considered various short statements that denied any wrongdoing. Once he settled on a statement with his lawyer, he decided he also wanted to email it to Lenny Spiegleman.

"Lenny, I have to resign," he told his supporter on the phone. "Please look over what I'm emailing you and give me your input."

The statement read as follows:

"I hereby resign as Rabbi of the Jewish Center of Destiny County. I wish to thank the community for their support. I am very proud of what we accomplished during the last seventeen years, and I sincerely wish the community well in the future."

Lenny called Rabbi Dreidel back as soon as he read the email. For the first time in many days, the call did not go to voicemail.

"Rabbi," said Lenny, "you don't have to do this."

"I have to do this before Shabbos."

"No, you don't. Let Adam Habbibi lead Shabbos services. There is nothing wrong with your statement, but don't rush to send it out."

"I just wanted your take on it. I have to resign or be fired," the rabbi said. "This has to go out."

As soon as Harold emailed the resignation statement to the newspapers, his office phone and his cell phone rang off the hook. Harold took all the calls from the press. He wanted to emphasize that the rabbi denied wrongdoing and was stepping down for personal and family reasons.

When asked who would take control of the synagogue, Harold told the reporter that the rabbi had not resigned from the board of directors and would participate in planning for the future.

"KISSING RABBI RESIGNS AFTER NEW ALLEGATIONS," read the headline of the *Destiny Dispatch* announcing the news. The article also noted that it was not clear if Rabbi Dreidel was also stepping down as director.

Hezekiah and Lacey rejoiced on social medial for all to see. Hezekiah also posted his suspicions that Rabbi Dreidel and his wife were going to stay on in the background, like "leeches sucking off the good people of Destiny County."

SEVERANCE

Unlike a normal mortal who had just been humiliated on the worldwide internet and was now out of a job, Rabbi Dreidel did not fall into a funk of inactivity after his resignation. Quite the contrary, he called supporters, consulted additional lawyers, and scratched and clawed, demanding a generous severance package from the Jewish Center of Destiny County. He also asked his lawyer, Harold Bernard, to demand a severance package from the TUCAS regional office under the auspices of Rabbi Yitzak Yosef.

Rabbi Dreidel found old news articles about the money paid to other rabbis who had left the pulpit under cloudy circumstances. He found cases of financial settlements for rabbis who committed offenses that Rabbi Dreidel considered far worse than his misbehavior. The rabbi's conclusion: the community should provide him a severance package. His contribution to the community should not be forgotten. He had nine mouths to feed. He needed to pay out-of-state tuition for the oldest girls so they could attend a proper high school. He was supposed to walk away with nothing? That wasn't going to happen!

Hezekiah and the *trayf* (un-kosher) forces of evil had succeeded in getting him tossed out. He didn't need to suppress the strong feelings in his *kishkas* any longer, as he did when he politicked for reinstatement. He could now act on his instincts. In other words, rather than taking time to contemplate his misfortune and consider where he went wrong, the rabbi was like a rabid dog fighting for a last bone. He was *gornisht helfn*, beyond help—his inner dog was completely unleashed.

All of this energy helped the rabbi come up with a genius idea. Clearly, no one but he would have thought of such a reasonable solution.

True, the Jewish Center of Destiny County was dead broke owing to his suspension and lack of fundraising during the last several months. However, he thought, the synagogue, whose mortgage he paid like clockwork, could easily afford a higher mortgage payment of, say, another $500 per month. A second mortgage on the synagogue would free up cash to Rabbi Dreidel and his family—perhaps as much as $400,000, a win-win for all involved! The community could absorb the costs over time. Such a substantial amount of funds would allow the rabbi a chance to relocate, afford new housing, pay the family's bills, and give him time to get his bearings.

Rabbi Dreidel had a special relationship with the local bank's president, a born-again Christian, who was instrumental in approving the original synagogue construction loan. That loan was approved without a track record of any payments. Rabbi Dreidel, in applying for a second mortgage on the synagogue building, could demonstrate an excellent record of timely mortgage payments. Loan approval should be easy-peasy.

The rabbi started to sound out members of the community

in regard to his "severance package" and his solution to finance it—a second mortgage on the synagogue.

Thanks to a very favorable increase in property values, the rabbi and Abigail also enjoyed as much as several hundred thousand dollars of equity in their family home. But that was their private residence and was not on the table for discussion.

No one in the community knew the amount of equity in the personal residence. Some thought that there was very little, based on a rumor that the rabbi repeatedly refinanced his home to pay the family's living and travel expenses. In fact, during favorable months of fundraising, Rabbi Dreidel frequently made a double payment on the home mortgage. Thus, he was not surprised when a realtor he knew gave him a high valuation on the house based on comparable sales.

Rabbi Dreidel emphasized to the realtor that the amount of equity in the residence was no one's business. He also complimented himself for having the foresight to transfer ownership of the residence to himself and Abigail early on, when the *tsuris* began. He felt that the equity in the house was a windfall that he and Abigail richly deserved, even though the years of payments on it came entirely from community contributions.

The rabbi's oldest brother flew into town. Together, he and Rabbi Dreidel drove to the homes of various supporters to lobby for a severance package. The brother, also a rabbi, explained to anyone who would listen that, under Jewish law, Rabbi Dreidel was entitled to one month's salary for every year he worked for the Jews of Destiny County. The problem with the formula was that his supporters never knew what his salary was; it was never discussed or disclosed.

The board of the synagogue consisted of himself, his father, and his wife. They never had a single board meeting, other than the one to transfer the personal residence from the Jewish Center of

Destiny County to Mishegas and Abigail Dreidel. The board never set Mishy's salary. He drew whatever money was available when convenient to do so. He paid the organization's bills and his family's expenses without any oversight.

They hadn't grown rich or funded a retirement account. They had no savings put away. Abigail was never paid a salary despite all that she had done with women's classes, Friday night dinners, the preschool, holiday events, and Shabbos luncheons.

Didn't she also deserve a severance deal?

Certainly, thought Mishy, *the community would fund a severance package.*

After all, he was handing over a synagogue built from scratch, and he never had missed a mortgage payment. He deserved *gelt* and lots of it. He wasn't chopped liver. He had a family to relocate and feed. Nine kids weren't cheap.

Rabbi Yitzak Yosef was willing to listen to what Harold Bernard had to say about money for Rabbi Dreidel. He already had told Abigail that he was in her corner and that he had an emergency fund that would always be available to her and the children during a crisis.

He let Harold know that he was not opposed to gifting some money to Rabbi Dreidel; after all, it would cost the family money to move back to New York or wherever they wanted to go. The sooner that happened, thought Rabbi Yosef, the better for everyone.

The point was to get the rabbi on his way and turn the page. Rabbi Yosef rationalized that Rabbi Dreidel was an industrious and creative fellow. He would figure out how to land on his feet. No use crying over spilled milk, business was business. TUCAS needed to get back to business in Destiny County.

Rabbi Yitzak Yosef had already fielded calls from other rabbis asking if the position was open. He needed to select a good candidate. He would take his time and involve the most active members of the community—the heavy hitters with a track record of generous donations.

There was one slight problem, though. Other than the small emergency fund he had mentioned to Abigail, Rabbi Yitzak Yosef didn't have any *gelt* that he personally controlled; each synagogue was its own separate entity. His synagogue had a board of directors, a financial committee, a bookkeeper who issued the checks, and a tax accountant who reviewed the books. He couldn't just reach into some account flush with cash and write a check to Rabbi Dreidel.

To compound the problem, when Rabbi Yitzak Yosef sounded out Harold about what Rabbi Dreidel wanted, the demand started at $25,000 then skyrocketed. Now they were asking for $200,000.

Maybe, just maybe, thought Rabbi Yitzak Yosef, if he called on some old friends of TUCAS and was vague about what the money was for, he could quickly raise $10,000 or $15,000.

How much did it cost to hire a mover these days? The old rabbi had no idea, so he made some inquiries. A mover, a storage facility, and first and last month's rent on a four-bedroom apartment in the old neighborhood in New York might come to $20,000. He'd offer something a little lower than that to start.

He talked to his wife about dipping into their family's savings, which consisted of an inheritance from her parents. This was a touchy issue. Rabbi Yitzak Yosef and his wife had their own children who were either rabbis or married to rabbis all over the country. They frequently needed gelt.

Rabbi Dreidel's excessive demands raised the old rabbi's blood pressure again, but he reminded himself that getting rid of Mishy and hiring a replacement was a process. Nothing was ever going to be easy with Rabbi Dreidel, but the worst was over. He had resigned as rabbi, and now he needed to resign from the board. The sooner he left the area, the better.

Rabbi Yitzak Yosef decided he could make a loan to TUCAS from his wife's inheritance to give himself time to raise money for Rabbi Dreidel. In the meantime, he would start calling some of his contributors. The old rabbi tried to lower Rabbi Dreidel's expectations by explaining to Harold Bernard that he would do his best, but that the amount he could come up with was in the low twenties, if that.

Back in New York, Rabbi Dreidel's father could no longer contain himself. He heard from his son that the community reaction to taking a bigger loan on the shul was meeting resistance. The Jews of Destiny County seemed lukewarm to the idea of adding debt to their already precarious financial situation.

Rabbi Dreidel's father, as the patriarch of the family, decided to write a letter. It couldn't hurt. His son had the emails of all the people who needed to be contacted. The letter said:

Dear kind friends and community members,

Although many of you already know me, I am Rabbi Mordechai Dreidel of New York, father of Rabbi Mishegas Dreidel, father-in-law to our beloved Abigail, and grandfather to their nine children. I am also on the Board of Directors of the Jewish Center of Destiny County. Your lovely community has lost its wonderful and energetic Rabbi who built such a beautiful synagogue. You will also soon lose Abigail and the children, all of whom were beautiful sons and daughters of the community. I always appreciated the love and support shown to the Dreidel family over the years. I will never forget you, nor will Rabbi Mishy, Abigail, or the children.

As the community addresses the future fundraising for the beautiful shul Rabbi Mishy built for you, you will surely see how hard it is to keep everything going and undoubtedly more fully understand the rabbi's contribution to your community. He built something that many said could never be done, dedicating himself completely, as did Abigail, without ever putting even a shekel in their own pockets for a rainy day.

Now they have no source of income and no home to move to. They are obviously deserving of a generous severance package. Otherwise, where will they go, penniless and destitute? I would certainly invite them into my house, but I am already bursting at the seams with another son's family who moved in during a remodel of their home that is not yet complete.

The question is this: does the community of Destiny County have a heart and soul? If the answer is yes, please do not let the Dreidel family become beggars. Yes, the community was hurt, but if we look at the last two decades of contributions and balance the scales, doesn't all the hard work and good that my son did for you dramatically tilt the scale in favor of him and his family?

I believe you to be good people who will not say to the Dreidel family, "There's the door and may the devil take you!" I have met so many of you over the years. I cannot conceive that you will let the Dreidels leave with only a "Goodbye and good luck!" They should be given a severance package of at least $350,000. This is a very modest number compared to what they brought to you individually and to the community.

As a father and grandfather of this family, I urge you to do what's right under Jewish law and what you must do regardless of the recent negativity in the newspaper. As a member of the Board of Directors, and as a Rabbi, I bless each and every one of you and tell you honestly that there is always a caring and reasonable solution to any problem.

With great regret that I need to send you this directive instructing you to do what's right and in accordance with Jewish law, sincerely,

Rabbi Mordechai Dreidel

The father's email, although heartfelt, went over like a lead balloon. After the rabbi's scandal, suspension, reinstatement, salacious news stories, and resignation, the community was in no mood to entertain a demand for money.

The rabbi's loyal supporters felt bad for the rabbi, but what could they do? How was the shul even going to survive?

Others thought and sometimes said to each other, "$350,000! C'mon. He resigned because of his own misconduct.

"He embarrassed and betrayed the community. We don't owe him anything under any law, Jewish or secular."

When someone forwarded the father's email to Hezekiah, he stoked the flames on social media with posts ridiculing "The Kissing Rabbi's" demands for money. Hezekiah urged his followers to call Rabbi Yitzak Yosef, once again posting the old rabbi's phone number on the internet. Hezekiah also demanded Rabbi Yosef immediately "defrock" Rabbi Mishegas Dreidel for sexual misconduct. He called the congregants who continued to support Rabbi Dreidel sheep led astray by a "pervert" and said they would never reach *Gan Eden*, paradise.

With the resignation, Harold Bernard thought he could finally close the door on his pro bono activities for the rabbi. Instead, he found himself in the middle of the negotiations between Rabbis Dreidel and Yosef. The two bounced accusations, insults, and threats back and forth like a pinball machine.

Finally, Harold drafted a document he titled "SEPARATION AGREEMENT," with sufficient legalese about *whereas, non-*

disparagement, and *confidentiality* that the rabbis soon got down to brass tacks. For once, Harold seemed to wear down the rabbis with multiple drafts of the proposed written agreement rather than the other way around.

The lawyer eventually learned what each rabbi really wanted.

Rabbi Yitzak Yosef wanted Rabbi Dreidel off the board of directors. This wasn't a problem for Rabbi Dreidel, because his wife and father were still on the board, so he could maintain control of the Jewish Center of Destiny County. He needed control to assure himself a severance package (lots of gelt!) funded by a second mortgage on the shul.

He also wanted some sort of permanent recognition for his contributions to the community. He suggested a sign in the foyer of the synagogue in large letters that read, "THE JEWISH CENTER OF DESTINY COUNTY," on the top line, and, "FOUNDED BY RABBI MISHEGAS DREIDEL," on the bottom line.

Rabbi Yitzak Yosef wanted Rabbi Dreidel to have enough gelt to get out of Dodge, if not before sunset, as soon as practicable. Any signage would be left to the next rabbi and the congregation. He had no objection to a severance package paid for by the Destiny community. He had a final offer for the rabbi—$25,000. That was the most he could come up with as the TUCAS regional director.

"By the way," he told Harold, "this is borrowed money. Rabbi Dreidel shouldn't expect a shekel more."

Rabbi Yitzak Yosef also insisted that the funds would be paid directly to the airlines and moving company, rather than to Rabbi Dreidel. He also told Harold that his legal advisors in New York said the money should not be called a severance payment.

Harold suggested that they call the funds "moving assistance."

Rabbi Dreidel found the direct payment provisions insulting, but at the end of the day, after they nudged up the amount a little bit more, he agreed.

Rabbi Yitzak Yosef sent a check for $28,750 to Harold's trust account for the Dreidel family's moving expenses. In exchange, Rabbi Dreidel signed a document resigning from the board of directors of the Jewish Center of Destiny County.

THE EPIPHANY

R abbi Yitzak Yosef proposed Harold Bernard as the temporary executive director and board member replacement for Rabbi Dreidel. Someone had to stand in until a new rabbi was chosen, and Harold seemed a logical choice. Given how loyally he had represented him, without charging a single kopek, Rabbi Dreidel authorized his father and wife, the two remaining board members, to approve Harold's appointment.

Harold immediately appointed a congregant who had thirty years of experience as a government accountant to head a financial committee, a first for the Jewish Center of Destiny County. Its finances had always been held close to the *tallit* (prayer shawl) of one man, Rabbi Mishegas Dreidel. Harold charged the committee with reviewing the synagogue's finances, fundraising, and proposing a severance package for Rabbi Dreidel.

Rabbi Dreidel met with the accountant. He wouldn't fork over any financial documentation, but he went on and on for hours about various ways to fund his severance package, including refinancing the synagogue. He didn't give the accountant anything but the most basic, verbal information about the organization's income and expenses.

After several hours, the accountant had to get back to work. He arranged to meet the next day with Rabbi Dreidel, but the same thing happened. The accountant asked questions, and the rabbi changed the subject. Rabbi Dreidel demanded the accountant focus on his family concerns: out-of-state tuition for his older kids, housing costs back in New York, health insurance, and how long it might take him to find a job.

The accountant called Harold asking to be replaced. He complained that his time was wasted. The rabbi, he told Harold, would not release the password to his computer or any of the monthly lists of donations. He claimed the information was private and confidential. He would not turn over bank statements, loan documents, or checking account statements—he would only give general, verbal descriptions. The rabbi, the accountant said, would only turn over the information to the next rabbi.

Harold tried to intercede. The financial committee, he explained to the rabbi, earnestly wants to do something for you and your family. They are calling it "transition funding," and they aren't under any legal obligation to pay you anything. Rather, they want to do something for you out of love and compassion.

"Until they know what the shul has, they can't make a plan," Harold said.

He told Rabbi Dreidel that Lenny Spiegleman and Anna Habbibi were independently trying to raise money for him, too. "They say community support for you has dropped off since the second newspaper article and your resignation.

"Your insistence on a severance package is working against you. You are never going to get anything from this committee if you don't turn over the accounts."

"Are you for me or against me, Harold?" Rabbi Dreidel responded. "Now you sound like another Hezekiah trying to throw me under the bus. Transition funding? What's that? I am entitled to a severance package under Jewish law. I will accept nothing less.

"Don't you understand that I am fighting for my family?" Rabbi Dreidel said.

"After all I've done, do you think the board is going to just turn over everything to you or that snake of a rabbi, Yitzak Yosef?

"I've talked to other lawyers, Harold. I know that what I am asking for is reasonable. You should be helping me get it."

"That's what I'm doing," Harold replied.

"No you're not," Rabbi Dreidel said.

"Yes I am," Harold replied.

"No, you are stabbing me in the back!" the rabbi said.

"That's ridiculous!" Harold shouted.

"Dear God, how much can one man endure?" the rabbi *shried*.

And so it went.

Lenny Spiegleman and Anna Habbibi got frantic phone calls that afternoon from Rabbi Dreidel complaining that Harold was making a "power grab." The rabbi claimed he had provided all the information the accountant needed, but Harold and his committee wanted to audit his books. Did they want to turn him over to the IRS?

"Everyone knows," complained the rabbi, "that if you look at financial records long enough, you can always find something to pick on."

The information they were demanding included confidential details about all the donors, the rabbi said. It should only be turned over to the next rabbi.

The rabbi ranted that Harold and his stupid, so-called financial committee had turned into his worst nightmare. Lenny and Anna listened and did their best to calm down their beloved rabbi. Hearing how distraught he was broke their hearts.

They called Harold Bernard to voice their concerns about the rabbi's mental health. What was going on? The rabbi was so upset. He seemed to be deteriorating mentally.

Harold confirmed their worst fears. "The rabbi is out of his gourd. Now, he's demanding interim salary payments in addition to a severance package.

"He also is after me to approve property tax payments on his house from contributions to the shul."

Harold Bernard was worried about his lack of access to the shul's finances. He called Rabbi Yosef and asked whether the TUCAS organization would please hire a lawyer to get control of the synagogue's records and bank accounts.

Rabbi Yosef said they wanted to avoid hiring a lawyer and going to a civil court at all costs. If they were going to go to court, the Beis Din, the Jewish court, is where they would go. However, he warned, that was risky. Those courts had a tendency to make compromises between the positions of opposing parties.

"You might get your records, Harold, but Rabbi Dreidel might get a financial award that no one can afford."

The next day, Abigail called Harold, Anna Habbibi, Lenny Spiegleman, and Gloria Epstein to let them know the family was flying to New York to celebrate the rabbi's father's birthday and to take a "time out." The rabbi, she admitted, wasn't doing so well, but she assured Harold that he would pay the current month's bills.

In response to Harold's protests about the rabbi withholding needed information from the financial committee, Abigail said that she wasn't getting involved. It didn't matter that she was on the board of directors, she had to take care of the rabbi and her family. They had been through a lot.

The Dreidel family, with all nine kids, flew to New York. There, they stayed at Abigail's sister's house in the old neighborhood, camping on the floor during their "vacation."

Rabbi Dreidel's mood did not improve. He kept explaining to anyone who would listen that he had been wronged by the community he built. He consulted lawyers in New York who were experienced with 501(3)(c) organizations to "learn his legal rights." He went to the shul of the Grand Rabbi of blessed memory to pray. He walked the streets of the old neighborhood. Each night, even on Shabbos, he came home to his brother-in-law's house exhausted but unable to sleep.

After Shabbos, Rabbi Dreidel sent emails to his banking friend, the born-again Christian bank manager in Destiny County, to see what was needed for a second mortgage on the synagogue. The bank manager thought an additional loan of $300,000 would get approved. Rabbi Dreidel worked non-stop on the loan application. He failed to disclose that he was no longer on the board of directors.

As the weeks passed, Rabbi Dreidel's extended family saw that he wasn't right. His eyes were glazed, he laughed too much, and he wouldn't stop talking about his situation. Making matters worse, people avoided him and his family. Abigail wasn't surprised, because she knew how insular the ultra-orthodox community was in the old neighborhood. But the cold shoulders were still painful.

Abigail and her sister tried to make things fun for the kids. But when the two sisters talked, usually late at night, with all the kids finally asleep and with Mishy walking the streets, Abigail was able to unburden herself. She didn't see how she and her family were ever going to be accepted in the old community. Mishy wasn't in any condition to get a new job. And she missed her house in Destiny County. They couldn't afford anything like it in the old neighborhood. She didn't see any light at the end of the tunnel.

Rabbi Dreidel, while focused on himself, also saw how miserable he made his wife feel. He could see how his wife suffered. He let her down terribly, which was all the more reason he had to squeeze a decent severance package out of the godless Jews of Destiny County.

His unhappiness snowballed, even though he thought he had already reached the depths of despair. Abigail took pity on her husband and tried to act like everything was more or less normal. But they couldn't avoid seeing each other's discontent and hopelessness.

One sleepless night, wandering the streets of New York, Rabbi Dreidel had an epiphany. Why did they have to move? Wasn't his problem simply a question of public relations? He hadn't done anything criminal. What did the politicians and big corporations do after a scandal? They hired a PR firm, a high-class one, which organized a PR campaign. Why couldn't he do the same?

Now, I can see what the so-called victims want, the rabbi said to himself. *No one had sued me. They just wanted an apology. I can do that. I'll arrange to see them one-on-one. I'll apologize. If they need a little gelt too, I'll raise it. I'll do whatever it takes. Nothing is impossible, thanks to the Almighty, blessed be He.*

Mishy tried out his latest, genius idea on his rabbi father, his brothers, his brothers-in-law, and Abigail. Everyone listened politely, and no one rejected the idea out of hand. Abigail was skeptical, but she would love it if things could only go back to how they were. The family consensus was that, if he had enough community support, things could be worked out.

Rabbi Dreidel booked a red-eye flight back to Destiny County. He strategized how to talk to his congregants on the way. He decided that he would level with everyone about his epiphany: The Master of the Universe had told him not to leave Destiny County.

The first person he talked to was none other than Harold Bernard. Harold summoned all his lawyer skills to limit his immediate, disdainful reactions to what he was hearing. After two hours of listening to the rabbi's self-described epiphany, Harold seemed utterly unconvinced. Instead, he pressed the rabbi for the financial documentation.

"Rabbi," Harold told him, "you are no longer in charge of the Jewish Center here. You have to turn all the bank accounts over to me."

The rabbi stormed out of Harold's office.

Next, Rabbi Dreidel tried the Habbibis. They didn't reject the idea of the rabbi's return out of hand. But they warned him about how toxic the community might be, and they said he should consider the well-being of his kids. Of course, the Habbibis said, they loved him, Abigail, and the kids, but was an attempt to return really in his family's best interests?

Lenny Spiegleman also suffered hours of listening to his broken friend. Rabbi Dreidel detailed his epiphany and how he could return to Destiny County as the rabbi, even though it wouldn't be easy. Only he, Rabbi Dreidel told Lenny, knew how to fundraise in this community. Only he could heal it.

Lenny, exasperated and frustrated, told the rabbi that he could not resign and then expect the community to rally for his reinstatement a second time.

"As much as I love you," Lenny told Mishy, "as much as I hate to lose you, I think you need to relocate and start over.

"I realize the money from TUCAS and what Anna and I raised isn't much. But if you cooperate with the financial committee, they can really help."

This led to another heated hour of Rabbi Dreidel explaining why he deserved a severance package. He also declared, yet again, that he wouldn't release financial information to anyone but the next rabbi.

And so it went, on and on.

Usually, an exhausted congregant would call Harold Bernard, Lenny Spiegleman, or Anna Habbibi to tell them he had just met with the rabbi for several hours. The rabbi made the congregant swear to keep their conversation under wraps, but he had said he had an epiphany. What was going on? Did the rabbi really think he was coming back to Destiny County?

The chopped liver hit the fan, again, when the bank manager called Rabbi Yitzak Yosef. The old rabbi had introduced several of his younger colleagues to him after Rabbi Dreidel's success in getting the construction loan. The bank was willing to help the other local synagogues, too. A good relationship had formed.

The bank manager thought he would just share the good news that the second mortgage on the synagogue in Destiny County was likely to be approved. Rabbi Yitzak Yosef had heard about Rabbi Dreidel's idea through the grapevine, but he never suspected the rabbi would proceed without an agreement from Harold Bernard or anyone else in the community.

The old rabbi played it cool. He told the bank manager to hold things up, that the loan might not be needed, and to talk to him before finalizing anything.

As soon as he ended that cordial conversation, Rabbi Yosef called Harold Bernard. The lawyer told Rabbi Yosef that he also had heard Rabbi Dreidel's idea about the loan, but he had no idea it was actually being processed.

Harold felt dread and shock. How could Rabbi Dreidel do this without telling him? Harold was now the executive director. He was responsible for the synagogue's finances. As a lawyer, he also had fiduciary duties. The board hadn't approved anything; they hadn't even met. Harold absolutely needed to get control of the bank accounts.

A lightbulb went off in Harold's *yiddishe kup*. *This must be why Rabbi Dreidel won't transfer the bank accounts!* Harold thought. *He's afraid, if he does, he won't be able to get the loan for his severance package.*

Once ignited, Harold's suspicions skyrocketed.

On a hunch, he searched the county auditor's website for tax information about the Dreidels' house. It showed the property taxes for the second half of the year had been paid. As an attorney, he also had a password to access additional information from the website. He found that, despite the lack of approval from anyone, the rabbi had paid his property taxes with a check from the Jewish Center of Destiny County.

Clicking around, Harold then discovered that, in the same week Rabbi Dreidel was suspended, the Jewish Center of Destiny County had transferred the house to Mishegas and Abigail Dreidel. The lawyer wasn't an expert in 501(3)(c) organizations, but he knew a charitable organization couldn't transfer a valuable asset to two members of its three-member board of directors.

Harold wanted to crawl under a rock. His beloved rabbi, and possibly the rabbi's wife, had committed a fraudulent transfer of real property. Also, his beloved rabbi likely had committed Class B Felony Theft when he used community funds, without any authorization, to pay personal property taxes. What else had he done?

THE BEIS DIN

In many religious traditions, we are told over and over to avoid judging our fellow human beings. Clichés abound about walking in another man's shoes, judging books by their covers, foregoing judgments "lest ye be judged," etc., etc., *ad infinitum*. Yet, in reality, we are constantly judging our fellow human beings.

Think of our many courts: superior court, district court, municipal court, traffic court, small claims court, bankruptcy court, the court of appeals, and of course, the state and federal supreme courts. Many judges who populate these courts sit up high, in elevated chairs, survey their large courtrooms, and command respect. They are quite busy. You have to wait in line a long time to see a judge. They wear black robes and spend their days judging one case after another. That's their job. In fact, you can't have a court unless you have a judge. Where did this longstanding religious idea about not judging each other come from, when we have so many judges?

But it is not only the professional judges who are judging all the time. We all contribute to and participate in the court of public opinion, political polls, TV ratings, social media, and surveys. We like to count, categorize, describe, compartmentalize—a day doesn't pass when we don't judge something. From the mundane choices between ten different toothpaste brands and thirty different shampoos to important choices, such as which career to pursue and with whom to partner, when aren't we judging, preferring, eliminating, and deciding?

And of course, doesn't every monotheistic religion believe in an omnipresent Creator who sees all, misses nothing, and ultimately serves as the Great Arbitrator, the Final Judge who can't be fooled? In Judaism, the rabbis foretell the Day of Judgment after the coming of the Messiah, when one's destiny in the afterlife will be written and sealed.

With all this judging going on, is it surprising that highly observant Jews also get in on the act? They operate a rabbinical court called the *Beis Din*, the House of Judgment. Who needs a rabbinical court? Why the rabbis do! They can't go to a secular court. A secular court cannot decide matters of Jewish law. They need a Jewish Court. That's how, after all was said and done, Rabbi Dreidel invoked the Beis Din, a rabbinical court in New York, New York, to plead his case.

How do you sue in rabbinical court? You write your complaint, pay your filing fee, and fill in the particulars on the forms. This allows the court to give notice to your adversaries—simple as a pimple! You get assigned to the rabbi who administers your case. Each side picks a rabbi from a list of esteemed old rabbis who sit on the court. Those two rabbis pick a third, and as soon as you can say *amen*, everyone is summonsed to tell the rabbis, on such and such a date, who's who, what's what, and pay up.

The great sages also tell of the Heavenly Court, a court none of us can avoid. There, everyone's case is examined, not just after we breathe our last breath, but every second of every day. All the holy angels, born from each person's good acts, and all the dark angels, born from each person's sins, continuously gather together before the Heavenly Court. In Rabbi Dreidel's case, many luminous angels appeared for many years, one by one, born from his numerous good deeds.

In fact, Rabbi Dreidel's holy, luminous angels had impressively outnumbered his dark angels, until he was overcome by sin. Then, giant-sized dark angels began to appear, barking like hungry seals. In Rabbi Dreidel's tragic case, although the barking, dark angels were clearly outnumbered, the Heavenly Court could not ignore the cacophony. The court granted the floor to the biggest and most energetic of all the dark angels who cried and *shried*, shrieking in tears, "Pay attention to me! I made a mistake, big deal! I admitted it! Isn't that enough?! I don't deserve this! I accomplished more than anyone else! I am special! I was thrown under the bus! No one is listening! I need to feed my children! Where is my severance package? I am not giving over my shul for free! I have been cheated; my achievements stolen! I have been shamed and suffered more than anyone can endure! I am a prince, not a pauper!"

The Holy Judges listened attentively, but eventually started to feel sick and suffer headaches. They asked the shrieking dark angel to calm down. The giant dark angel was having none of it.

"Calm down? Lower my voice? How can I calm down? I was born of sin, but now I am being threatened and vilified. The truth is, everyone knows that I am better than the other angels. I was thrown under the bus! Under the bus! Under the bus! My reputation is ruined! I have no income! I gave everything, and now I have nothing!"

The Holy Judges finally heard enough. There was no ibuprofen in heaven. Their heads were pounding. They went into an inner chamber to escape the noise of the giant, dark angel who wouldn't quiet down. Their nerves frayed, they needed to regain their bearings.

SCHMUCK!

Without community support for his epiphany, Rabbi Dreidel flew back to New York to rejoin his family. Neither Harold nor the financial committee had gained access to the synagogue bank accounts.

Harold was in an awful quandary. He recognized his fiduciary responsibility to the organization as a board member. He also knew that he had to withdraw as a board member, because he was now aware of criminal acts toward the organization by Rabbi Dreidel while Harold was representing him. A lawyer can't represent both the victim and the offender.

Harold also realized that the rabbi's wife and father had to leave the board. Abigail never performed any board duties and did not want to start now. Her priority was her family. The rabbi's father lived in New York. They simply acted as straw men for the rabbi, an entirely fraught situation.

The rabbi, who had resigned in disgrace from the pulpit and then resigned from the board, after extracting a price for his resignation, still controlled the organization's finances. Worse yet, Rabbi Dreidel intended to leverage that control to extort money from it.

Harold wondered whether the rabbi's laser focus on money and his epiphany were part and parcel of a narcissistic personality run amok.

Who does a lawyer call first when he has ethical problems as a lawyer? Why, another lawyer, that's who.

His colleague concluded that Harold needed to disclose the conflict of interest to the financial committee, notwithstanding his prior representation of the rabbi. He would not be disclosing his client's confidential information, the lawyer friend rationalized, because he learned of the criminal behavior only after his representation had concluded. Further, he had a duty to disclose it; the members of the committee, as representatives of the Jewish Center of Destiny County, also had fiduciary duties.

Second, Harold called Rabbi Yitzak Yosef to tell him that he had an ethical conflict that required his withdrawal from the board and as executive director. Rabbi Yitzak Yosef told Harold that he could not resign from the board until a new rabbi was chosen because that would add to the turmoil and upheaval. Creating a vacuum now, while Rabbi Dreidel still controlled the board, would play into his hands.

Rabbi Yosef understood Harold's ethical and fiduciary dilemma. After all, the Talmud devoted many pages and commentaries to conflicts of interest for judges and witnesses. It also addressed the sanctity of community funds. However, Rabbi Yosef remained steadfast—Harold could not resign, at least not now. He told Harold that he should delegate the issues that caused the ethical problems to the finance committee and recuse himself from those deliberations.

Rabbi Dreidel had agreed to substitute Harold for himself on the board because he thought he could control him. Subsequently, he fought Harold's most basic requests—access and control of bank accounts, bills, and donor lists. Rabbi Dreidel would not make the same mistake twice. He would not agree to any new board member that he couldn't control. The other board members—Rabbi Dreidel's wife and father—wouldn't agree to anyone Rabbi Dreidel didn't approve.

Third, Harold called Abigail in New York. He told her about the property tax payment, which, Harold hoped, was news to her. She didn't act at all surprised or concerned. Harold worried that she was complicit in her husband's underhanded dealings, and he kicked himself for assuming she wasn't. Harold also discussed the transfer of the residence with her.

"It was our house," she told him. "I don't see anything wrong with what we did."

But when Harold explained that it was illegal self-dealing for the board of a charitable organization to transfer a valuable asset to a member of the board, Abigail ended the conversation.

"My family is all I care about," she said. "Please leave me out of the synagogue business. The rabbi's business is the rabbi's business."

Not five minutes after the call with Abigail, Harold got a call from Rabbi Dreidel. Harold tried to keep calm and discuss things rationally, but it was impossible. The rabbi kept interrupting, accusing Harold of disloyalty. He called his former lawyer and loyal friend names that took the Lord's name in vain, and he threatened to sue him in the *Beis Din*.

Harold finally said, "Rabbi, you committed felony crimes. The conveyance of the house was fraudulent self-dealing. Payment of the property taxes was felony theft."

"So, you and Rabbi Yosef think you can steal our house and charge me with crimes now that I'm back in New York?" Rabbi Dreidel shouted into the phone. "First, they take away my synagogue, and now you want to take away my house?

"You know, very well, that the only reason the house was in the name of the Jewish Center was to save on taxes."

Rabbi Dreidel went on to claim that he had given all the information he could to the financial committee.

"I can only turn over the records to the next rabbi; otherwise, I would be violating the contributors' confidentiality," the rabbi said.

Harold had heard it all before, but this time he cracked. He finally let fly with a "Fuck you!" and slammed down the phone. He was shocked that he had cursed the rabbi, a man he had loved and fought for.

The rabbi, now hysterical, called Lenny Spiegleman and Adam Habbibi. He explained again, after he stopped hyperventilating, that he was entitled to an ongoing severance salary (in addition to a severance package), and he explained that he deserved to have his property taxes paid, but that Harold was crazy, threatening him with criminal prosecution.

"Could you please call Harold and find out his intentions?" he asked each of them.

Harold told the rabbi's friends that he had no intention of referring anyone to the local prosecutor. He simply needed the financial records without any further delay, and before any more damage was done.

Adam and Lenny each called back the rabbi to assure him that no one was going to jail. Harold just wanted the synagogue records and bank accounts.

Rabbi Dreidel decided that he wasn't going to be pushed around anymore. How dare that rat, Harold, threaten him with criminal prosecution! The only crimes were what Harold, that traitor, and Rabbi Yitzak Yosef, that dog, had done to him.

For two days, Rabbi Dreidel walked the streets of New York, notebook and pen in hand, stopping only to draft and redraft his complaint to the *Beis Din*. He would show them. As stated in the holy Torah, "Justice, justice, you shall pursue…"

When Harold received a certified letter from Rabbi Dreidel with the return address of a *Beis Din* in New York, he suspected that he had just been sued. He had learned some rudimentary Hebrew when he was a bar mitzvah boy, but that was decades ago. Unable to understand the contents of the document, he called Rabbi Yosef for help.

The old rabbi told Harold he also had received his envelope in the day's mail. He explained that Rabbi Dreidel was suing both of them in the *Beis Din* in New York for damages consisting of back salary and reinstatement of his position, or, in the alternative, a severance package of $1 million.

The complaint alleged that Rabbi Yitzak Yosef threatened Rabbi Dreidel and his wife with slander, coerced a wrongful resignation, and torpedoed a bank loan intended to fund a severance package. The complaint accused Harold of pure "*mesirah*," threatening to report his conduct to the police under circumstances forbidden by Jewish law. Specifically, Rabbi Dreidel claimed, Harold Bernard wanted to report alleged financial improprieties, all of which Rabbi Dreidel vehemently denied, to the IRS and sue for expenditures the lawyer claimed were inappropriate, even though the board of directors—his wife and father—had approved every payment.

Rabbi Yitzak Yosef and Harold commiserated with each other about this new turn of events. They worried mightily about having to travel to New York to defend themselves, even though they were confident they would prevail. Rabbi Dreidel was making a fool of himself. Did he really want a *Beis Din* to know everything about all the victims and all the lies?

On the other hand, a Jewish court could take pity on Abigail and the kids. She had a valid claim about her years of service to the community. She hadn't done anything wrong. A *Beis Din* might award the Dreidels some real gelt. Rabbi Yitzak Yosef told Harold that they had to take the complaint seriously.

Meanwhile, Abigail knew her husband's mental state was a mess. He was carrying around papers all the time, *hocking a chinik*, sounding like a boiling tea kettle, to everyone on his cell phone. He wasn't sleeping, and he was constantly scribbling like a mad *Rashi* or *Rambam*, great Jewish scholars, in his spiral notebook. When she finally saw the complaint to the *Beis Din* hidden under a bunch of books she was trying to straighten up, she hit the roof. She could read Hebrew!

Abigail found her husband in the kitchen with the kids.

"We are not suing Rabbi Yitzak Yosef. Period. You are out of your mind!" she shouted.

Rabbi Dreidel was too shocked to respond.

Abigail wasn't finished. She told her husband, "I am not allowing this! You will withdraw this craziness in the *Beis Din* immediately. I won't be a party to it."

"I will decide!" Rabbi Dreidel yelled back. "I am fighting for our family. We can't let them throw us under the bus. I am seeking justice for us, and you can't stop me!"

The *kindeleh* were shocked to see their parents yelling at each other.

In defense of Rabbi Dreidel's complaint to the Beis Din, there were some precedents, though rare, of rabbis bringing TUCAS disputes before a religious court. However, as word spread among the rabbi's parents, siblings, and in-laws, they all condemned the lawsuit.

Rabbi Dreidel's father took the lead.

"We will help you in every way we can," Rabbi Mordechai Dreidel told his son, after calling him one afternoon to meet in the older Dreidel's musty study. "But you have to get better, mentally. Get some counseling. And you have to withdraw that lawsuit from the

Beis Din. The *schande* (scandal) is bad enough already!"

Mishy, feeling cornered, alone, and rejected by his own family, took to the streets of the old neighborhood, absenting himself completely from his wife, children, parents, and in-laws.

Although the family had grown accustomed to his agitation and his frantic comings and goings at all hours, they were afraid for Mishy when he didn't come home for two nights. No one knew where he was, and Shabbos was approaching.

Like a petulant child who threatens to eat worms and die, Rabbi Dreidel's frothy anger toward his wife and father turned into a severe depression. His body couldn't sustain the rage. When the anger subsided, he felt completely broken and discarded.

After two days of walking the streets and sleeping on a bench in the synagogue, his footsteps led him to the shul. Sullen and disheveled, he took his place next to his father, who welcomed him with a kind, "*Gut Shabbos.*"

That Shabbos was tense, with everyone careful not to say anything touchy. Mishy knew he was defeated. The first thing after Shabbos, he withdrew his complaint to the *Beis Din* for the sake of *shalom bayis*, family peace and marital harmony.

Abigail proposed that Mishy's father request a meeting with the leader of TUCAS, the Grand Rabbi's former secretary, Rabbi Megillah, who now served as administrator for TUCAS and all its rabbis worldwide. He lived across the street from Mishy's father. Years ago, Rabbi Dreidel's grandparents had rented an apartment in the same building as Rabbi Megillah's parents. Rabbi Megillah and Mordechai Dreidel used to play with each other as kids.

Old Rabbi Megillah was elderly, overweight, diabetic, and suffering from heart disease. But the TUCAS organization and the inspiration he gained during his many years of service to the Grand Rabbi, may his memory live forever to bless the Jewish people, were his entire life. He loved his job and the respect he enjoyed from all the other rabbis. He also believed in his mission and that of TUCAS—to spread Judaism worldwide. He would never retire.

Rabbi Megillah presided over an annual convention of all the TUCAS rabbis from around the world. Thousands of them came for the convention and to visit family and friends. They would recharge their batteries, attend seminars, and listen to first-rate speakers at a large white-tablecloth banquet. It was filled with so many tables of rabbis that they had to project the dais on giant movie screens throughout the convention hall.

When he granted Rabbi Dreidel the meeting, old Rabbi Megillah already knew about his misguided lawsuit in the *Beis Din*, his suspension, reinstatement, the articles on the internet, and his resignation. He had spoken to Rabbi Yitzak Yosef regularly throughout the ordeal.

His decades of experience had taught him how to listen and propose practical solutions to seemingly unsolvable problems. He concluded that Rabbi Dreidel's behavior did not qualify as an emergency for TUCAS funds. This situation fell into another category entirely. He had already turned down Rabbi Yosef when he asked for money to expedite Rabbi Dreidel's exit from Destiny County.

Rabbi Megillah met with Mishy and Abigail, and with Mishy and Mishy's father several times. Rabbi Dreidel increasingly alienated the old rabbi by *hocking a chinik* about being thrown under the bus and stridently making monetary demands.

Abigail's words, on the other hand, spoken from the heart and with humility, resonated with the old man every time she spoke. Finally, the old rabbi asked for some time to investigate. He wanted to speak directly with some members of the community. He also asked to talk to Abigail alone. He correctly surmised that their marriage was on the rocks. She didn't want it to be that way, but what was a mother with nine kids supposed to do?

Abigail, thought old Rabbi Megillah, had devoted herself to TUCAS and the Destiny County community for years without a salary. Her claims were legitimate. She and her children should not be kicked to the curb. Also, Rabbi Dreidel needed time to become himself again. He was so full of himself that he couldn't stop *kvetching* and wouldn't take responsibility for his misdeeds. Rabbi Megillah could see that Abigail was entirely correct when she told him, one-on-one, that she and her husband needed some time to make a transition to the secular world.

She requested that Rabbi Megillah assist their claim for a severance package, not for Mishy, but for her and the children. She would abide by whatever Rabbi Megillah recommended.

When the old rabbi called the Habbibis, Lenny Spiegleman, and other community members, he was impressed by how much they loved and cared about the Dreidels. Their spontaneous efforts to raise money for the family spoke volumes, he thought, as did the community's intentions to come up with a modest severance package for Rabbi Dreidel. He understood why, in the face of such generosity, Rabbi Dreidel's refusal to turn over the shul records had created a tremendous schism.

Clearly, shul members needed to know where they stood financially, before giving Rabbi Dreidel any money, Rabbi Megillah thought. The young rabbi should not have taken money, without authorization, to pay his property taxes, and he shouldn't have transferred the house to himself in secret. His epiphany also had alienated his best friends in the community.

The old rabbi granted Rabbi Dreidel's request for a one-on-one audience. He told him, unequivocally, that he needed to turn over all the records immediately to the financial committee. Rabbi Dreidel had the *chutzpah* to tell Rabbi Megillah that he didn't understand the governance of charitable corporations.

"I've talked to lots of lawyers," Rabbi Dreidel said, "I know my legal rights!"

He attempted to school the old rabbi about severance packages, but Rabbi Megillah was having none of it.

"You should be on your knees thanking these fine people from the community, instead of giving them so much *tsuris*, Rabbi Dreidel. You *hocked them a chinik* with demands and epiphanies. You acted brazenly.

"A quiet, humble approach would have served you better.

"Turn over the records, apologize and everyone will help you. It won't be as much as you want, but you'll get something."

Rabbi Dreidel wouldn't stop arguing. Finally, the old rabbi asked him to leave. Rabbi Dreidel said he wasn't done and wasn't leaving. This led to the following exchange:

"You will see yourself out the door now," Rabbi Megillah said.

"I am not leaving!" Rabbi Dreidel shouted.

"You are leaving. Goodbye," the senior rabbi shouted back.

"I have more to say," Rabbi Dreidel insisted.

"I listened to you," Rabbi Megillah said, "and I'm done now. Goodbye."

"You need to listen to me!" Rabbi Dreidel insisted.

"I listened. Goodbye," the older rabbi repeated.

"I'm not leaving," Rabbi Dreidel said.

"Schmuck! What's wrong with you!" Rabbi Megillah shouted. "Get out of here!"

"I'm not a schmuck," Rabbi Dreidel responded, "you're a schmuck!"

"You're calling me a schmuck?" Rabbi Megillah said, getting up from his chair. "I'm going to pick up this phone and have the staff outside this door forcibly remove you."

"Okay, I'm leaving. Thanks a lot. Thanks for nothing," Rabbi Dreidel shouted, as he walked toward the door.

After a few minutes to catch his breath and let his anger subside, Rabbi Megillah called Rabbi Yosef and told him that he couldn't influence Rabbi Dreidel and couldn't work with him.

Still, Rabbi Megillah saw a possible solution. He asked Rabbi Dreidel's father and Abigail to meet with him and proposed that Rabbi Dreidel turn over the bank accounts to the financial committee. The committee could then meet, review the records, and propose a severance package. They also could consider funding the package with the loan on the synagogue that Rabbi Dreidel already had gotten approved.

"True, he went about it the wrong way," Rabbi Megillah said. "Because of that, the community could agree to something less than Rabbi Dreidel demanded."

Abigail and Mordechai would sign written resignations from the board of directors, but he, Rabbi Megillah, would hold the resignations until the severance package was forthcoming.

Abigail and Rabbi Dreidel's father readily agreed to the proposal. Rabbi Dreidel threw a tantrum when they explained it to him, but he was outvoted.

Mordechai said that he felt any mention of money worsened Mishy's psyche. The sooner the family got whatever they were going to get, packed up, and left Destiny County, the better for everyone. Abigail agreed.

Rabbi Dreidel still refused to sign over the accounts, declaring, "even if the Almighty Himself threatened to re-flood the earth," he wouldn't give in to the ungrateful Jews of Destiny County.

So, Harold consulted with the bank manager and the bank's legal department to create a document that allowed him, as executive director, to access the records. Rabbi Dreidel wouldn't sign the document, but his father and Abigail did. Harold, respectful of his own conflict of interest, immediately turned over the accounts to the financial committee.

The reason Rabbi Dreidel wouldn't turn over the accounts became abundantly clear. Despite his resignation, the rabbi had continued to write himself checks and pay the family's credit card bills from the synagogue account.

Without the credit card statements, the committee couldn't decipher just how much Rabbi Dreidel had paid himself after his resignation. But clearly, it was many thousands of dollars of community funds.

The financial committee now demanded a full audit and access to the credit card bills. It also demanded that Harold Bernard withhold payment of the money that Lenny Spiegleman and Anna Habbibi had raised for the family until they could determine exactly how much money Rabbi Dreidel had taken. In the meantime, the committee decided to limit disclosure of the damning information to avoid more bad publicity and jeopardize the few monthly contributions still coming in.

GOD'S
INTERVENTION

Jews have been wedded to their calendar for millennia. The Jewish New Year, Rosh Hashanah, always falls after the end of summer. The blessing of the New Year begins the High Holy Days, culminating in Yom Kippur, the most solemn day of the year. It is devoted to self-examination and the chance to shed one's sins and start anew. On the heels of Yom Kippur comes the holy week of Sukkot, commemorating the Jews' wanderings in the wilderness before receiving the Torah. That week ends with Simchat Torah and the annual conclusion and beginning, anew, of the reading of the Torah.

Rabbi Yitzak Yosef wanted a rabbi in place for the County of Destiny by Rosh Hashanah. *Those poor Jews,* he said to himself, *have suffered enough. They need a new rabbi.* Rabbi Dreidel was history. It was time to start over. Rabbi Yitzak Yosef called his friend and mentor, Rabbi Megillah, who knew more about promising, young TUCAS rabbis than anyone.

As Rabbi Yosef expected, his old friend immediately came up with an idea. "I just talked with Rabbi Koveh Hagadol in Houston," he said. "He had an opening in Amarillo.

"Three wonderful, young rabbis spent Shabbos there in the last few weeks, and one already has been chosen for the position.

"Shall I ask the others to visit Destiny County? I think one has a connection in your area."

So, it came to pass that the Jewish Center of Destiny County welcomed Rabbi Asher Baruch, a young, handsome rabbi with a full black beard.

He just happened to know all about what had happened in Destiny County. His younger sister had given him a blow-by-blow history of the events. She had just spent a year helping her first cousin at a TUCAS preschool. The first cousin was none other than Rabbi Schvitzerman's wife.

Rabbi Asher Baruch looked at the places where his other brothers and sisters had recently established their TUCAS shuls, all smaller communities than Destiny County. In comparison, Destiny County, with its beautiful shul, was a gold mine. The infrastructure for the next, fortunate rabbi already was in place.

Rabbi Baruch had a Jewish sense of humor. Rabbi Dreidel's problems had reminded him of a joke about a young man who was full of himself. The young man took a beautiful young lady to a restaurant for a first date. He couldn't stop talking about himself during drinks, the salad, the entré, and even the dessert. He went on and on about his family, his education, his job, and his hobbies. He chatted non-stop and only about himself. Finally, when the server brought the after-dinner coffee, the young man said, "Okay, enough about what I think, what do you think about me?"

When Rabbi Dreidel heard Rabbi Baruch was coming to lead services, he called to give him "advice" on things to say in his sermons, including pointed references to Jewish law about severance compensation. Rabbi Asher listened politely, but he couldn't help but remember the joke about the self-centered young man.

The loyal congregants of Destiny County were going to go to High Holiday services even if Mickey "Moishe" Mouse was the rabbi. They went. They congregated. They prayed. They ate apples and honey with Rabbi Baruch after Rosh Hashanah services. They fasted with him on Yom Kippur. Together, they ate lunch with Rabbi Baruch in the *sukkah*, a temporary hut built for the holiday. Joyfully, they danced holding the Torah and drank kosher whiskey with him on Simchat Torah. Jews are Jews, and rabbis like Asher Baruch know their stuff.

He started each sermon with a good Jewish joke. Not having much time to prepare, Rabbi Asher's *spiels* were much shorter than the Jews of Destiny County were accustomed to—making it much easier to stay awake. This was a refreshing change. By the time the marathon of holidays and services concluded, the young man was almost like a member of the family. The congregation of Destiny County had found its new rabbi.

Back in New York, unemployed and forlorn, spinning his wheels and cursing those he blamed for his misfortunes, Rabbi Mishegas Dreidel also attended High Holiday services. Sometime in the middle of the fifth and closing service for Yom Kippur, Rabbi Mishegas Dreidel had another epiphany. He realized that he wasn't going to get reinstated. As soon as the holidays were over, the rabbi decided, he would return and clear out the house, hire a realtor, arrange for movers, cash in on the sale of the family residence, and turn his back on Destiny County.

Unfortunately, there was still one little problem. The financial committee wanted to see the credit card bills to find out how much money the rabbi had appropriated after his resignation.

The committee reminded Harold Bernard not to release the money in his trust account for the Dreidels until it could figure out how much community money was missing.

Another round of frantic phone calls ensued between Rabbi Megillah, Rabbi Yitzak Yosef, Rabbi Schvitzerman, Rabbi Finklestein, Lenny Spiegleman, Adam and Anna Habbibi, Abigail Dreidel, and Mishy's father. Rabbi Dreidel was not on speaking terms with anyone, even though his financial misdeeds were the centerpiece of the conversations.

Finally, Rabbi Megillah, building on his proposal to Abigail and Mishy's father, worked out a deal almost as complicated as what the Talmud said about who had to pay if you went on a trip and your cow got stolen.

Both Rabbi Dreidel's father and Abigail would resign from the board of directors, effective immediately. The community would not turn Rabbi Dreidel over to the local constables. In fact, all members of the financial committee would sign a release forgoing all claims against the Dreidels on behalf of the Jewish Center of Destiny County.

Rabbi Mishegas and Abigail Dreidel would sign a promissory note in favor of the Jewish Center of Destiny County, described as the repayment of a "loan" for the sum of $50,000. It would be secured by a deed of trust on the family residence.

Rabbi Megillah would hold the note and deed of trust unless the loan went unpaid. Abigail intended to get a personal loan from her uncle to repay the Jewish Center within a month's time. If that date came and went without a payment, Rabbi Megillah would forward the promissory note and deed of trust to the chair of the financial committee. The committee could file the documents with the county auditor, and the money would be paid from the sale of the family residence. The money in Harold Bernard's trust account would be disbursed to Abigail Dreidel. Abigail desperately needed money to live on, and Harold needed to get the money out of his trust account.

Was everybody happy? No one was happy. The negotiations left a bitter taste in everyone's mouths except those of Rabbis Megillah and Yitzak Yosef, who approached the negotiations like a business transaction. There was a problem that needed to be resolved, and the sooner the better.

Everyone, despite their distaste for this dirty business, signed the documents—except Rabbi Mishegas Dreidel. He'd withdrawn his lawsuit from the *Beis Din*, but asking him to sign off without a severance package was like rubbing a dog's nose in poop. Abigail could sign what she needed to sign. But even with his own father's approval and encouragement, and his understanding of the need to put the entire affair behind them, Rabbi Mishegas Dreidel would rather suffer torture at the hands of persecuting Romans than pay a dime back to those half-witted Jews of Destiny County.

Meanwhile, Rabbi Dreidel found that Rabbi Asher Baruch was a pleasure to deal with on the sale of his residence. They quickly agreed to an inflated price. Rabbi Asher didn't worry that he might be paying top dollar or even a little more. He loved that he could buy a house next door to the synagogue. His wife and young kids could easily walk back and forth and fully participate in the religious life of the synagogue.

In the big scheme of things, sure, he was overpaying for the house, and, let's face it, the house wasn't in good shape. But *nu*, he was moving his family to a gold mine, the County of Destiny, where he would serve for the rest of his life as the esteemed head rabbi. He would dedicate himself to Judaism, loving his fellow Jews, teaching Torah, and growing the community. And let us all say it together, "Amen!"

After the papers to sell the house were signed, sealed, and delivered, Rabbi Dreidel tried to start up again with Rabbi Baruch about a severance package. But the new rabbi told him that he couldn't get involved and directed him to the financial committee. Rabbi Dreidel didn't like it, but that was that. One rabbi moved out. Another rabbi moved in.

GLOSSARY

Aliyah – the honor of going up to the Torah during services

Amen – a word everyone says after the rabbi finishes a prayer that means, "That's right!" or "Oh yeah!"

Beis Din – a Jewish Court, usually composed of three rabbis, or, if in heaven, angels as the both prosecution and defense, and God as the judge

Bima – the stage or platform where men crowd around while the Torah is read

Boychik – a young boy, a term of endearment for a young man

Bris – the Jewish ceremony of circumcision

Chazzer (or Hazzer) – a pig

Chutzpah – guts, nerve, gall, cojones, balls

Daven – to recite the prescribed liturgical prayers

Dreidel – a spinning top

Dybbuk – a ghost that possesses a dislocated soul of a dead person

D'var Torah – a spiel, often too long, on the weekly Torah reading

Eretz Yisrael – the land of Israel—once thought of as an earthly paradise, but now overwhelmed by cell phones

Farkakte – covered in excrement

Farmischt (or Famischt) – confused, mixed up, disoriented, like everyone feels after fasting on Yom Kippur

Frum – devoutly, and sometimes irritatingly, observant

Gan Eden – the Garden of Eden, former residence of Adam and Eve

Gelt – money, or, on the festival of Chanukah, something even more valuable— chocolate candy wrapped in gold foil

Geshrey – like a shrey, but louder, to shriek, cry, shout or hoot

Gornisht helfn – beyond help

Goy – a non-Jew, often used pejoratively, as in, "…something only a goy would do"

Hazzer (or Chazzer)– a pig, or food made from a pig, like bacon and ham

Hazzarai – junk food that is non-kosher or kosher food that is junk

Hocking a chinik – "to sound like a boiling teakettle," to rattle on and on

Kaddish – a prayer of mourning recited during services, but only with a minyan, ten men

Kashrut – the detailed laws of kosher foods, including rules about meat from animals with cloven hooves, fish with fins and scales, and not mixing meat and dairy

Kibitz – to speak informally, usually with unwanted advice or commentary

Kinder – children

Kindeleh – little children

Kishkas – guts, intestines, generally tied up in knots

Kosher – foods that conform to Jewish dietary rules or a metaphor for things Jews will accept

Kugel – a baked casserole of noodles or potatoes that bubbe always made better than anyone else

Kvetching – complaining, whining, often about over-stressed *kishkas*

Macher – a big shot, a person who gets things done

Mamzer – a bastard

Mechitza – a partition to separate men and women in the shul, but easy to see through

Megillah – a long, involved story

Mensch – a real human being, a good person

Mesirah – where one Jew rats out another Jew to the non-Jewish authorities

Mezuzah – a decorative case with a prayer inside that is hung on a doorpost

Mikvah – a ritual bath for purification used regularly by orthodox Jews

Mincha – afternoon prayers

Minyan – a quorum of ten men required in orthodox worship services, but often difficult to obtain—or ten men and women, often just as difficult to obtain—at conservative synagogues

Mishegas – craziness, nonsense, foolishness

Mitzvah – a commandment, a good deed, often forgotten about, notwithstanding Yom Kippur resolutions

Moshiach – the Jewish Messiah who will usher in an era of peace and redemption despite the *mishegas* going on in the world

Mushugganah – crazy, as in, Moshiach was driven *mushugganah* by the *mishegas* of the men and women praying for his arrival

Naches – the glow of pride a parent feels towards his or her child anytime the kid does anything even remotely good

Nebbish – an ineffectual, weak man, sometimes a *mushugganah* who lacks the chutzpah to commit the *mishegas* he imagines

Nu – so? Or, so what?

Nudged – push a little, annoy, much like the English word

Oy vey – "Oh no!" Or, "Oh woe!"—an expression of dismay

Oy vey iz mir – "Oh woe is me!"

Pushke – an alms box, usually a tin can: *When pushke comes to shove, a Jew should give a little tzedakah!*

Rachmones – compassion, pity, mercy

Rambam – another name for Maimonides, a famous Jewish thinker, writer, and codifier of Jewish laws. His books were, at one time, burned by the rabbis for being too rational.

Rashi – an acronym for an oft-quoted, highly acclaimed rabbi who provided commentary on the Torah and the Talmud, often illuminating but sometimes confusing readers

Rebbetzin – a rabbi's wife, mother of his many children, chief cook for his congregation and family—also serves as co-counselor and teacher

Schande far di goyim – "a disgrace before the gentiles"—a scandal so embarrassing that it reflects poorly on all Jews, but is often not even noticed by the gentiles in question

Schlemiel – a dumb, awkward, or unlucky person

Schlep – to carry, generally while complaining about the burden

Schlepper – a foolish person wandering around, an ambulatory schlemiel

Schlepping – to carry clumsily—a schlemiel with a heavy backpack

Schmeer – a spread of cream cheese or some other substance applied with a broad brush

Schmoozing – talking casually in a friendly way

Schmuck – a prick, a detestable person

Schvitz – to sweat, perspire; ex: the *schlepper* was *schvitzing* as soon as he stumbled out the door

Seder – the traditional Passover feast that includes eating bitter herbs, drinking four cups of wine, and retelling the story of the Exodus from Egypt

Shabbos – the Sabbath, Judaism's day of rest requiring intense preparation and exhausting prayer

Shalom bayis – marital harmony, family peace, something that does not exist

Shiksa – a derisive term for a woman who isn't Jewish, often an attractive blonde; the opposite of a *shaina maidel*, a compliment that means a pretty girl

Shofar – a ram's horn used for religious purposes and almost impossible to blow

Sh'ma Yisrael – "Hear oh Israel," the first words of a famous Jewish prayer

Shidduch – a marital match, if the couple is lucky

Shried – cried or shouted in an ear-piercing way

Shtick – a modus operandi, a routine, one's (often comedic) thing

Shul – synagogue, a building in which people often are lulled to sleep by long spiels or sonorous, endless chanting

Spiel – a talk, a speech, sometimes a lengthy monologue if the listener can't get away

Tallit – Jewish prayer shawl worn even when it's really hot inside

Tallit katan – a fringed garment worn by orthodox men under their clothes

Talmud – learned volumes of Jewish laws with explanations and commentaries by famous rabbis of long ago

Tefillin – black leather boxes with straps that are worn by orthodox men when reciting weekday prayers

Teshuvah – "return" as in returning to God, repentance. Not to be confused with Tenuvah, a producer of dairy products

Tsuris – troubles, heartache, woe, aggravation often accompanied by *shrying* without *rachmones*

Trayf – non-kosher food, applied metaphorically to anything Jews don't like

Tzaddik – a righteous spiritual master, a holy person, with sightings as rare as a hairless opossum or a blue whale

Vershimmelt – shook up, rattled, *famischt*

Yartzeit – the anniversary of the death of a parent or close relative requiring the recitation of kaddish if a minyan can be found

Yeshiva – an orthodox school where the boys study the holy books

Yetzer hara – the evil inclination, often used to explain doing something that's fun but not exactly kosher

Yiddishe kup – a Jewish head, smart, a good head—think Einstein, Ginsburg, Heifetz, Rambam and Rashi, but not Madoff, Epstein, or Shylock

ACKNOWLEDGMENTS

A thousand thank-yous to Ben Hershberg who is a talented editor and wonderful friend. His repeated expressions of delight in this novel were a constant uplift. A very special and heartfelt thank you as well to Howard VanEs and his outstanding publishing team at Let's Write Books, Inc.

I also want to thank my family: my wife Donna, my sons, Matt and Sam, and my brother, Steve, whose suggestions were invaluable. Lastly, I want to thank the early readers who read the manuscript unedited and provided their input, Giovanna Franklin, Larry Fowler, and of course, Donna. Lastly, sincere thanks to members of the tribe far and wide for their community, support, and fellowship.

ABOUT THE AUTHOR

Andy Becker is a writer, gardener, and lifetime learner who lives in Gig Harbor, Washington with his wife Donna and their two dogs, Nova and Splash.

His first published book, *The Spiritual Gardener: Insights from the Jewish Tradition to Help Your Garden Grow*, is an illustrated gift book coupling spiritual themes with gardening tasks to inspire gardening and well-being.

Andy's second book, *Cracking an Egg*, is a humorous and heartfelt look at early childhood experiences from growing up in the 1960s.

Andy's author website is found at: **www.andybecker.life**

PRAISE FOR 'THE SPIRITUAL GARDENER'

When you open this book, you will be amazed at the wisdom of author Andy Becker, who combines profound knowledge of gardening skills with a deep love of Jewish wisdom and spirituality. The quotations that he shares from the Torah, *the* Midrash, *and the* Chasidic Masters *blend in seamlessly with the pragmatic suggestions on how to improve your horticultural skills. The* Torah *begins with Adam and Eve in the perfect Garden; with the help of this book, you will find yourself transported to that primordial setting, or at least closer to it. Digging in the earth is holy work. Enjoy this wonderful book and give it as a gift to like-minded friends and family members. Highly recommended.*

Rabbi James L. Mirel

Author of *Stepping Stones to Jewish Spiritual Living*

Becker's prose reads without resistance, plying between the natural present and centuries of wisdom with insightful ease. His words slip into the reader's soul as deftly as pumpkin or squash seeds or are nested in sentient soil like carrot grains on fertile seed tape. Here flower these meditations nurtured from Jewish roots and insightful horticultural dexterity. The book is divided into sections as natural and rhythmic as planting; its fruit bursts forth, cultivated, verdant, and ripe. As words are seeds themselves, this book offers from its leaves a bounty of horticultural wisdom, practical tips, spiritual inspiration, and a bounteous harvest.

Dr. Loss Pequeno Glazier
Digital Poetics (Alabama University Press) and *Anatman, Pumpkin Seed, Algorithm* (Salt)

This is the perfect read for anyone who continues to wonder why he or she sticks fingers in the dirt and prays that a seed will grow. This inspirational miracle of horticultural prose is accompanied by evocative watercolor illustrations and meaningful religious quotations. I will gift this book to others who continue to ask me why I do what I do. It puts words to every gardener's life and experience since Adam graced Eden.

Kirk R. Brown
Award Winning Garden Designer, Speaker, and Dramatist

With wry humor, earthy spirituality, and practical advice, lawyer and amateur gardener Becker tells the story of his own garden and entreats readers to plant, tend, harvest, and share their own soil in this fine debut. Explaining that he tries to live his life by the commandment of bal tashchit ("do not waste or destroy"), Becker explores different aspects of gardening and how they relate to his own spiritual thinking. He doles out tales of tending his garden, making peace with moles, slugs, and his neighbors who feed the rabbits he is determined to eject from their burrow under his garden.

In an age when one can feel tethered to a phone and bombarded by information and news, Becker argues that tending to a garden allows for "sanctified time." For Becker, troweling, watering, mulching, and seeding provide time to relish life and present opportunities for him to muse about the value of humility, how to divide chores in a marriage, and the ethics of hunting, among other topics. In uncomplicated, clear prose, Becker pleasantly urges readers—even those with just a balcony—to make a space where their home can be "infused with the Divine Presence." Green-thumbed spiritual readers will relish Becker's welcoming memoir.

Publisher's Weekly Booklife

PRAISE FOR
'CRACKING AN EGG'

In this charming compilation of vignettes, Andy Becker shares belly-laugh stories about growing up in the 50s and 60s. With a keen sense of irony, he describes fond and not-so-fond memories: fishing with his mom, dad, and siblings when smothered by mosquitoes; Thanksgiving Day when relatives squirted each other in the eye with lemons; and the annual Seder, when Andy studied rigorously to memorize all his lines. Becker includes fascinating scenes, such as when his grandfather, the owner of an upholstery factory, brought coffee and donuts to the workers who were all striking against him. A delight for readers of all ages, this engaging collection is not to be missed.

E.C. Murray
author and founder of Writersconnection.org

Follow the adventures, mishaps, and tribulations of a boy growing up in suburban America in the 60s. You will laugh, tear up, and sigh with nostalgia as you recall the days of playing with little green soldiers, jumping hedges, and going to the neighborhood bakery with Mom. This heartwarming book humorously recounts memories guaranteed to remind you of your own childhood.

Kerry Stevens
author of *Blood Ties*

Quotes ; '65. You can't make a statement
of faith

30 ch. / 257 pps ≈ 8.3/pm

This book was a hit $$. What did
I hope to get from it? I know that there
are a huge number of Rabbis that, in spite of
their structures had problems controlling their
Sluggy boys. (Troppen. Freundel, Moshe Zahavi
Kolko. Abrahemson). I just wanted an
idea of what the p thought process was
like from their side. This is a thinly
fictionalized retelling of actual events.
from _____ community.

Author's cword play, Mishegas Dreidel.   (p68).
                         , TUCAS. Moshe Cohnmenn
p68. Lunacy Dorums
A lot of these guys are scholars but REAL LOW
uncommon sense. If you wanted to know about
women's must sets  why not go
to a titty bar? Or why not consult with a
hooker?

Made in the USA
Columbia, SC
27 September 2021